WRESTLING with the Angel

Women Reclaiming their Lives

edited by
CATERINA EDWARDS
& KAY STEWART

RED DEER
PRESS

RED DEER PRESS
813, MacKimmie Library Tower
2500 University Drive N.W.
Calgary Alberta Canada T2N 1N4

Cover and text design by Duncan Campbell
Cover image Superstock/Ivy Bigbee
Editor for the Press: Aritha van Herk
Printed and bound in Canada by Kromar Printing Ltd. for Red Deer Press

Financial support provided by the Canada Council, the Department of
Canadian Heritage, the University of Calgary and the Alberta Foundation for
the Arts, a beneficiary of the Lottery Fund of the Government of Alberta.

Canadian Cataloguing in Publication Data
Main entry under title:
Wrestling with the angel
ISBN 0-88995-201-9
1. Canadian essays (English) – Women authors.*
2. Women authors, Canadian (English) – 20TH century – Biography.*
I. Stewart, Kay L. (Kay Lanette), 1942–   II. Edwards, Caterina, 1948–
PS8235.W7W73 2000   c814'.5408'0352042   C00-910203-5
PR9194.5.W6W73 2000

5 4 3 2 1

CONTENTS

Reconstructing Experience

Reexamining Rituals

To the women who are family by blood and by choice.

—Caterina Edwards & Kay Stewart

Acknowledgments

A collection like this takes shape through the cooperative efforts of many people. Foremost among these are the writers who responded so generously to our call for submissions, who made changes when asked (or resisted them with energy and strong arguments!), who kept the faith through the long process that ends with this publication. Our thanks not only to the contributors whose essays appear in this anthology, but also to those we were not able to include.

Carolyn Lee, our editorial assistant in the early stages, made our work easier by her efficiency, good judgment and sense of humor. Astrid Blodgett, Carol Kleckner, Kari Scarlett, Lynda Schultz, and Kathy van Denderen provided invaluable secretarial help. Our thanks to these women and to the Department of English, University of Alberta, for making their assistance available to us.

We are also grateful for the financial assistance given to individual writers (Yasmin Ladha, Alberta Foundation for the Arts; Ann Atkey, The Canada Council for the Arts) and to us as editors (Alberta Foundation for the Arts). Without the support of such organizations, both writers and readers would be the poorer.

The final shape of this book owes much to the keen editorial eye of Aritha van Herk, whose warm support came at a crucial time. To family and friends, thanks for bearing with us.

Introduction

Life writing can be an outpouring, a catharsis, a testament, a celebration, a lamentation, and a search for order and knowledge. It is personal, private, even intimate. Once life writing is printed, once indulgence is disciplined by shape and brevity, it moves several degrees along the continuum of private to public and becomes the essay, personal or autobiographical. Michel de Montaigne called the essay "the book of self," and in the traditional sense of the genre, such writing should not simply be instructive or informational. Forged by the writer's observations and experiences, the essay, as opposed to the diary, speaks to others. It creates a space for the personal story in the discourse of common concerns.

Just as the autobiographical essay looks inward and outward with an active rather than a passive gaze, its writer does not simply relive or record her life experience. She must wrestle with the limitations and imperatives of both memory and form. The title of this collection evokes the image of Jacob wrestling with the angel until daybreak and not letting go until the angel blesses him. The writer must also wrestle for a moment of grace, never giving up until she is blessed with a gift of light, which is insight.

Wrestling with the Angel refers not only to the biblical Jacob. In her seminal essay "Professions for Women," Virginia Woolf warns us that what stifles a woman's ability as a writer is the role of the Angel in the House. If a woman excels in the "difficult arts of family life," if she becomes what she is expected to be—sympathetic, charming, and unselfish—she will not excel at the art of writing. The angel can "pluck the heart out of [your] writing." In order to write honestly, particularly about her bodily experience, the writer must not attend to what husbands, lovers, parents, or children wish her to say. Part of the job of a woman writer is to deny expectations, to wrestle with the Angel in the House.

This act of engagement is a common thread that runs through this collection of essays: the writers reject any outside influence that defines them, whether tradition, convention, or family. Each one wrestles to define, to reclaim, her self and her life.

We did not begin with the theme of women reclaiming their lives or women writers reclaiming their art. Instead, we began with the idea of putting together a collection of autobiographical essays by contemporary Canadian women. Kay Stewart found herself parenting again almost ten years after her son left home. Her experience led her to think about how often she and her women friends seemed to start over: a new marriage, a new career, a new loss to grieve, a new sense of self to celebrate. She suggested we ask writers to reflect on encountering such life experiences the second time around.

The two of us had put together a previous collection of women's essays and enjoyed it. As with other instances of recurrence, our experience this time around was different. The first time, we waited apprehensively for submissions and opened every envelope with excitement. This time we again found exciting new voices but also the quiet satisfaction of renewing ties with women writers who had contributed to the previous collection, *Eating Apples: Knowing Women's Lives*. This interplay between repetition and variation echoes through many of the pieces in this collection. As Gail Scott says in her essay on her search for artistic nourishment in Paris, there's no such thing as repetition. Looking for the Paris of Hemingway and Stein, Scott discovers the difficulty of seeing for one's self. The exiles she encounters are not the wealthy Americans of the twenties and thirties, but African immigrants hounded by police. Likewise, in "supermom," Lea Littlewolfe realizes that although she has been heroic in her mothering of a stepson, and she is expected to do the same for a step-granddaughter, she cannot. "I am not solving all the problems of the world in one child." Circumstances, people, and landscapes all change, and the awareness we bring to them also changes. Repetition with variations: to each new experience we bring a different self, a greater awareness of the larger world around us, and a more realistic sense of our own desires and limitations.

Caterina Edwards suggested we broaden the focus of the collection to include the way in which events are re-envisioned, seen again. Memories elude us; they change or slip away. Sarah Murphy writes "The Night the Thirty-Ought-Six Got Shot Through the Ceiling" as part of her attempt to recall buried, traumatic memories, discovering that she can recapture the emotions even when the events elude her. Sandra Birdsell, investigating her connection to Winnipeg in "Why I Live Where I Live," describes a shifting land symbolic of elusive memory and history that does not support granite monuments but can throw up "the pelvic bone of an ancestor." In "Archaeology," Myrna Kostash examines photographs, poems, and letters for "confirmation and elaboration of memory," her bittersweet relationship with three lost friends. She finds only artifacts, only "shards of familiarity" from a distant time.

Inevitably, the younger self grows into a middle age that is more skeptical, more reflective, and more aware of how ambiguous an experience can be. Emma Pivato recalls in "Lost Connection" her decision to stop breast-feeding her third child. But her memory of the intensity and joy of the mother–daughter connection has been changed by her experience of her daughter's many handicaps. Jean Horton celebrates not taste but memory in "Eating a Jonathan Apple," an essay that contemplates nostalgia and loss.

We write to give form to experience, and in the process of writing, we can deform that experience or even create a false synthesis. Ann Pearson, in "Never the Same River," writes of her return to an area of France she visited in her youth, and becomes aware of the difficulty of avoiding distortion or falseness in the portrayal of earlier trips and marriages. "Verbalization objectifies, solidifies the fluid and elusive into a fixed shape, an 'I' not me and yet mine, like all my past selves."

Still, writing can also lead us to see or understand an experience clearly for the first time. Kay Stewart found that in writing "Mother–Love, Mother–Loss" she came to understand the connection between the ways in which we feel abandoned by our mothers and the ways we abandon ourselves. Likewise, writing about her family history in "Home is Where They Have to Take You In" caused Caterina Edwards to see why Venice for her has always seemed a refuge and an imaginative home.

Ideally, writing helps to define the self, and many of the essays deal with the writer's desire to be herself in relation to other people. Janet Lundman tells an aging roué in "Swimming the Gaps," "this is the last act . . . we can be who we are," while in "Re-Covering," Dianne Linden wishes she had the confidence and self-possession to be a "sumptuous" couch rather than a straight-backed chair. Both Sharon Butala and Janice MacDonald look back on their divorces to understand how to begin again. "The Day I Got My Divorce" chronicles the courtroom drama or farce in which Butala attempts to play her role in what is clearly someone else's ritual. In "Starting Over," MacDonald invents new rituals of family life, and rediscovers her twenty-four-year-old self.

Several of the writers find that reexamination of their past involves acknowledgment of other selves, lost or forgotten. In "Me and My Shadow," Lorna Millard explores the conflict between the self she is and the one she might have been if she had been raised by her birth mother. Michelle Alfano in "A Stone's Throw Away" revisits the limited and submissive self her family created. Both Rebecca Luce-Kapler in "Wise Blood" and Lindy McIntyre in "Tracing Elements" find that their heritage has a darker side. Whereas for Marguerite Watson in "Symptoms," the darkness in her body, a large tumor, keeps her whole. And Yasmin Ladha finds that she has misunderstood or misinterpreted much of what she knows of the friend she grieves. But misinterpretion is an aspect of wrestling with the angel. The writer holds fast until blessed with understanding.

All the writers in this collection have looked back and forward, have looked inward and outward. They offer their provisional insights to the community, helping to form that very community with words and dialogue. In "No Time to Die," in contrasting the two times she has been widowed, Eunice Scarfe writes, "And if I tell you this story of loss, it's because I know you have one too." Margaret Atwood celebrates her mother and her aunts in

"Great Aunts," tracing the relationship between the stories they told about themselves and each other, about the family, their animals, and the community, and about her development as a writer. Atwood writes that her essay, like her mother's stories, has no clear moral: "What was being passed on was the story itself: what was known and what could be told.... The permission to tell the story, wherever that might lead." It is in the shaping of our memories of places, people, and events into stories like these and sharing them with others that we keep the world alive.

This collection has no simple message. With its diversity of topics and voices, it highlights differences. The writers range from women students who have never published before to those who are firmly established. But they are all writing about incidents of their personal, daily life. Ordinary women, sharing the extraordinary. Blessed by the angel.

Reevaluating Relationships

Great Aunts

MARGARET ATWOOD

IN THE EARLY PART OF MY CHILDHOOD, I did not know any of my relatives, because they lived in Nova Scotia, two thousand miles away. My parents had left Nova Scotia during the Depression because there were no jobs there; by the time I was born, the Second World War had begun, and nobody traveled great distances without official reasons and gas coupons. But although my two aunts were not present in the flesh, they were very much present in the spirit. The three sisters wrote one another every week, and my mother read these letters out loud, to my father but by extension to me and my brother, after dinner. They were called "letters from home." "Home," for my mother, was always Nova Scotia, never wherever we might be living at the time; which gave me the vague idea that I was misplaced. Wherever I actually was living myself, "home" was not there.

So I was kept up on the doings of my aunts, and also of my great-aunts, my uncles, my cousins, my second cousins, and many other people who fitted in somewhere but were more distantly related. In Nova Scotia, it's not what you do or even who you know that is the most important thing about you. It's which town you're from and who you're related to. Any conversation between two Nova Scotians who've never met before will begin this way, and go on until both parties discover that they are in fact related to each other. So I grew up in a huge extended family of invisible people.

But it was not my invisible aunts in their present-day incarnation who made the most impression on me. It was my aunts in the past. There they were as children, in the impossible starched and frilled dresses and the floppy satin hair bows of the first decades of the century, or as shingle-haired teenagers, in black and white in the photograph album, wearing strange clothing—cloche hats, flapper coats up over the knee—standing beside antique motorcars, or posed in front of rocks or the sea in striped bathing suits that came halfway down their legs. Sometimes their arms would be around one another. They had been given captions, by my mother, in white pencil on the black album pages: "We Three," "Bathing Belles." Aunt J. was thin as a child, dark-eyed, intense. Aunt K., the middle sister, looked tailored and brisk, in a Dutch cut. My mother, with huge pre-Raphaelite eyes and wavy hair and model's cheekbones, was the beauty, an assessment she made light of: she was, and remained, notorious for her bad taste in clothes, a notion she cultivated so she wouldn't have to go shopping alone. But all three sisters had the same high-bridged noses; Roman noses, my mother said. I pored over these pictures, intrigued by the idea of the triplicate, identical noses. I did not have a sister myself, then, and the mystique of sisterhood was potent for me.

The photo album was one mode of existence for my invisible aunts. They were even more alive in my mother's stories, for, although she was no poet, my mother was a raconteur and deadly mimic. The characters in her stories about "home" became as familiar to me as characters in books; and since we lived in isolated places and moved a lot, they were more familiar than most of the people I actually encountered.

The cast was constant. First came my strict, awe-inspiring but lovable grandfather, a country doctor who drove around the dirt roads in a horse and sleigh, through blizzards, delivering babies in the dead of night, or cutting off arms and legs, or stitching up gaping wounds made by objects unfamiliar to me—buzz saws, threshing machines. Under his reign, you had to eat everything on your plate, or sit at the dinner table until you did. You had to go to church, every Sunday. You had to sit up straight. ("Father laid down the law," said my mother. And I could picture him laying it down, on the dining-room table, in the form of two great slabs, like those toted around by Moses; only his were of wood.)

This larger-than-life figure, who resembled in my mind the woodcut of Captain Ahab in our copy of *Moby-Dick,* once threatened to horsewhip my mother for "making moon eyes at the boys." ("Did you?" I said. "I don't know," said my mother.) Although he never actually did any horsewhipping, the word made a vast impression on me. I didn't know what a horsewhip was, and such a punishment had the added attraction of the bizarre.

Then came my distracted, fun-loving, bridge-playing grandmother, and my Aunt K., a year younger than my mother but much more intellectual and firm of will, according to my mother. Then Aunt J., sentimental and apt to be left out. These three were "the girls." Then, somewhat later, my two uncles, "the boys," one of whom was an inventor and blew the stove lids off the country schoolhouse with some homemade explosive hidden in a log, the other a laconic ironist who frequently had everyone "in stitches." And the peripheral figures: hired girls who were driven away by the machinations of my mother and Aunt K., who did not like having them around; hired men who squirted them while milking the cows; the cows themselves; the yearly pig; the horses.

The horses were not really peripheral characters; although they had no lines, they had names and personalities and histories, and they were my mother's partners in exciting and, it seemed to me, life-threatening escapades. Dick and Nell were their names. Dick was my favorite; he had been given to my mother as a broken-down, ill-treated hack, and she had restored him to health and glossy beauty. This was the kind of happy ending I found satisfactory.

THE STORIES ABOUT THESE PEOPLE had everything that could be asked for: plot, action, suspense—although I knew how they would turn out, having heard them before—and fear, because there was always the danger of my grandfather's finding out.

What would he find out? Almost anything. There were many things he was not supposed to know, many things the girls were not supposed to know, but did. And what if he were to find out that they knew? A great deal turned, in these stories and in that family, on concealment; on what you did or did not tell; on what was said as distinct from what was meant. "If you can't say anything good, don't say anything at all," said my mother, saying a great deal. My mother's stories were my first lesson in reading between the lines.

My mother featured in these stories as physically brave, a walker of fences and also of barn ridgepoles, a sin of horsewhipping proportions—but shy. She was so shy that she would hide from visitors behind the barn, and she could not go to school until Aunt K. was old enough to take her. In addition to the bravery and the shyness, however, she sometimes lost her temper. This was improbable to me, since I could not remember any examples. My mother losing her temper would have been a sight to behold, like the Queen standing on her head. But I accepted the idea on faith, along with the rest of her mythology.

Aunt K. was not shy. Although she was younger than my mother, you would never know it: "We were more like twins." She was a child of steely nerves, according to my mother. She was a ringleader, and thought up plots and plans, which she carried out with ruthless efficiency. My mother would be drawn into these, willy-nilly; she claimed she was too weak of will to resist.

"The girls" had to do household chores, more of them after they had driven away the hired girls, and Aunt K. was a hard worker and an exacting critic of the housework of others. Later on in the story, Aunt K. and my mother had a double wedding; the night before this event they read their adolescent diaries out loud to one another and then burned them. "We cleaned the kitchen," said Aunt K.'s diary. "The others did not do an A-1 job." My mother and Aunt J. would always laugh when repeating this. It was, as Matthew Arnold would have had it, a touchstone line for them, about Aunt K.

But there was even more to Aunt K. She was a brilliant student, and had received her M.A. in history from the University of Toronto at the age of nineteen. My grandfather thought my mother was a flighty, pleasure-bent flibbertigibbet until she saved her own money from schoolteaching and sent herself to college; but he was all set to finance Aunt K. for an advanced degree at Oxford. However, she turned this down in favor of marrying a local Annapolis Valley doctor and having six children. The reason, my mother implied, had something to do with Great-aunt Winnie, who also had an M.A., the first woman to receive one from Dalhousie, but who had never married. Aunt Winnie was condemned—it was thought of as a condemnation—to teach school forever. She would turn up at family Christmases, looking wistful. In those days, said my mother, if you did not get married by a certain age, it was unlikely that you ever would. "You didn't think about not marrying," said Aunt J. to me, much later. "There wasn't any *choice* about it. It was just what you did."

Meanwhile, there was my Aunt K. in the album, in a satin wedding gown and a veil and a cascade of lilies identical to my mother's, and later, with all six children, dressed up as the Old Woman Who Lived in a Shoe in the Apple Blossom Festival Parade. Unlike the stories in books, my mother's stories did not have clear morals, and the moral of this one was less clear than most. Which was better? To be brilliant and go to Oxford, or to have six children? Why couldn't it be both?

WHEN I WAS SIX OR SEVEN and my brother was eight or nine and the war was over, we began to visit Nova Scotia, every summer or every second summer. We had to: my grandfather had had something called a coronary, more than one of them, in fact, and he could die at any moment. Despite his strictness and, to me, his fearfulness, he was loved and respected. Everyone agreed on that.

These visits were a strain. We reached Nova Scotia from Ontario by driving at breakneck speed and for a great many hours at a time over the postwar highways of Quebec and Vermont and New Brunswick, so that we would arrive cranky and frazzled, usually in the middle of the night. During the visits we would have to be on whispering good behavior in my grandfather's large white house, and meet and be met by a great many relatives we hardly knew.

But the worst strain of all was fitting these real people—so much smaller and older and less vivid than they ought to have been—into the mythology in my possession. My grandfather was not galloping around the countryside saving babies and sawing off limbs; he was not presiding over the large din-ing-room table, laying down the law. Instead he carved little wooden figures, chess pieces and apple-blossom pins, and had to have a nap every afternoon, and his greatest exertion was a stroll around the orchard or a game of chess with my brother. My grandmother was not the harried although comical mother of five, but the wispy-haired caretaker of my grandfather. There were no cows anymore, and where were the beautiful horses?

I felt defrauded. I did not want Aunt J. and Aunt K. to be the grown-up mothers of my cousins, snapping beans in the kitchen. I wanted them back the way they were supposed to be, in the bobbed haircuts and short skirts of the photo album, playing tricks on the hired girls, being squirted by the hired man, keeping dire secrets, failing to do an A-1 job.

MUCH LATER, when I thought I had grown up, Aunt J. took me to my first writers' conference. That was in Montreal, in 1958; I was eighteen, and bent on being a writer. I had already produced several impressive poems; at least I was impressed by them. They had decaying leaves, garbage cans, cigarette butts, and cups of coffee in them: I had been ambushed by T.S. Eliot several months previously, and had wrestled him to a standstill. I did not yet know that it was the done thing, by now, to refer to him as T.S. Idiot.

I had not shown my seedy poems to my mother, who was the oldest of the three sisters and therefore pragmatic, since it was she who'd had to tend the others. She was not particularly literary; she preferred dancing and ice-skat-ing, or any other form of rapid motion that offered escapes from domestic duties. My mother had only written one poem in her life, when she was eight or nine; it began: "I had some wings, / They were lovely things," and went on, typically for her, to describe the speed of the subsequent flight. The beau-ty of this was that whatever I came out with in the way of artistic production, my mother would say, more or less truthfully, that it was much better than she could do herself. But by this time I wanted professional advice. I knew that if I forced her to read my butt-and-coffee-grounds free verses, she would say they were very nice, this being her standard response to other puzzlements, such as my increasingly dour experiments with wardrobe. Clothing was not a priority of hers either.

But Aunt J. had written reams, according to my mother. She was a romantic figure, as she had once had pleurisy and had been in a "san," where she had made flowery shellwork brooches; I had received several of these treasures for Christmas, as a child, in tiny magical boxes with cotton wool in them. Tiny boxes, cotton wool: these were not my mother's style.

Aunt J. had to be careful of her health, an infirmity which seemed to go along with writing, from what I knew. She cried at the sad places in movies, as I did, and, as a child, had been known for impractical flights of fantasy. Her middle name was Carmen, and to punish what they thought to be her inordinate pride over this, her two older sisters had named the pig Carmen.

By now, Aunt J. was no longer lanky. She was rounded in outline, myopic (as I was), and depicted herself as a sentimental pushover, though this was merely a convenient fiction, part of the self-deprecating camouflage adopted by women then for various useful purposes. Underneath her façade of lavender-colored flutter she was tough-minded, like all three of those sisters. It was this blend of soft and hard that appealed to me.

So I'd shown my poems to Aunt J. She read them and did not laugh, or not in my presence; though on consideration I doubt that she laughed at all. She knew what it was to have ambitions as a writer, though hers had been delayed by Uncle M., who was a bank manager, and by their two children. Much later, she herself would be speaking at conferences, sitting on panels, appearing nervously on talk shows, having authored five books of her own. Meanwhile she wrote children's stories for the weekly Sunday-school papers, and bided her time.

She sent my gloomy poems to second cousin Lindsay, who was an English professor at Dalhousie University. He said I had promise. Aunt J. showed me his letter, beaming with pleasure. This was my first official encouragement.

The writers' conference Aunt J. took me to was put on by the Canadian Authors' Association, which at that time was the only writers' organization in Canada. I knew its reputation—it was the same tea-party outfit about which F. R. Scott had written: "Expansive puppets percolate self-unction / Beneath a portrait of the Prince of Wales." It was rumored to be full of elderly amateurs; I was unlikely to see anyone there sprouting a three-day beard or clad in a black turtleneck pullover, or looking anything like Samuel Beckett or Eugene Ionesco, who were more or less my idea of real writers. But Aunt J. and I were both so desperate for contact with anything that smacked of the world of letters that we were willing to take our chances with the CAA.

Once at the conference, we opted for a paper to be given by an expert on Fanny Burney. I goggled around the room: there were a lot of what I thought were middle-aged women, in flowered dresses—not unlike Aunt J.'s own dress—and little suits, though there was no one who looked like my idea of a writer: pallid, unkempt, red-eyed, poised for the existential jump. But this was Canada and not France, so what could I expect?

Up to this time I had seen only one Canadian writer in the flesh. His name was Wilson MacDonald and he'd turned up in our high school auditorium, old and wispy and white-haired, where he'd recited several healthy-minded poems about skiing, from memory, and had imitated a crow. I had a fair idea what Jean-Paul Sartre would have thought of him, and was worried that I might end up that way myself: wheeled out for a bunch of spitball-throwing teenaged thugs, doing birdcalls. You could not be a real writer and a Canadian too, that much was clear. As soon as I could, I was going to hit Paris and become incomprehensible.

Meanwhile, there I was in Montreal, waiting for the Fanny Burney expert with Aunt J. We were both nervous. We felt like spies of a sort, infiltrators; and so, like infiltrators, we began to eavesdrop. Right behind us was sitting a woman whose name we recognized because she frequently had poems about snow-covered spruce trees published in the daily Montreal newspaper. She was not discussing spruce trees now, but a hanging that had taken place the day before, at the prison. "It was so dreadful for him," she was saying. "He was so upset."

Our ears were flapping: had she known the condemned man personally? If so, how creepy. But as we listened on, we gathered that the upset man was not the hanged one; it was her husband, who was the prison chaplain.

Several gaps opened at my feet: the gap between the sentimentality of this woman's poems and the realities of her life, between the realities of her life and her perceptions of them; between the hangers and the hanged, and the consolers of the hanged, and the consolers of the hangers. This was one of my first intimations that, beneath its façade of teacups and outdoor pursuits and various kinds of trees, Canada—even this literary, genteel segment of Canada, for which I had such youthful contempt—was a good deal more problematic than I had thought.

YEARS LATER, I went on a literary outing with both of my aunts.

This took place in the early seventies, when I was over thirty and had published several books. Aunt J.'s husband had died, and she'd moved from Montreal back to Nova Scotia to take care of my aging grandmother. I was visiting, and the aunts and I decided to drive over to nearby Bridgetown, to pay a call on a writer named Ernest Buckler.

Twenty years before, Ernest Buckler had written a novel called *The Mountain and the Valley*, the Mountain being the North Mountain, the Valley being the Annapolis Valley. He'd had some success with it in the States, at that time, in Canada, a surefire ticket to hatred and envy—though because he was an eccentric recluse, the hatred and envy quotient was modified. However, his success in the States had not been duplicated in Canada, because his Toronto publishers were United Church teetotalers, known for throwing launch parties at which they served fruit juice. (Modernization came finally with the addition of a bottle of dreadful sherry, doled out in a separate room, into which those who craved it could slink furtively for their hit while the fruit-juice drinkers pretended not to notice.) These publishers had discovered that there were what my mother referred to as "goings-on" in Buckler's book, and had hidden it in the stockroom. If you wanted to actually buy one, it was like getting porn out of the Vatican.

(My grandmother, before word of its depraved nature had spread, had bought this book as a birthday present for my grandfather, but had taken the precaution of reading it first. She took it out behind the barn and burned it. "It was not fit for him to read," she had remarked, which cast as much light on her opinion of my grandfather—veteran of dissecting room and childbed—as on her opinion of the book.)

I had read this book at the age of thirteen because somebody had given it to my parents, thinking they would like it because it was about Nova Scotia. My mother's comment was that it was not what things were like when she was growing up. This said a lot. I snuck this book up onto the garage roof, which was flat, where I swiftly located the goings-on and then read the rest of the book. It was probably the first novel for adults that I ever did read, with the exception of *Moby-Dick*.

I remembered Ernest Buckler's book with fondness; and by the seventies I'd become involved in a correspondence with him. So over we went to see him in the flesh. My Aunt J. was all agog, because Ernest Buckler was a real writer. My Aunt K. drove. (My Aunt J. never drove, having scraped the door handles off the car on one of her few attempts, according to her.)

Aunt K. knew the vicinity well, and pointed out the places of interest as we went by. She had a good memory. It was she who had told me something everyone else had forgotten, including myself: that I had announced, at the age of five, that I was going to be a writer.

During this drive, however, her mind was on other historical matters. "That's the tree where the man who lived in the white house hanged himself," she said. "That's where the barn got burned down. They know who did it but they can't prove a thing. The man in there blew his head off with a shotgun." These events may have taken place years, decades before, but they were still current in the area. It appeared that the Valley was more like *The Mountain and the Valley* than I had suspected.

Ernest Buckler lived in a house that could not have been changed for fifty years. It still had a horsehair sofa, antimacassars, a wood stove in the living room. Ernest himself was enormously likable and highly nervous, and anxious that we be pleased. He hopped around a lot, talking a mile a minute, and kept popping out to the kitchen, then popping in again. We talked mostly about books, and about his plans to scandalize the neighborhood by phoning me up at my grandmother's house, on the party line, and pretending we were having an affair. "That would give the old biddies something to talk about," he said.

Everyone listened in on the party line, of course, whenever he had a call, but not just because he was a local celebrity. They listened in on everyone.

After we left, my Aunt J. said, "That was something! He said you had a teeming brain!" (He had said this.) My Aunt K.'s comment was: "That man was oiled." Of the three of us, she was the only one who had figured out why Mr. Buckler had made such frequent trips to the kitchen. But it was understandable that he should have been secretive about it: in the Valley, there were those who drank, and then there were decent people.

Also: there were those who wrote, and then there were decent people.

A certain amount of writing was tolerated, but only within limits. Newspaper columns about children and the changing seasons were fine. Sex, swearing, and drinking were beyond the pale.

I myself, in certain Valley circles, was increasingly beyond the pale. As I became better known, I also became more widely read there, not because my writing was thought of as having any particular merit but because I was Related. Aunt J. told me, with relish, how she'd hidden behind the parlor door during a neighbor's scandalized visit with my grandmother. The scandal was one of my own books; how, asked the outraged neighbor, could my grandmother have permitted her granddaughter to publish such immoral trash?

But blood is thicker than water in the Valley. My grandmother gazed serenely out the window and commented on the beautiful fall weather they were having, while my Aunt J gasped with suppressed giggles behind the hall door. My aunts and my mother always found the spectacle of my grandmother preserving her dignity irresistible, probably because there was so much of it to be preserved.

This was the neighbor, the very same one, who as a child had led my aunts astray, sometime during the First World War, inducing them to slide down a red clay bank in their little white lace-edged pantaloons. She had then pressed her nose up against the glass of the window to watch them getting spanked, not just for sliding but for lying about it. My grandmother had gone over and yanked the blind down then, and she was doing it now. Whatever her own thoughts about the goings-on in my fiction, she was keeping them to herself. Nor did she ever mention them to me.

For that I silently thanked her. I suppose any person, but especially any woman, who takes up writing has felt, especially at first, that she was doing it against an enormous, largely unspoken pressure, the pressure of expectation and decorum. This pressure is most strongly felt, by women, from within the family, and more so when the family is a strong unit. There are things that should not be said. Don't tell. If you can't say anything nice, don't say anything at all. Was that counterbalanced adequately by that other saying of my mother's: "Do what you think is right, no matter what other people say"? And did those other people whose opinion did not matter include the members of one's own family?

With the publication of my first book, I was dreading disapproval. I didn't worry much about my father and mother, who had gracefully survived several other eccentricities of mine—the skirts hand-printed with trilobites and newts, the experiments with beer parlors, the beatnik boyfriends—although they had probably bitten their tongues a few times in the process. Anyway, they lived in Toronto, where goings-on of various kinds had now become more common; not in Nova Scotia, where, it was not quite said, things were a bit more narrow. Instead I worried about my aunts. I thought they might be scandalized, even Aunt J. Although she had been subjected to some of my early poems, coffee cups and rotting leaves were one thing, but there was more than dirty crockery and mulch in this book. As for Aunt K., so critical of the shoddy housework and drinking habits of others, what would she think?

To my surprise, my aunts came through with flying colors. Aunt J. thought it was wonderful—a real book! She said she was bursting with pride. Aunt K. said that there were certain things that were not said and done in her generation, but they could be said and done by mine, and more power to me for doing them.

This kind of acceptance meant more to me than it should have, to my single-minded all-for-art twenty-six-year-old self. (Surely any true artist ought to be impervious to aunts.) However, like the morals of my mother's stories, what exactly it meant is far from clear to me. Perhaps it was a laying-on of hands, a passing of something from one generation to another. What was being passed on was the story itself: what was known, and what could be told. What was between the lines. The permission to tell the story, wherever that might lead.

Or perhaps it meant that I too was being allowed into the magical, static but ever-continuing saga of the photo album. Instead of three different-looking young women with archaic clothes and identical Roman noses, standing with their arms around each other, there would now be four. I was being allowed into "home."

MARGARET ATWOOD *is the author of several novels, most recently* The Robber Bride *and* Alias Grace. *She has also published short stories, nonfiction, and poetry.* "Great Aunts" *first appeared in* Family Portraits *(1989).*

Taking the Plunge

SUSAN DRAIN

WHAT I REMEMBER MOST is the green and white rush, water and air foaming and crashing about my head. All senses swept into one wet, noisy pummeling.

And panic, crashing upward like the water.

Then the colors and the noise settle into separate spheres, sun above and water all around, and blessedly, no rocks—thank God, no rocks—just the smell and push of water, and the bewilderment of nerve endings registering the leap from sunshine to the froth of chill water.

I'm alive and striking for the bank.

Scrambling into the tranquillity of air, I stagger; you reach for me. The sun glances off your hair—and down again I go, into the pool of shadow where you bend over me. My blood foams and crashes against the barrier of skin—mine cold and wet, yours smelling of the sun.

You told me later that you wanted to laugh when you saw me flailing in the air above the millrace. How ridiculous and vulnerable I was. I waited to hear you say, How dear and precious, too. But you'd said that once, traced the letters on my wet back, let me read them on your lips as we stood on the bank. You never confessed much, and you never repeated yourself.

(You never said, How brave. You didn't know. It may have been the bravest thing I'd ever done.)

I was twenty that summer; you were twenty-eight, I think—it was a much bigger gap then. Could it possibly have been sunny for four whole months? You and Simon were both teaching summer courses. I was working on campus: shepherding convention goers to and from their residence and meeting rooms, finding things for them—flip charts, tee times, restaurant recommendations. I was supposed to anticipate their needs and fend off their advances. It was a satisfying time: I had both work and leisure, there was plenty of company, and the campus was beautiful. While I waited for guests to register, I embroidered flowers like Matisse cutouts and worked through the reading list for my honors year. When I wasn't working, I went to the riverbank to read my books, and sunbathe, and swim. I savored the order of my days. I began to dream beyond that degree and that campus.

You and Simon used to meet on the riverbank after class. Sometimes you'd race each other across the current, stroking upstream in order to reach the bank opposite. Sometimes you'd go up to the dam and leap into the millrace, to be swept downstream and emerge laughing from the turbulent water. It seemed like craziness to me, but I laughed, too, as I watched. Afterward, my days seemed dull.

After your swim, you'd go to Simon's for a beer. Simon (whom I knew) used to stop to ask what I was reading and eventually he invited me to come, too.

I did. You pretty well ignored me, both of you—showed me where to drop my towel and books, passed me a beer ("you don't want a glass, do you?")— and plunged into a conversation that had been going on for days. You were reading and discussing your reading—you stayed up late to talk (then complained that even afternoon classes began too early). One would open a bottle, and the other would make grilled cheese sandwiches; you'd argue, and you'd quote, and you'd laugh. You'd just finished *The Female Eunuch*—it was brand new—and wanted to know what I thought. I shook my head, and the talk swirled quickly past and onward. When I got up to leave, you held out the book to me, an invitation to two new worlds.

I thought it was heaven. I'd never seen ideas worked through before: my intellectual life had been in the classroom, where ideas were the polished artifacts of my professors or the half-formed notions of my peers. This was like the squash games I saw you play later: competitive but collaborative, fast, hard, and exhilarating. Once you showed me some of the letters you and Simon wrote each other that summer. They were different from the conversations. In the letters the abstract sometimes became personal and argument became intimacy. "How could I keep my thoughts straight," Simon complained in one letter, "with Susan sitting beside you? All I could think was, if she would just lean forward a little, I could see the curve of her breast."

It was heaven, and I was there. I'd never imagined that ideas and grilled cheese sandwiches, friendships and swimming, books and sex, arguments and love could be so inextricable. My heart lurches clumsily just at the memory, and the little compartments and parcels of my life rattle emptily. For one summer, I was one of the lucky ones: we were bright and passionate, beautiful and strong; we were gentle and exultant. I know we were self-absorbed. I hope we were generous. People turned to watch us as we passed, and they smiled, the same involuntary acknowledgement that babies draw.

(How do you remember it? We make and remake our pasts, but I would grieve, even now, if our stories had diverged too much.)

There was a fortnight that summer when you went away, taking some friends to Georgian Bay. You left me your keys, and when I wasn't working, I haunted your flat: wore your sweater, leafed through your books, drank your beer, and slept in your bed. It rained for the first time all summer. I wrote a lot, cobwebs laid over the gap in my days. When you came back, I threw out every word (I've written them all again since then, every one a hundred times. Perhaps this is the last version.)

It was after you came back, I think, that I decided I, too, would jump off the dam. I'd thought it crazy when you and Simon first did it, but over those weeks, I began to see it differently. You loved games: tennis, squash, rugby—the more strenuous the better. Swimming was not exciting, but in the millrace, there was a current to be fought, a tumult to ride. You knew something that I'd forgotten, how to be fully present in the physical. Childhood over, I'd learned to live in my head; my body had become an intimate stranger. You lived fully in both body and mind: I wanted that as I wanted you. I was desperate to jump.

It was quite simple really. I thought about it for days. Then one afternoon, when you and Simon were heading upriver, I announced that I was going to jump, too. You both looked a little nervous. Simon stationed himself on the bank. You stayed with me until I stepped into the air and fell into the river.

You laughed, but I had jumped. It was my triumph. I didn't ride the tumult as you did, but I was briefly part of it, sense and senses all engaged, if overwhelmed. With that plunge I staked a claim on the heaven I'd visited with you. I wanted a life that challenged and celebrated, embraced and integrated all that I was or could be. And I wanted it on equal terms.

It was impossible, of course, but it lasted far longer than anyone could have expected—well into winter. We argued books and tramped the riverbank in the snow. Ice hemmed the river; the current churned dangerously out of sight. It grew more and more difficult. We broke too many rules. But I had renounced safety for a chance at heaven, and you abetted me. Our great accomplishment for those few months was that we would not acknowledge the impossibility; we lived resolutely in the moment. All that winter we rode the millrace: your lectures, my essays, the clamor of our blood. Through it all I waited to hear where I would go to graduate school. That I might not go was a possibility neither of us entertained. I would not settle for secondhand heaven.

Sometimes my resolve faltered, but I had taken the plunge, and no midair flailing could restore the old equilibrium. I wish I could have been more graceful. Two or three times I panicked; it scared you. The moment we inhabited finally burst. You came ashore quickly. When I found my feet again, it was on an entirely different shore.

SUSAN DRAIN *is associate professor of English at Mount Saint Vincent University in Halifax, Nova Scotia. The local ocean is too cold for literal plunges, but she is still taking metaphorical ones.*

Blood Turn

PAULA JOHANSON

THE DISTINCT ODOR OF FRESH BLOOD on her breath is bothering me. I don't expect a small, plump grandmotherly woman to smile proudly at her husband at the lectern and confide to me in a stage whisper that she's pleased how we young people react to his lectures, while the cloying smell of blood clots rolls forth with her every breath. She makes me think of meat, blue-rare. Instead of the lecture or the conference, I think of menstrual blood spiraling down the legs and around and down the shower drain, of hospital visits for my new babies' vaccinations, and of the blood clinic at this conference, with first-time donors leaving very white.

I know blood donors from both sides, friends at the clinic down the hall and remembering that rush of other-blood in my veins: a trickle where the flow should be loud, hard, and long. Where the pulse should hammer, it fluttered weakly and the *drip drip drip* was no substitute. There was a golden-skinned nurse at my side, measuring and soothing and cooling me with her hands, but the *drip drip* was somehow not antiseptic enough. I could smell it. Or was it my own blood? I remember the hemorrhage and the dizzy darkness and the splash from crotch to ankles. Surely they changed the bed after I spiraled down into the dark. Then I smelled it; I still smell it. This old woman brings back for me the memory and smell of the fresh gush, and clots of bright and dark, and the mushy, salty odor like the harbor at my door.

That's the tag that got this memory started, I realize. I live by the ocean; I smell it all day. Perhaps this grandmotherly woman in the next seat has a personal scent that's briny and compelling like homesickness. She could even be wearing a perfume that's like my grandmother's. But then she leans forward again to whisper in my ear that her husband loves doing these talks, though it's such a bother to bring her along and so little for her to do at these conferences. I want to wipe my ear of the clot and the trickle running from it. Her lips are unstained, even by lipstick. She has no need for it; her color is high, even florid. Her hand grips a purse with no tremor, an easy strength in hands unknotted by arthritis.

She's like my grandmother: no arthritis. Strength in old age. I let the lecture run past me again and wonder how I can keep this friendly woman from unnerving me. Maybe I can get her to talk about herself and tell me stories like my grandmother does, my memory person, whom I am too much like already at the end of my youth. Last time I saw her was at Christmas, carving the turkey and setting out the bread and glasses of red wine at every place along the table. She held my babies and told me of her own mother putting binding bands on *her* children. She put no binding bands on my twins, but she wrapped me up tight. She told me stories while I wrapped twists of her white hair into curls around my finger.

The smell of blood is becoming distressing.

The plump woman eases herself forward again to whisper of her husband's joy in these talks. She's glad it's something they can share, that we all can share, even if she really isn't sure what all is going on. The sweat is starting out on me, and *I* don't know what all is going on. The milk pricks in my breasts and sweat gathers to trickle down my side, salty and sharp, but without that copper tang that is madness and release.

I knew release, I remember it from when my children were born—first one, then the other—release, and an openness like I'd never known as the bewilderment and panic of labor burst from me and flowed away. The man was on my right hand, the woman on my left hand, and my children, male and female, turned small heads to follow their voices. I was unable to hold them, open to the world as I went down into that twisting dark.

The plump woman turns and strains to reach a dropped pamphlet. She wonders aloud if young people really have respect for the aged anymore. I mutter something affirmative, thinking of my grandmother. When she said grace, our heads were bowed, but she looked upward with eyes open. I wipe my hands with a tissue and remember what my grandmother told me to eat to keep the milk flowing sweet and free for the babies, and how to wrap them warmly, for they came from a warm place. The blood scent is there still, and damn the conference, the lecture, and the people crowding the room and my space. I want to track that scent to its source. It's not my time, and that woman must surely be past it. But as she hands me the pamphlet, she whispers again the hot smell of hunger and distress and comfort.

I can't face that need, that distress and hunger and need for comfort, for contact, binding around me and holding me. There is a moment of silence from the speaker at the lectern. In that quiet comes a rustling from the clothes and bodies of the people around me in the room, like when my grandmother said grace or when I told my family of the children I was carrying. When I look up, I see the change coming in this old woman as she lifts her face to me like a priest lifting the Host. She is old, so old, but her eyes are young as a child's, and there is comfort in the set of her mouth. When she takes my hand, I feel the touch moving in me like the twins turning inside me while I sang hymns in church at harvest. With that, I know who this stranger, this old woman, is for me: she is the Old Woman for me, Fate and Crone and Goddess for me, speaking in the flesh and the touch of hands. I know the comforting that I must begin to give and what she has just said that I did not hear. I twist out of the grasp of those strong, untrembling fingers and watch the white curls turn as I back out of the room, away from the crowded lecture and away from her words and unsettling breath.

At the end of the hall, the young people move away from the phone for me. The coin drops, the dial turns under my hand, and I will soon know if I can be there for my old woman, my grandmother, when she needs me like I needed her at the end of my youth.

PAULA JOHANSON, *author of* No Parent is an Island, *spends winters writing in Victoria and summers working a market garden near Edmonton. She co-edited* Tesseracts 7 *for Tesseract Books. "Blood Turn" won the* Edmonton Journal *literary contest.*

Archaeology

M Y R N A   K O S T A S H

Shard

when we love
god
dreams in us
a certain hunger

Signed g dillon slater, from the Xeroxed and initialed copy of a poem written in 1967 and kept folded around two of Rochelle's poems, written a little earlier. How a poem of George's written in 1967 came into my hands I do not remember. Perhaps in 1969, on Hydra, my hot bare feet slapping on the cool white stone of the floor in George's house, his poems drifting off the table in the breeze from the unshuttered window. But I am making this up.

Excavation One

IN SEPTEMBER 1965, I was alone in Seattle. Alone in the sense that I had not yet met Sharon, Rochelle and George—in that order, and in reverse order I will lose them. I was a student at the University of Washington and everything was about to happen to me.

I was always taking pictures with my little Kodak and conscientiously assembling them in precise chronology in an album. This is how I know that one evening in 1965, dressed in a man's blue cotton shirt and holding a cigarette, my elbow propped on an open textbook, I was lying on the wicker couch in my living room, holding hands with someone outside the frame. Perhaps we were recovering from the All-Cause Protest Folk-Rock Concert of the night before. A yellowed newspaper advertisement inserted into the album exhorts us to bring our own protest sign and, sure enough, there in the little photo, propped in the corner behind the couch, is a bundle of stakes bearing placards, although the only letters I can make out are INSTR. I have no idea what they mean.

Another picture shows my bedroom door which I had transformed into a kind of *iconostasis* hung with the images that meant so much to all of us at the time—the album cover from *Highway 61 Revisited*, a *Vogue* magazine portrait of the Beatles in their mop-top phase, the famous study of Jean-Paul Belmondo with the Gitane in the corner of his mouth, and the front page off the *Edmonton Journal* in November, 1963, "Prime Suspect Held in Kennedy Killing"—although the only one I still have in my possession is *Highway 61 Revisited*, back on the record shelf.

First Artifact

"There's a girl, Sharon Jacobs, in two of my classes who's befriended me. She's about twenty-three, worldly, and very nice to me. Tomorrow I'm going with her to a teach-in at the university." *From a letter to my sister, October 2, 1965, Seattle*

So that's how it began. I had met Sharon.

"If things don't swing too much here, she suggests we go to the Athens Cafe in the evening. Rochelle, her best friend, works there. I think she's a belly dancer."

I thought Rochelle looked like Nefertete, only fatter, and by my standards she had already, at twenty-five, lived a full life, from Brooklyn to Phoenix to San Francisco and Seattle, progressing through marriage, divorce, abortion, and trays of beer and bottles of ouzo near Skid Row.

The three of us spent a lot of time at the Athens Cafe, especially after Sharon had fallen in love with Nick, a lumberjack straight out of the Oregon woods and out of some Peloponnesian village before that. And I had got the hang of the dance and enough wine into my belly to fling myself around in the only abandon I knew, including sex. When I was with Rochelle and Sharon, and especially with Rochelle, I felt always that I had been summoned to an adventure I would never have set off on alone. Rochelle and her buddies would come crashing through my door after the Blue Moon had closed for the night or they'd ring me from the Moon, telling me to get my ass on over there, or Rochelle and Sharon and Nick would come tapping at my door at midnight, saying, "Hey, we're going to Vancouver." And we did go to Vancouver, drunk and stoned and back again, stopping at the border to take our picture just north of the forty-ninth parallel, in UnAmerika.

I know all this because I have the letters I wrote to my sister describing it all. But the letters also forget. From September 1965 to April 1966, when the letters stop, there hasn't been a single reference to George Dillon Slater.

Are there letters missing? How could I leave George out of the story of Sharon and Rochelle and me? It's like one of those Soviet photographs from which Trotsky or Bukharin have disappeared.

How Rochelle met George I remember very vividly, although I don't know now whether the vividness is due so much to recollective clarity or to the embellishment the story has acquired over several tellings. On the other hand, of course I remember: I'm the one telling this.

In a pool hall not far from the Blue Moon one night about eleven o'clock, a big, blond logger attacked a lanky, mustachioed poet with a cue stick to the left eye. Had Rochelle not stopped in a few minutes earlier to buy a pack of cigarettes, George need never have crossed our path. However, bleeding and howling, the poet was transported in Rochelle's Volkswagen to the nearest Emergency ward. She spent days and nights at the hospital and when the poet, George Dillon Slater, was released, patch-eyed, she took him home.

She told me about him before I met him: about his playful fingers and his life in the Merchant Marine (but what about it?) and his poems. I wondered in dismay if she had relinquished her typewriter to him but she had not.

Instead, they wrote poems together. I could see this when I went over to visit them, the two typewriters back to back on the Formica table pulled up alongside their bed-in-the-wall plump with Indian cushions and draped with Indian cottons, the holy of holies, and I imagined them at midday, curtains drawn, sitting naked and cross-legged on this bed, smoking hashish and stroking each other's shoulders and leaning over from time to time to punch something into the typewriter.

Is he a good lover? I asked, for I was young and curious about these things, and she seemed taken aback, eyeing me sideways before she answered. "Of course he is! I'm in love with him!" I imbibed a lesson right there about adult female sexuality, for I had not so long ago still been a virgin and believed that all sex was like mine, self-absorbed. Rochelle was older, and I wondered that under all her vagabond layers there was this woman who liked to be in love, and I longed for her, yes I did.

Second Artifact

Watching you
wend your way
through impossible
days of glaring brightness
and oblivious nights of
furious empty passion
I think about
the time I sat . . .

I don't remember receiving it; perhaps it's one of those poems Rochelle or George would leave on my kitchen table. This one has been written on a corner torn off a larger sheet. Did I save them all?

She was in love with one-eyed George and because she was so was I, for I wanted to see the world of men the way she did, and if she loved this poet with the silky black hairs along his arms, then I adored him, as he sat across from Sharon and me in the pub at the farmers' market, his straw cowboy hat pushed back on his head, rolling a cigarette and telling us stories of . . . ?

There were hours and afternoons and days and nights of George and Rochelle and Sharon and me, but what do I remember? A bright and breezy Saturday afternoon with a spring wind blowing through the screen door while George lies sprawled on my wicker couch and I vacuum the floor under the din of the Paul Butterfield Chicago Blues Band.

Where was everybody else?

Eventually, George made love to me and to Sharon, too.

He began with me at a birthday party where Sharon and Rochelle were lurching across the room in a Greek dance while I banged away on a tambourine and George, squatting against a wall, stared at me one-eyed. Later that night he crawled through my bedroom window. I lay naked under the sheets and told him he had no business here, that he should go home, meaning to Rochelle. But to have his long brown body laid out the length of mine was, as far as I was concerned, part of my ceremonies with Rochelle. He returned to her the next day with half the remorse I felt when I feared she would not see things my way.

He then made forays to Sharon's house. Of all our relations, hers with Rochelle were the oldest, and once when I dropped in on her she was dancing around in her bathroom, slicing a razor in the air around her wrist. "She hates me!" she shrieked. "She's laughing at me!" Then George was back in my bedroom where, after the fourth or fifth time, he began to leave behind little crumpled balls of angry verse.

Third Artifact

black hair stuck
wet to her
neck my lip
twisting quiet

and grinding the

bite goes on

What did we think we were doing? Rochelle visited me alone one after-noon and, declaring she was no longer in love with George, gazed mournful-ly at me and put her arms around me and there we stood, my nose buried in her kinky, dusty hair, a round gold hoop tickling my lip, her sweat and musk and cigarette smoke wafting up my nose, her broad hands pressing against my ribs while she murmured that it was friends who counted, with friends one could talk about a future.

Two weeks later she went to Mexico on a boat with George. Sharon and I got postcards.

He was back in three weeks, she somewhat later. The only thing she had to say about their trip was that it had been crazy. But George, lying on their pillowy bed and pushing back the curtain so he could look at me from his right eye while I peered discreetly into the little bowl of jasmine tea, intimat-ed in his elliptical way—he was the kind of poet who wrote "yr" for "your"—that they had had a nasty quarrel and Rochelle had refused to return with him, saying she wanted to court a fisherman in his stead. I could believe that if I wanted to, Rochelle seemed to say, seated with her back to us at the type-writer, and I did. Why wouldn't it be true?

That was February. Very soon after, Rochelle and George went to New York and in the spring I returned to Canada. Sharon stayed in Seattle. We were never all together again.

Excavation Two

IN THE SUMMER OF 1969, I was in George's house on Hydra. I can prove this with three kinds of evidence: my letters home; letters that followed me to England from Hydra; letters addressed to me in Hydra. All these letter-writers assumed I was there, so I didn't make it up, obviously. Also, of course, I remember being there.

I was in George's house for weeks but I can remember only two little moments of him in action. Like bits of film edited out of the main tape. In one, I am lying in a delirium of fever when George, who has been away sailing for a few days, steps into my room. I recognize his form in the doorway, backlit by the sun. Does he step forward to touch my brow or does he back out, into his garden, away from the heat of my fever? I don't remember.

In the other, I am seated at a taverna table outdoors under a vine, in the company of George and several of his island friends, mainly women. George is seated at my right, at the foot of the table, and so I have a good view of the friend who is seated to his right, the poet Leonard Cohen, who has materialized from a side street after a visit to the barber. His hair is much too short and he talks to George about Scientology. I catch only snatches of this—about "going clear"—because, loath to seem overly impressed by Cohen's presence among us, I have turned my attention to the women.

For the next several years, however, I will periodically ransack the Cohen *oeuvre* in hopes of coming across some confirmation and dilation of this little scene. So far, nothing.

Hydra, August 1969. Nothing happens. Thus I wrote in a letter home. "Nothing happens. Typical day: get up at 10, stroll over to a cafe for a breakfast of Turkish coffee and yogurt, go buy some fruit and walk over to the rocks, lie there all day in the sun, return to town at sundown, have a leisurely supper of stuffed vine leaves, salad and retsina, stroll around some more, go back to George's house and sit on the roof, watching the stars, talking quietly, playing the guitar." So I was not alone. But who was playing the guitar? I do not play the guitar.

Who was on the roof watching the stars? Five months later, a letter follows me to London from Athens. It is from a Harry Louis, a Greek physician. I had been recuperating from my illness on Hydra when he prescribed sea water for my legs and so I was plunged, Harry's hands under my arms, into the sea. He refers to this in his letter but I no longer remember why he would be writing me at all. He mentions, with punctuation, that "Killer of course told us all the news about you and Bar (!) and the party. He turned up here holding a bottle of champagne in each hand!!" Who the hell was Killer? Bar? And what in God's name was the news?

Excavation Three

from a letter from Sharon, April 1972

" . . . ROCHELLE NO LONGER IS FRIENDLY—she simply dropped out again. Last three times I talked to her on the phone, she responded with long silences and her characteristic close, 'Well, guess I'd better hang up now.' Very weird. And who cares, anyway? Oh, I heard through the grapevine (Rochelle, 3 months ago) that George Slater got married in London. Don't know any more about it. She'd better be rich!"

And suddenly they are all back, rounded up in the hand of Sharon, with whom it had all begun in the first place. Sharon, writing frantic and disconsolate letters from various lairs in rainy Seattle, telegraphing the news, corralling Rochelle who had emerged from the photo booth in New York City onto the streets of Seattle and relaying the story of George who had managed—the trickster!—to leave Hydra for a bride in London by way of San Francisco. And how would Rochelle know?

For two years Sharon wrote me letters, outlining all the improvements which she hoped to make in her unsatisfactory life, followed by recriminations of her sloth and reclusiveness. Letters populated thinly by a divorced husband (the logger from the Peloponnesus) and a Spanish-speaking lettuce picker who arrives on the page only to disappear before the sign-off, and otherwise she has the society of ghosts. Ours. Sharon, in a basement room, huddled in rain and "planning" an organic garden, long bike rides, and evening classes in auto mechanics, living on unemployment insurance after having quit a "moronic" office job which she blames herself for finding "draining and tedious." It was, after all, only an office job; how could it have felt so bad? (She was reading Solzhenitsyn.)

She tries to win me back, mentioning articles in *Ms* magazine, films from

Red China and the novels of Margaret Laurence, as though sensing that, were we to meet now, in 1972, for the first time, I would not be her friend. She tries to woo me, too, with nostalgia, for the good old days of 1965 and 1966, clutching my sleeve, as it were, and drawing me, as she had done in those "swinging days," to the Athens Cafe, the Pink Pussycat Disco, the Blue Moon, the parties with "our SDS friends," and tantalizing me with glimpses of Rochelle and George.

George is married. Rochelle has gone to San Francisco to live and cook in a Buddhist monastery where her guru lives. George isn't answering her, Sharon's, letters because he is so damn selfish and, frankly, a true MALE CHAUVINIST PIG, but he couldn't care less, of course.

Sharon travels to Greece and writes me from Athens in November 1973. It is an extraordinary document written from Athens "in a state of siege" during the days of the student occupation of the Polytechnic, "violent clashes between students and workers and the police, tear gas, many wounded, some killed, tanks appear after midnight, guns aimed at the Polytechnic, the U.S. Sixth Fleet presiding over the waters at Piraeus (how embarrassing to be an American in Europe)."

But it is no use. It is years before I will be interested in this story and I have stopped writing to her. She asks, plaintively, for a letter, but I am not to "bother" if I don't want to. She is, after all, depressed, and all she can do is pray that this will pass over. She is losing all her friends. And can only offer me rumors now: Rochelle may be in Lisbon and George has headed for "outside of USA on borrowed money."

Fifth Artifact

from a letter from Rochelle, May 1972, on her way to the Buddhist monastery to cook for her guru

" . . . a poet you are too. So here's a fan letter to beautiful, darkly brooding you, who(m?) I knew for a little while years ago. I guess I saw you through my own suffering, alcohol-veiled eyes and so now it is all different. I go now to work at chipping away some more of my backlog of desires, to meditate and to try to turn inward in my never-ceasing attempt to stop making waves and so end this absurd cycle of birth and death."

After this, Rochelle vanishes in a rumored Lisbon and I am left with the awful perplexity of one who knows she cherished only the figment of her imagination, the divine Rochelle being merely my own creation ("a poet you are too"), her own self being a suffering drunk.

Sharon: "I am unable to imagine myself thinking quickly and clearly or doing anything difficult." This is April 1974. There are no more letters.

George leaves a longer, if intermittent, trail. In 1977, when I am in Toronto having lunch with a magazine editor in a restaurant across the street from a downtown hotel, she catches sight from the window where we are seated of the figure of Leonard Cohen, slipping into the hotel in a long black coat. He looks, the editor says, Hasidic. Later, I leave a note for Cohen at the hotel reception desk, inviting him for a drink and mentioning Hydra and George in 1969.

Sixth Artifact

Thanks for the invitation but off to L.A. George is married and on Hydra.
signed L. Cohen

Seventh Artifact

In 1981, from Nafplion, the Peloponnesus, I send a letter to George Slater, Poste Restante, Hydra. Three months later it is returned, uncalled-for.

Then, in 1987, I visit an English-language bookshop in Athens. I am looking for translations of contemporary Greek poetry and so, crouched in the aisle, I look very carefully through the poetry section right down to the bottom shelf, a scarce inch off the dusty floor. And there, in dark blue and dust, is a volume, published in Athens in 1976, by George Dillon Slater.

I withdraw it gently and buy it and take it with me to my room where I examine it, word for word, forcing myself not to race ahead, prepared to read between the lines, if necessary, for confirmation and elaboration of my memory. Which is to say, of Sharon, Rochelle and me. Nothing. There are two shards of familiarity—a reference to Killer (whoever he was, but there he is again) and a note about how he, the poet, lost his eye at the end of a billiard cue.

But he does not say he lost it in Seattle and he does not mention his rescue in the Volkswagen of a drunken poetess.

One of us is making this up.

MYRNA KOSTASH, *a founding member of The Periodical Writers Association of Canada, also served as president of the Writers Guild of Alberta and as chair of The Writers' Union of Canada. She is the author of several award-winning books of nonfiction, including* Bloodlines: A Journey into Eastern Europe *and* No Kidding: Inside the World of Teenage Girls. *Her most recent book is* The Next Canada.

Love Letter to a Senior Woman Friend

YASMIN LADHA

The "Good-bye, and good luck" that the country girl or the tavern woman or the washerwoman or the mule driver gives, is a farewell forever, a lifelong farewell, a farewell laden with unrecognized sorrow. Their souls and all their five senses go into that "Good-bye, and good luck." –Camilo Jose Cela*

Mrs. Sharma

c-23 Shanti Bhawan

New Delhi

Dear Mrs. Sharma,

The chair feels warm. I finally meet your daughters, Meenu and Neelu, at Shanti Bhawan, before they bring me over here, to the farm. How many times you told me, "Go and see Sunil's farm. Go see my temple there." Every Delhi itinerary of mine included the cheese farm, honest, only I never made it. There wasn't the need to scurry up here. We could make it, together. Sometime soon, we both promised each other.

How is your son?

Sunil is in Italy now. How is he holding up, Mrs. Sharma? I get it, then I don't, that I'll not see you in your motley brown sari early in the mornings, washing the steps.

The moo-moo *of the cows*

The sun is affectionate. My chair, toasty. The moo-moo of the cows passes over my shoulder into fields shimmering like emerald paddy, and the slender cosmos flowers tint the breeze candy-pink. My heart isn't broken. It's gone dry and spacey. This rompy, languorous season hones it fine—that you are gone, forever; that the beacon-red baseball cap on Meenu's head is a tender favor, a kindness come my way. It's also a farewell. I know I won't pass here again.

Ganesh with panache

You will like what Meenu and Neelu are doing at the farm today. They have residenced a brick-red Ganesh among toothy new plants. But he isn't the oldie podgy Ganesh whose trunk sways leniently, comfy as a quilt to his devotees. Parts of this Ganesh have been to Nutri-System. These days in bazaars, the elephant god's rump loose belly and rotund arms are sliced off at fleshy points, so he is ample and lean together. Folksy Ganesh has gone zany hip in the '90s boom-Asia-boom prosperity, where formal Miss Eves, reliant on husbands, sons, and surly rickshaw drivers, are now Ms. Durgas, warrior she-gods astride mopeds, shrewd, and zippy and lean on chancy Indian roads. This boom-Asia-boom prosperity, where a small farmer's bullocks as well as Nokia cellular are essential farm implements, where eating with hands in *haute* joints (taken over by stiff brown *sahibs* and *sahibas*) is chic and sucking loud.

Miss (India) Universe 1995

On our way to the farm, Meenu, Neelu, and I leave her perched on a billboard, pouty and giraffe tall. We also leave behind the blare of earthy, bawdy film songs—wild, heaving superhit thumpers.

> Q: "What's behind the *choli?*" (wickedly cropped, sari-boob
> blouse)
> A: "In my *choli* is my heart." (My foot! Behind her pert *choli*
> are her goblet-sized swillers.)

The Moguls came, then the British, now it's the hefty American *padshahs.* Advertisements of Coca-Cola–Pepsi–Coca-Cola–Pepsi–Coca-Cola–Pepsi persist for eternal stretches on the mantra-land highway, or call it the cantankerous, nutty, and soulful Indian road linker between towns and cities: the Grand-Trunk Road. (Hip to say GT Road.) We leave behind posters of Samsung of Korea, and "Gypsy can Groove on Wrangler" ads, in which a pair of sexy Wranglers gyrate over a rough-&-tumble Indian Jeep called Gypsy. For me, the name doesn't summon a stud in tight (but) scruffy jeans who has jeeped the scorching Thar and polar Alaska, all in one day of course, but a woman swaying around a fire on the cover of a *Mills & Boon* paperback. She wearing thick, gold loops (the kind Punjabi women favor). Her dark, long hair (swaying too) *purdahs* her cheekbone, just so. As a twelve-year-old, I sneaked two things to bed: a *Boon* romance and definitely two bars of Kit-Kat.

Still on GT Road, we leave belching lorries packed to the skies—on their behinds, two humble requests done up in floral: "Use Dipper At Night" and "Please Horn—Okay?" We leave the tiger glamour of five-star ritz. Finally, the Indira Gandhi International Airport. We whoosh past it, make a sharp turn off, and suddenly, we are in dark green glitter. Just lush green for miles, just sharp, wet distance.

On the farm

Here, everything is sweet and edged, like Sunil's cheese, like Delhi's red soil, which my five senses, my hair, want to loll in, smart from. Everything is sweet as unchilled—there isn't the techno, metallic taste of things out of the fridge. And everything is moving on. It's really a farewell, sifting away unblemished—only you don't get it. Like when does India haul OXFAM into the attic? I don't even notice. I don't even know your first name. I never asked. This day is a postcard, it stings.

You will never be at Shanti Bhawan again, Mrs. Sharma.

I don't even know your first name

Some say it's a rabbit pounding rice on the moon. Some say it's mother's brother on the moon. From where you are, do you see the bluish puffy bites inside the moony-moon? As if a snake has bitten that evasive white face. There is the burn of puffy bites on this postcard day, and I am not—what's the silly word? No, I am "dolorous," but why the hell didn't you tell me that Mr. Bhu is not your husband. At the farm, Neelu sets the record straight:

your husband, a pilot, has been dead for years. Mr. Bhu, his younger brother. That your roaring construction enterprises had always been a combo: Mr. Bhu, the engineer; you, the one with gumption. You could get a carpenter even in the middle of a mean monsoon pour. Neelu leaves it at this—these anecdotes with a wondrous smile for her amazing mom. I want to prod: but Mrs. Sharma and Mr. Bhu also shared a bedroom. I crave this grit. This love story. But I can't ask a daughter intimate questions about her dead mother. Mrs. Sharma, you and I shared five years or perhaps, only I shared my life with you.

The first time I come to Shanti Bhawan, I don't heed your explanation—a guest at a licensed bed and breakfast has to be registered at some Indian government bureau—that you need my passport for a single business day. A-ha, a claptrap! (On wintry Sunday afternoons in Calgary, munching on a bowl of Quaker Harvest Crunch cereal, I sat through myriad Indian movies about filched passports. Hoteliers in cahoots with gangs, smooth as balm.) Say, how do you register me that year? Slowly, however, an arm-in-arm relationship ripens between us, doesn't it? A warm feeling like herbs darkening a moist garden patch. Bewitch it all for me again, just once. Like you in a cut-sleeved blouse and muck-dull sari, hosing down the steps of Shanti Bhawan, your braid drenched. And when the sun does a shimmy, glinty stars trail along your braid.

I am hurt by Hindu temples

There are cosmos and purple irises gushing, exploding around the outdoor temple you built on Sunil's farm. The temple, seductively near the bedrooms. You wake up and pad over to prayer. Neelu tells me the temple burnt in your kidneys, your very liver for a long while. And when you let the construction begin, you anguished over every detail like a deranged artist. Who lives in your temple? I hope you made room for Gauri, malleable as tofu. Only pliant Gauri, the rural and tender goddess, can massage gentleness back into Hinduism. But count me out. Just this Sunday, a Hindu mob, not outsiders, but neighbors you send newly made mango pickles to, from whom you borrow a couple of chairs for a birthday party, burn a young Muslim woman's diplomas and certificates. As if a Muslim woman doesn't have enough on her plate already. India is a raging Ayodhya town. Centuries back, Muslims hounded their temples, built mosques over them, and now, saffron-clad Hindus are set to re-historisize newly: they demolish the sixteenth century Babri Masjid in Ayodhya. The season has set. It's Saturday night on the town to bump off Muslims. Suddenly, I find auspicious Hindu colors of saffron and mendicant-ochre repulsive. Has Ganesh, who sits on my study table, begun to grow sly eyes? Is his trunk grinding my hand shut as I write all this?

I would have gone tizzy with throb

Mrs. Sharma, at one time, I would have peeked in your impetuous, madly beautiful temple, plump with purple irises and grass such a slashing green, like razors under my feet. Gone tizzy with throb, I would have washed my hair over and over, worn holy white, jaws soggy from prayer, crazed prayer bouncing, spilling, rotting in my mouth. But now my heart sneers. I reach for my copy of the Koran, purchased from the University of Calgary bookstore awhile back, for a REL 201 "Introduction to World Religions" course. The salient parts I highlighted in yellow, to get me through tests. Now, I even wrap my Koran in a red silk scarf. I've never done this before. Neither do I visit Sunil's cows. I like the heat of this chair, the soxy reek of cheese on my fingers, this basket of tree-warm tangerines.

Tyranny from the death bed

Why did you extract from Sunil a promise that he won't marry his love, even if she gets a divorce? Promise. Promise. Promise. So what else is new at the edge of death? Febrile life, I guess. Though there are no papers between us, crisp with dark signatures, I have declared to my waiting mother, who shields me still, and I am close to forty, that even if she were dying, I wouldn't, wouldn't leave the man I have loved for fourteen years, a married one. There is no place to put the tangerine peel, so I stuff it in my shirt pocket. It's hard to ask Meenu and Neelu personal questions about you and also ask, "Oh, where is the bin?" Why didn't I ask you anything? For fourteen years, I have lived apologetically, outside sanctions, not asking unless confession selects me. With you, I should have. I missed the boat.

Things move on

The dogs have gotten used to me in the half hour I have been here. Though the most fierce one is tied up. Things moves on. These pesky farewells, light and wily, it doesn't dawn on you they are finalities.

The sun is toasty on one side of my neck. I slathered on enough Keri-Daily UVB/A in the shower this morning. Mrs. Sharma, whenever I stayed with you, we split Keri-lotion and socks.

Do you know Neelu prayed to the Saint?

Neelu prays and prays to Sai Baba of Shirddhi, save my mother, save my mother. Sai Baba comes and picks you up. Neelu thinks it is a sign that the holy man has lifted out your disease. Such an unsubtle sign from the Baba of Shirddhi and Neelu takes home hope. Even teases you, "Don't worry, Mummy, upstairs, God will have some construction work for you," damned sure you will make it. I love her then, her blinkers, her punchy hope. After Daddy dies, the first time I place my hand over my mother's nose, she almost chokes in fright. When she discerns it's only my hand, she tucks it in her warm, fighty armpit. I am seven, and since then, never skirmish about hope, fierce hope.

Fierce Tulips

Do you have perfunctory marigolds in your temple? Temples should have fierce red tulips for fierce hope—utterly nirvana-obtuse. Ah, forget it! Today, I don't care to bicker with the gods. Today is a day to love. I should wash my hair, whisper all my love for my mother and my brother into this brightness, keep fast for you, breathing you in, breathing you out, loving the shimmy in your braid. I sit in my warm chair. I hope this is prayer.

Bozo Question

He is an elderly steward. A Jack-of-all-trades, including accounts. Everyone calls him Father, out of respect for his age. Right now, he is planting the toothy plants around the Nutri-System Ganesh. I have never met this elderly caretaker until today. He ignores me. Maybe someone from the family should tell him my letters surrounded you, the last days. Neelu says he has been with the family for ages, always at the farm. The old man's legs are long like poles, and from the back, he looks gangly as a seventeen-year-old with the broadest feet. It's only when he gets up, a crusty thicket of wrinkles patch over each knee. Meenu administers over how he plants the flowers. "You are planting too close," "No that's too far." "This plant is too fragile, Father, the sun will kill it." In India, blue-collar jobs come with backseat drivers. One person to do the job and seven to show how. Only artisans are left alone. You don't screw with their moods or craft, passed down callus to callus, from one generation to another. The most ferocious of the three dogs is tied up. He won't back off from strangers and cobras. Meenu raised him. Meenu has the blackest hair without any split ends. She is testy with chatty questions and long telephone rings. "Do you think she is around?" I ask her. Perhaps it's a bozo question, but I want her to catch the heart of it—to talk fast and fierce about you. But Meenu is direct and very busy. Wafflers grate on her. "Well, we would like to believe it," the end "THE END." What's wrong with heating up the sweetness, that maybe you are with us on this postcard day at the farm? I forget that Meenu and Neelu have lost their mother. They have to endlessly comfort Mr. Bhu, resentful of life, resentful of them. I dearly want to grow closer to the two sisters, the two strangers. I know I won't.

Good-bye Mr. Bhu

Mrs. Sharma, Mr. Bhu doesn't eat. It's Meenu who coaxes and muscles him about and shrieks when he mixes sugar in water to speed up the poison in his bloodstream. At Shanti Bhawan, she takes me to your bedroom before we leave for the farm. Mr. Bhu sleeps on the same side where you passed away. He, you, and I watched television in this very personal chamber. Later, Sunil would pop in from the farm, and I helped him wrap the cheese in the back room. Mr. Bhu's eyes are huge as ever (the only thing unchanged, his Krishna-huge eyes), but he has no body.

> *Once upon a time, there was a large man who didn't talk much but had a surprisingly gigglish laugh and wide Krishna eyes. He and I would walk around the South Ex. market after ten p.m. when the hawkers were packing up their scrawny wares and the night had got into swing for the young in designer jeans swanking in lantern-lit Chinese restaurants. Sometimes, Mr. Bhu and I got out of the way of a bony cow. He was dreamy about you, Mrs. Sharma, even after so many, many years togeth-*

er, as if always, his first time, forever, scooping down to catch your words, putting a cup of tea in your hands, stilling your whirl for a moment. (It didn't click in then that such a sharp love, sweet with shards, should have blunted by now, in the cornflakes and vinegar reality of a husband and wife.)

This man is a bony pillow. He doesn't cry tears but weak water slips out of the corners of his eyes. His mouth, a dark rectangle, opens with "Baa! Baa!" mutter. I watch the dark rectangle close, catching the shards, "She's gone! She's gone!" The plight of a lovesick goner. Will this be my plight, too, if my love dies before me? If my love leaves me?

The next time I see Mr. Bhu, Sunil, Neelu, and I are drinking beer at Shanti Bhawan. I have come to visit Sunil. Meenu is with her family. Mr. Bhu gives us a windish nod, a slur, and wheels himself into the bedroom. Sunil and Neelu's bodies prickle up. He won't let them ride out the mourning. Your children have bodied together, clenching you in each other, one way to fathom without you. Neelu's voice is fatigued. "At least, he can be strong for us." No way. Mr. Bhu has sabotaged himself completely. Done himself in, full gear: no food, no speech, no legs. He won't live on without you.

I gain Sunil. I lose Mr. Bhu

When Sunil returns from Italy, he rings me up for a beer at Shanti Bhawan. I give him a bear hug. A truthful, desperate hug. Sunil and I, involved in wacky, impossible loveships, and one fine day you pop out with, why can't we two get together, and whirl away. Since then, Sunil and I are friendly, but terribly cautious, polite eekers to one another. If we ever end up like two smashed up countries driven to merge, we would certainly die.

I write you ringy on-top-of-the-world letters, always leaving space for him, "Next time Sunil, you and I should have a beer together, shoot the breeze." Today, at Shanti Bhawan, we split a couple of bottles of Kingfisher right from the heart and snack on cubes of his Delhi gruyère in a bowl of dark tomatoes. I gain Sunil. I lose Mr. Bhu.

It wasn't a rented room at Shanti Bhawan

Thank-you for giving me the room with the front porch. Do you remember the arrangement? In the afternoons, the Laundry Babu took over the porch to do the ironing. His wife's bangles tinkled as she separated the clothes. What if you visit me in my room at Shanti Bhawan? It would spook the shit out of me. But then, how does that Mogul courtly verse go?

If someone comes toward you, take a step forward

If that someone leaves, close your eyes and recite a gentle *du'a.*

I will never live at Shanti Bhawan again. That's over

It wasn't a rented room. Every January for five years, I brought Pledge and Pine-Sol from Calgary for rooted smell, familiar clean. I placed Ganesh on top of an empty wood-crafted Saskatoon Berry Chocolate box (a splurge of nine dark *bouchees* of wanton chocolate, each wrapped in palatial purple, from Calgary's jazzy, *nouveau riche* 17th Avenue). Then I wrote.

It doesn't matter that at home I drink juice, gin, whatever, from a jam jar. That I don't change my sweater for a whole dirty week, only wash my hands when I throw garlic and onions into the *dal* pot. But writing away from home demands a cleanliness, imposing habits, so you don't crack up, flying out of the window in uncharted ecstasy or fright.

Love me Tender, Love me True

Mrs. Sharma, the Laundry Babu recognizes me but withholds his razzmatazz. His wife has forgotten me.

During the afternoons, the hot smells of pressed clothes roll out of the porch. The Laundry Babu's museum iron has coals blazing like red sockets—he presses immaculate creases on my pants, immutable as tattoos. His hunch-backed wife's tinkling bangles. Their radio bloody loud, I lift the girlie red phone in my room and holler at you, I can't possibly write! Then the Laundry Babu knocks on my door, *"Bibiji,* your pen is so much powerful than this thing of an iron" and brandishes a bow as if he belongs to His Highness Mogul Akbar's Court. The volume immediately decreases. Only now, I can't write. This time, I open the porch door, "Please *Babuji,* increase the volume, my pen's gone dry." He shakes his head as if to say, "Ah well, if these aren't the ways of the la-di-da uppity," his skinny body sigh-sighing and a trifle mean. His wife's bangles continue to tinkle busily, but her eyes on me are bouncy. Her eyes, lined with rich dark kohl and mirth, especially when the joke is on the monied, the privileged.

My writing canned and feeling flighty as lingerie, I listen to Mohd. Rafi and Lata Mangeshkar crooning on their BPL transistor radio. Sometimes, I lift my girlie phone again, this time to request if you wouldn't mind delaying tea. For I am in the thicket of a syrupy Delhi afternoon, swaying, simpering to, "Beloved, these are my first footsteps in love." I string along Elvis's "Love me tender, love me true." Both songs whiny, so trembly sexy, so full of beans.

Letting go of Shanti Bhawan

You sit on the divan, always. I, on my bed, tell you gibberish and pain—you have an incredible number of chances to let on about Mr. Bhu and you. You don't.

Long distance, Sunil tells me my letters were around you when you were ebbing. I ask him now, here at Shanti Bhawan, and he can't recall exactly. I want details. He asks me, "What kind?" I tell him, "I don't know—you tell me, Sunil." But neither can I remember. Things are growing feeble. Without warning, I can't remember if you parted your hair in the middle or to the side. I clearly see the spiky stars in your braid, but not the parting. Things move on, but what about this goddamned pain?

So much has whisked by in these last ten months. Just ten months since you passed away.

Shanti Bhawan looks like some brigadier general's abode; dogs with shiny coats roam about the rooms. Actually, most of Shanti Bhawan has been converted into a girls hostel. Neelu runs the place. Sunil has been to Italy for more cheese machines and back. Meenu pitches in all her time at the farm, and with Mr. Bhu. The phone rings. A long ring. It's Meenu's daughter to remind her mother to take her to the dentist today. Meenu tells her she will be tied up at the farm. She hasn't an ounce left to give. The courtly Laundry Babu's smile is fatigued—I am with the past. His wife still wears rich dark kohl in her eyes, but they aren't spicy. She stands behind her husband, uncomfortable with an outsider. Neelu, a gentle stranger, continues to write me secretarial letters on behalf of the family. Only the paper is informal: yellow and lined. I am grateful for this lapse. And Mrs. Sharma, I did see a ghost at Shanti Bhawan, I saw Mr. Bhu, living and disappearing, simultaneously. I am writing fast because you are fading, but wait, I want you to know this: that night at Shanti Bhawan, Sunil and I split the beers from our hearts. That night, I hug your son truthfully, desperately. For a sweet, eternal moment, both of us mete out all we have, inside out.

May Allah, Ganesh, the shimmy and stars
dance in your plait, always.

Dearest Mrs. Sharma, all my soul, all my five senses go into this good-bye.
–Yasmin

*Cela, Camilo Jose. *Journey To The Alcarria: Travels Through the Spanish Countryside.* Trans. Frances M. Lopez-Morillas. New York: The Atlantic Monthly Press, 1964. 29.

Yasmin Ladha *is the author of* Lion's Granddaughter and Other Stories; *a chapbook,* Bridal Hands on the Maple; *and a book of prose, poetry, and essays,* Women Dancing on Rooftops: bring your belly close. *Currently, she teaches English at Chonbuk National University, Chonju, South Korea.*

supermom

LEA LITTLEWOLFE

O N THE WAY DOWNTOWN to the courthouse, via city bus, he announces, "By the way, I have custody of my seven-year-old son. Do you still want to marry me?" I'm twenty and I commit easily; I am not turning back now. A month later I am fed up with the bitter conversations between my new husband and his ex-wife regarding the kid. One afternoon, husband in tow, I take delivery of Ben. He is thin and smelly, his skin chapped, and black fissures accent his teeth. His mother has no clothes for Ben except the shorts and holey shirt he wears. The boy has been picking bottles and cans on the street to buy junk food for his stepsister and himself. He comes quietly. In the car he calls me Mom, and I headily scheme his rehabilitation.

A stop at Woolco provides Ben with a wardrobe. In the basement suite, Ben won't eat the beef vegetable soup I cook from scratch. Instead he sulks. I swing him over my knee, smack his bottom once, and am aghast at the tears. He tells me of not being fed by his mother, of being forced to stand in a shower stall in a lightless bathroom, of worry for his sister. Then he eats, without further fuss or trauma. I phone city hall, ask for a social worker, give Ben's full name and birth date. "I'll be there in twenty minutes, want to discuss the boy," she says. For several hours I am briefed on Ben's history. Put into foster care at two years because the parents won't care for him, six foster homes in five years, bed wetting, refusing to talk, stealing and lying, summer visits with birth parents that end in his running away. The province has been planning to put Ben in a psych ward for six months' observation before the next care strategy is mapped out. I tell the social worker I am taking responsibility for Ben. She recommends that I not return to university in September, instead give Ben parenting, let his father support us.

I played God to Ben till he was thirteen, when he went to live with his mother's sister. I ensured a stimulating cultural life, paid the bills, kept his father on track. I was supermom, even gave birth to a daughter after Ben had had four years of my undivided attention.

Second marriage. Twenty years later. Slightly diluted supermom mind. The stepdaughter shows up, drunk, with her four-year-old daughter, Bev. No clothes, no toys, no ID. Still in diapers. The child has been living in the back seat of a car, has seen a baby sister sicken with pneumonia and die, has been sexually molested and assaulted by her mother's lovers.

Bev and I enter a regime of quality care under my roof with protracted "visits" in her mom's care. Regularly I consult with social workers. When she's with me, Bev goes to school and is counseled by a psychologist. Bev is a brilliant kid. She can learn a new song on hearing it just once, excels at math, writes engaging stories well, and reads better than most high school students. Bev is now eleven.

She was in my house for three weeks last month, before her mother tearfully demanded Bev's return. I have been cool and detached, suggested ways that social services could rehabilitate Bev and her mother together, did not intimidate the mother. This week my stepdaughter went drinking. Both the white and native social workers want Bev in my care, with their full blessing. I'm not interested.

Maybe it's the bed wetting; every day Bev's bed has to be stripped and the bedding laundered. Or maybe it's having to remind Bev every half hour to go to the toilet. Otherwise she wets and/or soils her pants. Always there are instructions to use toilet paper and wash carefully. If Bev goes out with friends, inevitably she returns reeking of urine or worse. The cause lies in childhood molestation and recent rape. Counseling helps some, but mostly I have to think out toilet training techniques. For several days Bev wore long-skirted dresses, no panties, so she wouldn't have cloth to soak up urine. It worked. Bev made suggestions too. Always, before Bev is hauled back to her mother, Bev has settled into acceptable toilet behavior. I am weary of the cycle.

Perhaps more annoying is the stealing and lying. Car keys, CDs, clothing, jewelry, cosmetics, trinkets, and money are hoisted by Bev and handed over to other kids to buy their short-lived favor. Having her with us necessitates putting Bev under twenty-four-hours-a-day house arrest—which her grandfather and I must supervise. The R.C.M.P. officer calls Bev a "mixed-up kid" and names a psychiatrist. He decides not to interview her for another offense involving stolen keys.

A year ago I let Bev's mom "kidnap" her back, although I had convinced police and social workers Bev would be in danger with her mom. I finally had let go of the idea that only I could engineer safe environments for Bev. Blame it on hormone change or maybe public education that focuses on wellness as the panacea for societal woes. When I cared for Ben, the community wasn't peering at family dysfunction, jail inmates didn't participate in healing circles, clueless moms and dads weren't attending parenting courses. Nowadays the whole nuclear family works on straightening out its behaviors. Rehab centers, adult education programs, and halfway "safe" houses open to us their supportive arms. We can deal with issues and become psycho babblers with the help of court, church and radio talk show. So, Bev stays with her mom. And I am *not* solving all the problems of the world in one child.

LEA LITTLEWOLFE *has threads in the Cree, Odawa, Abenaki, Scots, Irish, and German cultural worlds. Home is Onion Lake Reserve on the Alberta–Saskatchewan border, though she teaches maths, sciences, and English for Ahtahkakoop Cree Nation. Lea emerged from the closet in 1996.*

Starting Over

JANICE MACDONALD

I AM THIRTY-SEVEN YEARS OLD AND STARTING OVER. This time I have two kids, a mortgage to pay, some ex-in-laws with whom I feel awkward, three gray hairs and a Zellers card. I also have something few eager graduates possess: experience. I have experience in spades, in droves, in bushel baskets stacked in the garage. If I could market all the experience I've stored, my worries would vanish, I could hire a landscaper, go to the hairdresser's, and give to the United Way.

Unfortunately, none of my experience seems of particular fiduciary value. No one pays for the ability to kiss away a sore finger, to hang wallpaper with a minimum of air bubbles, to create Halloween costumes from interesting items found around the house. There is little monetary value placed on the ability to shoulder and carry resentments quietly, or to smile with plastic bonhomie at staff parties twice a year in rooms full of people I have never met. I have kept house, added shaving cream and Y-fronts to the shopping list, wiped noses, and generally shifted various dreams and goals onto the back burner. None of these things can be put on a curriculum vitae. I've been Betty Friedan's secret nightmare, a Phyllis Schlafly dream.

I am scrambling back into the recesses of my mental cupboards, looking for the nuggets of useful knowledge and tools needed to make it in this increasingly competitive world. I continue to kiss sore fingers, I hang pictures over tears in the wallpaper, and I rejoice in the fact that I can ditch the plastic smiles. Most of my bankable experience is rusty, and I fight off feelings of panic by making jokes and drowning the mailbox in a flurry of query letters, applications, and grant proposals. I find myself practicing saying, "Would you like fries with that?"

Every two weeks, I have thirty-six hours to myself. I drive my children off to visit their father and drive away with both aching, empty arms and a sense of relief.

I have not yet managed to meld the sense of there being two different me's sharing the same air space. Every two weeks, I become solitary. I haven't been this way since I was twenty-four, so suddenly I feel twenty-four again. That is, I feel like a twenty-four-year-old with a low-grade flu, slightly slower and more tired than before.

At the same time that I know I should use my free time usefully and get all the things done that are impossible to do while minding and ferrying children from one activity to the next, I long to bask in the glow of limbo, knowing there is nowhere I have to be at any given time. I could browse in boutiques, I could call a friend and set up a coffee date, I could have a long bath, I could curl up under a quilt with a good book, I could split the atom and refine cold fusion.

I do none of these things.

Instead, I pull the doors to their empty bedrooms slightly closed and pad about the house feeling like a pretender or an intruder. I make lists. I fret about money. I drink from the same tea mug for a day and a half, bemusedly watching how the tannin stains its interior.

If I do venture out, I melt into the crowd, wondering if anyone can notice my missing appendages. I move faster, not because I have anywhere to be, just striding because I can without tiring out small legs that normally walk alongside me. If I find myself feeling at ease, I all at once feel guilty. If I come home late to find a good-night message from my girls on the answering machine, I berate myself for not being home to receive their call. I rent movies and wander away from them, returning them rewound and unwatched. I dither.

Conversely, on the other twelve days I find myself stretched and taut. There is not enough time to be a nurturing and inventive entertainer as well as search for work, mow lawns, and shovel sidewalks, on top of the regular loads of laundry and general chores. I snap at behavior that used to amuse me, I cut corners, I long for the magic hour when they are both finally asleep. I then lie awake at night, planning entertaining events and educational excursions that I know I will not follow through on. I buy concealer for the rings under my eyes.

Although the initial euphoria of waking up out of cryonic suspension has been beaten down by monetary worries, there is an underlying contentment to a life that doesn't have to be lived on eggshells. I no longer cringe at the sound of the telephone ringing as supper is ready, with the news that "work" again will keep him late. It is a relief not to have to listen to lies, telegraphed by his inability to look me in the eye as he speaks them. While there may not be much money, I no longer have to tug my imaginary forelock to receive household expenses. It took me several years to wrestle with whether I deserved happiness more than my children deserved a Dick and Jane family setting. The call from the spurned mistress was an ironic bonus.

And it's not all bad, despite the sober condolences from acquaintances who hear the news.

We are redefining ourselves as a family, but we are definitely a family. While we may still be dog-paddling in the wake of the familiar, we do not miss old patterns. And the twenty-four-year-old me, as tired and rusty as she is, is finding herself spurred on by the thirty-seven year old me, because now is no time to dawdle. I am starting over, and this time there are people counting on me. I shove the baskets of experience in the garage to one side to make room for new ones. Or maybe I'll have a garage sale.

JANICE MACDONALD *is a writer of mystery fiction and anything else that pays the bills. This has included songs, radio plays, canoeing manuals, history books, short stories and* The Next Margaret, *the first in her Randy Craig set-in-Alberta mystery series. She lives in Edmonton with her two daughters.*

Me and My Shadow

LORNA MILLARD

I WAS FLYING OUT TO CALGARY to visit my brothers. Nothing extraordinary about that, except until recently I didn't know I *had* brothers. As an adopted only child, I had understood that out there, somewhere, were my biological kin. Now I was about to meet them.

I was always curious about the things I didn't know about myself: what ethnic background I had, who my biological parents were and what their story was, whether there was somebody out there who actually *looked* like me. I am short and small-boned, with dark, curly hair and hazel eyes. Both my adopted parents are tall. Mum's eyes are blue and Dad's, though hazel, look totally different from mine. But my curiosity was stifled by concern for my adoptive parents' feelings—and dread of the unknown.

Mine had been a private adoption, and so Mum had been told things not normally passed on to adoptive families. She knew that my birth mother was one Elizabeth Stuber and that my birth name was Sharon Stuber. In my twenties, I visited the doctor who had arranged for my adoption. The first thing he said was, "You look a lot like Betty. And you have her awful laugh."

Betty. My birth mother had been a real person called Betty. I learned that she was a "free-spirited farm girl" who had come to Vancouver to have me, then returned to the prairies somewhere. The doctor would say no more.

Although I had enough information to search for her on my own, I was not prepared to take that step. But ten years later, when the BC Adoption

Reunion Registry came into existence, I screwed up enough courage to ask them to find her.

It could take up to six months, the adoption reunion counselor said. I read everything I could find, attended an adoption conference, talked with adoptees who had completed searches. I was ready for anything.

Then the counselor called back. "I have an update on your mother," she said, hesitating, "and it's not all good. I'm afraid your birth mother died a few years ago."

I had prepared for every eventuality but this one. My adoptive mother is in her early eighties and still going strong. She has been my model of a mother—indestructible both physically and spiritually. Mothers, in my experience, went on forever.

"How did she die?" I managed to squeeze the words from a throat suddenly constricted. "I'm sorry," she said. "I can't tell you that. It's against the Privacy Act."

"My birth mother died of something before she turned sixty, something that could be genetic, something *I* could be carrying, and you *can't tell me?*" I knew it wasn't her fault, but I could barely choke off the rage that swept in behind the initial shock.

After apologizing again, the counselor said that Betty had three other children, two boys who were my half-brothers, and their adopted sister. As Betty's "next of kin," they could release the information to me—or not. She would contact them for me.

Once off the phone, I cried. Then I kicked something. I tried to comprehend the astonishing discovery that, with Betty's death, I had lost a mother. She was not Mum. She never would be the mother who has seen me through first steps, piano lessons, the death of my first pet, my divorce and remarriage and everything in between. But Betty had still been mother to me in some sense. She was the mystery mother, the absent one whose unknown qualities I had inherited. I did not realize the extent to which I had breathed life into my construct of Betty Stuber until I lost her for this second, and final, time.

There is no blueprint for how a bastard child should grieve the mother she does not remember. My parents didn't want to hear anything beyond the facts—that I had found Betty too late. My husband and good friends comforted me, but even they could not comprehend what I was going through.

Still, there were siblings, and they were curious. The reunion counselor asked me to write a letter of introduction to my brothers. Not allowed yet to know their names, ages, or location, I sat down to write the most important letter of my life.

Soon, I had a newsy reply from Duane, the older brother. And photos. My husband, David, and I poured over the three-by-five snapshots. He thought my youngest brother, especially, had the same nose, chin, and mouth as me. There was one picture of Betty, taken about six months before her death. She was thin, her face deeply lined. David said we had the same bone structure in the face. I couldn't see it. I read the letter aloud. Then I hit the part about how Betty died. She had died of breast cancer. At only fifty-eight.

Having no genetic background information, I had always chosen to assume that I came from imperviously healthy stock. I took comfort in scribbling "N/A" on questions entitled "Family Medical Background." Confronted out of the blue with the threat of a deadly disease, I scuttled off to my doctor. But even her reassurances could not restore my former ignorant optimism.

Two more letters arrived, one from Wade, the youngest, the other from Shelley, my brothers' adopted sister. Shelley had sent an eight-by-ten photo of Betty as a twenty-year-old. This time I saw it: I had Betty's build, Betty's hair. Her cheekbones, her lips, her eyes. Now I knew where these features came from: I saw what Duane and Shelley and Wade must have seen in my photos.

We began to forge a connection. I learned that Shelley was married and lived on a farm. Duane and Wade shared a double-wide trailer they had inherited from Betty. They had always lived near the small town where Betty grew up. Betty herself had only left the area to come to Vancouver and work for a doctor—and have me. Duane, Wade, and Shelley had never known about me until the reunion counselor called them. Now, they were adjusting to the fact that they had an older sister, a stranger-sibling. Duane was displaced as the eldest; Shelley wondered if she had been adopted as the replacement daughter. Wade didn't know what to think.

As for me, the more I learned about them, the more I wondered who I would have been had I been raised as Betty's daughter. My brothers and I clearly had Betty's stamp on our features. And, long-distance, I liked all three of my newfound siblings. We shared a love of animals and the outdoors. They were avid campers and fishers, and I loved hiking and rock climbing. We all liked farm life, though my brothers assured me that twenty-four acres on Vancouver Island wasn't *really* a farm by their standards. But we were so different. Education was one of my life's passions, and I was working on a Master's Degree. None of them could fathom that interest. My career had always been an important aspect of my life. My brothers were unemployed and unconcerned. By tacit agreement, we never spoke of world issues, party or gender politics.

Who was Sharon Stuber? My doppelgänger. The person I would have become had I been raised with my siblings in the small Alberta towns where Grade 12 was a real achievement, especially for a girl, who really didn't need an education to become a farmer's wife. I joked about ending up a farmer's wife anyway in my current incarnation. But David and I are a far cry from the prairie version of farmers. We are rehabilitated yuppies who live in twenty-four acres of bush, blueberries, and garlic with David's family. We help prune bushes and tend chickens, but our off-farm jobs pay the bills. We had nothing in common with my new-found kin, whose lives and livelihoods were bound to section after section of crops and cattle.

My brothers invited us out for a visit. David was tied to work, and while I cherished his support, I knew I was most likely to glimpse Betty and Sharon if I went alone.

During the short plane trip from Vancouver to Calgary, the landscape altered drastically. Vancouver's familiar skyline, tree-clad mountains, and sparkling waters were replaced by gently rolling patchwork fields of green, some already striped with gold ribbons of swathed crops, drying in the sun.

The plane landed. En route to the baggage claim area, I spied a thin, slightly stooped figure eyeing the crowd. Wire-rimmed glasses framed deep-set eyes, a too-long nose and high cheekbones, a baseball cap pulled down over short brown hair. It was Duane.

We made small talk on the hour-long trip north and east to the small town where Wade was waiting for us, at the home they had shared with my birth mother. Finally, we pulled off the highway, took a dusty road past a water tower and grain elevators, and ended up in a quiet, treelined street. Duane turned up one of the driveways. We were home.

My first impression was doilies. Wade met us in an immaculate, wood-paneled living room where a doily rested on every tabletop and a gallery of family pictures hung on the walls. On our tour of their home, I saw no trace of my brothers beyond each of their bedrooms. But I saw Betty everywhere. This was still her house, six years after her death. We went into her bedroom so Duane, the family historian, could show me pictures of my maternal grandparents, uncles, and aunts. The bedroom was exactly as it must have been when Betty lived here. I had the uncanny feeling she had just stepped out and would be returning any minute from a shopping trip or a visit with friends.

In the backyard, lupines were in bloom, and suddenly I wanted to cry. I love lupines. Inhaling the peppery scent of the tall blue flower cones, I tried to conjure the woman who had planted these, tried to see her kneeling in the newly turned earth of her garden, patting new plants into place.

After dinner, I took a short walk. I needed to be alone. The end of their street intersected a ring road that separated the town from surrounding fields. I walked on the edge of a field that stretched endlessly into the distance, where it finally merged with a heat-shimmered sky. It was so different from where I grew up, the Fraser Valley, where all fields ended at the feet of mountains, and the blue, fir-clad mountains were topped by billowing clouds on most days.

How would this enormous sky and the unfenced expanse of green and gold have shaped Sharon Stuber? Would she, like her mother, have been termed a "free-spirited farm girl"? Would she have been taught by her mother to fish and to shoot a rifle, as Duane and Wade had? If her restlessness was anything like mine, I was sure Sharon must have taken up horseback riding. I could see her galloping away over the far-off hills to escape the small-town strictures that, if Sharon was anything like me, would have hemmed her in like a straitjacket.

Betty had been proud that Duane, Shelley, and Wade had attained a high school degree. She had supported Duane in taking a two-year college program. Would she have been as supportive of a daughter who wanted to go to university just to quench a thirst for knowledge? My own parents had supported my going to university—insisted on it, in fact—but even they had balked when I took Honors English just for the love of language. "Why can't you go to BCIT and take journalism? You can make a living from that." What would Betty have said to a pigheaded daughter with her head in the clouds?

Betty's daughter. That jarred me back to reality. Betty's only *acknowledged* daughter was Shelley. Sharon Stuber had existed only three days. On the fourth day, she was issued a birth certificate as Lorna Jean Millard and, with it, a whole new identity. What would Betty have thought if she had still been alive when I traced her? Would she have tried to explain her secret daughter to her other children, to her three remaining sisters? To their children and grandchildren? Or would she have kept the door firmly shut when I came knocking?

Worrying at this mental knot, I went back into the stifling house. Duane tried to call Shelley. No answer. He said she was working late all week. Shelley is an artist who also details vehicles. Right now she was pinstriping and painting logos on a fleet of trucks in another town. But was she really busy, or was it a good excuse to avoid me? I stared hard at Duane, trying to read his face, then gave up.

It was too hot to sleep. The three of us sat up into the night, exchanging stories of our separate childhoods. Duane, who had been quick with witty one liners all day, subsided, and Wade, who had been so very quiet, came alive. He told me about their father, how they lost him to illness years earlier, how Betty had taken over the family store, added an insurance business to it, and kept the family going. Smiling in recollection, Wade told story after story about their tiny, indomitable mother.

Duane pulled out his photo albums. He had captioned most of the pictures. I chuckled at his quirky sense of humor, so close to my own. There was a series of shots showing Wade wrestling with Puggy, the family dog. Duane's captions, told from Puggy's perspective, ended with the victorious canine sleeping on top of the supposedly vanquished Wade. Then we pulled out Betty's albums. She, too, had captioned her pictures. I saw at once that Betty and Duane shared this trait. And I realized, so do I.

"Do you think we look much alike?" I asked.

"You and Wade look most alike," said Duane. "You both take after Mom."

"Actually," Wade said, staring solemnly at me, "you look a lot like Mom. Seeing you is a little like seeing a ghost."

The next day we drove two hours to see Auntie Ida, the aunt who, when she first saw the pictures I sent to my brothers, announced that I looked nothing like her sister and that if Betty hadn't wanted to tell anyone about me, things were better left that way. She was also the aunt closest to my brothers, the one who had mothered them when Betty was gone.

I hung back and let the boys go first. Ida met us in the kitchen, hugging Duane, then Wade. She turned to me, saying, "Well, I guess I'm giving out hugs," and enfolded me in a quick embrace. Then she took a good look at me. One hand clutched mine hard. The other went to her mouth. Her sharp eyes filled with tears. "Oh. You look so much like Betty," she said.

All four of us sat stiffly in the living room, on the good furniture. I was to be treated as a guest. We made small talk about crops. Ida was a widow. Her only son, his wife and two young sons lived next door. Their farm was their livelihood. Crops were important, and this year, with a late season, everyone was anxious.

Finally, Ida offered coffee. With relief, I settled into the kitchen. The boys, who had obviously been hovering, excused themselves and escaped outside to tinker in the bowels of a truck with their cousin Jimmy. It was the chance I was waiting for, and I took it before I lost my nerve.

"Thank-you for giving me a chance to meet you," I said. "I know you weren't too keen on me at first, and I understand that. I know I was a total shock for everyone."

Ida said nothing for a moment, then smiled a tiny smile. "I had no idea what my little sister was up to," she said, her smile widening in recollection. "Betty was tiny but feisty. When she got an idea in her head, that was it. So when she up and moved to Vancouver, saying she got work with a doctor there, none of us blinked. Then, when Duane called and told me about you, well, you could have knocked me over with a feather. I had no idea Paul was that special to Betty."

My heart leaped. "Paul." My birth father had a name. He was real, too.

As we worked side by side preparing dinner, Ida said, "Too bad you didn't start looking for Betty sooner. She would have loved seeing you."

Wow, I thought to myself. I passed the test.

Ida went on. "The boys were devastated by Betty's loss. But Shelley was the real lost soul. She and Betty were more than mother and daughter. They were inseparable friends. Too bad she and Rick couldn't make it for dinner. She called this morning and said she was just too busy."

At that moment, in came my brothers, their cousin, his wife and two sons. Dinner—a huge spread of cold meats, salads, casseroles, and buns, followed by huge "tastes" from homemade peach and apple pies—was delicious, but stuck in my throat. Shelley was not here because of me. She and Betty had been soulmates, I remembered with a pang that felt like jealousy. How could I possibly threaten that? How could I convince her that I was not trying to take her place, but merely trying to find a small space of my own?

After supper, as the light waned, we piled into Jimmy's enormous farm truck and drove to the original Stuber homestead.

It was perched at the top of one of the rolling hills, and the view was sweeping. The old house had been rebuilt into three storage buildings. Jimmy's crop of wheat waved against them.

Even for this part of Alberta, the little farm house felt isolated. I wondered at the ethnic turmoil that had driven a young German couple with three babies to leave Romania, board a ship and follow a land agent to such a foreign and faraway place. I wondered as well at the confidence and adventurousness that might also have pulled them here to build a home and a life in this lonesome spot. A tight sense of family ran strong in their descendants, evident in the ties so visible between Ida and my brothers.

Two days later, we repeated the long, hot, dusty ride in Wade's tiny four-by-four. This time, I met Auntie Olga, her husband, two of her children and their respective families over another table groaning with food. Stuffed with prairie hospitality, I visited with Olga and the rest as they tried to fill me in on the whole Stuber history. It was an enjoyable time, marred only by Shelley's obvious absence.

Back at Betty's house—I couldn't help but think of it as her house, not Wade and Duane's—I tried for the umpteenth time to call Shelley. Once again, I got only an answering machine. The next day was my last full day. Time was running out. I spent the night restlessly composing letters to Shelley in my head.

Next morning, groggy with sleep, I stumbled into the kitchen. Duane looked up with a quick, shy smile. "I finally got Shelley on the phone," he said. "She's coming to dinner tonight."

We spent the day making perogies from Betty's handwritten recipe. We three made an efficient team: I mixed and rolled the dough and cut it, Duane made the filling, both of us stuffed the casings, and Wade carefully boiled the delicate packages.

At 5:00 P.M., Shelley arrived. She towered over the three of us, my sister the blonde Amazon. She was all smiles and hugs, even for me.

After supper, Shelley and I found ourselves alone in the living room. She seemed genuinely happy to see me, but I had to know, so I said, "I was worried you were avoiding me."

She sat thoughtfully for a moment, then said, "When I first heard about you, I wondered, am I the replacement daughter? Why did they adopt me? Mom told me it was because she miscarried after Duane, and the doctors said she couldn't have any more kids. Mom and Dad adopted me, and then Wade was a surprise. But I wondered." She looked at me and smiled. "But honestly, you let your imagination carry you away. I was working on a whole fleet of trucks, every day until two in the morning. Of course I wanted to see you. Couldn't you tell from my letters? Don't be silly."

The crisis was over. We could be friends as well as sisters. As if to seal this pact, Shelley told me a very private story about her last remembrance of our mother.

Betty had spent her final two weeks in the hospital, with Duane, Wade, and Shelley visiting constantly. Shelley said that although she and her mother were very close, they never told each other, "I love you." It was not their way.

The last evening, though, even with her brothers in the room, Shelley made herself say what was so evident. As she left, she kissed Betty and said, "I love you, Mom."

"I love you too, Hon," Betty replied, and those were her last words to her daughter.

Shelley had stayed at the hospital until very late that night. A few hours later, both she and her husband suddenly awakened. They watched as a presence became palpable and, finally, faintly visible in the room. It was not a particular shape, just a lightness, hovering beside Shelley. "But we both knew it was Mom, coming to say good-bye," Shelley said to me, her eyes awash with tears. As the apparition faded, the phone rang—the hospital calling to say that Betty had just passed away.

On the plane again, flying home to my own life, I take stock of the past week. What of me and my shadow? Who am I and who is Sharon Stuber? I have discovered some indelible prints of Betty in me, and where these occur, I intersect with my shadow twin. But glad as I am to visit it, the world that might have belonged to Sharon Stuber is clearly not my world. I loved the endless horizons of the prairie landscape, but for a woman of my temperament, those open spaces would have proven deceptive. Sharon Stuber's life would have been constrained by small-town conservative mores and limited opportunities. I think back to my cousin Jimmy's wife, a university graduate who gave up legal studies to marry her man and become a small-town librarian. I think of Shelley, who says she still flinches when she walks into the male bastion of a trucking fleet to do her job. I can't imagine how I would have turned out under those circumstances. And I am glad I will never have to know.

As the plane tilts down into its final descent into Vancouver, I think eagerly ahead to David, awaiting my arrival and my stories as we head from airport to ferry and our island home. I can now tell him that my prairie bachelor brothers and I share several traits—more than I expected after my initial impression and panicked phone call home on my first night in Three Hills.

"David," I had wailed long distance, "we have nothing in common. This is the meeting of two small-town, redneck, conservative, gun-toting Alberta boys and their leftist, feminist, gun-loathing lotus-land sister. What am I going to *do* with them for a whole week?"

Now, I can tell him that I like standing thigh deep in a muddy river, between my brothers, all of us casting our fishing rods again and again, and quietly storytelling while curious cows gaze at us from a nearby field. That Duane writes children's stories and hilarious doggerel, like the poem about Shelley's bull eating her garden. That Wade actually makes his own cheesecake.

I can tell him that my brothers, my sister, my aunts, and I have begun the process of becoming family. We have staked a claim to a small piece of each other's lives, by spending time together and making some memories. Not all of it has been easy, and from here it will be like any relationship, forever a work in progress. But we are, indeed, some strange but authentic kin.

I can hardly wait to tell him that, like Betty, I'm just a "tiny but feisty, free-spirited farm girl."

For a moment, a lump settles in my throat. With all my heart, I wish that I had had a chance to meet Betty. She is like a fragmented puzzle. Piecing her together creates only a collage of flat photographs, a wraith who dwells in other people's memories. When the people who knew and loved her point out the features, traits, and gestures she gave me, her ghost touches me. But the touch is ephemeral.

In an odd way, though, she did give me a specific gift, an entrée, even though I learned about it late. Shelley told me this, too: when Alberta allowed its adoptees to conduct searches for birth families, Betty told Shelley that she would help her search, if she wanted to. Shelley never wanted to. But perhaps this tacit permission spun itself westward, found Betty's other daughter, and perched on her shoulder until she was strong enough to take up that thread and follow it back to Betty herself. I'd like to think so.

Lorna Millard *shares a garlic and blueberry farm with her husband, David Olsen, and in-laws. When not weeding, Lorna instructs various courses at Malaspina University-College in Nanaimo, British Columbia, and researches and writes about adoption issues. She has two cats and a dog—all adopted.*

Lost Connection

Emma Pivato

IT IS MOTHER'S DAY TODAY and two days since I nursed Alexis, my last child, for the last time. I have had to supplement her constantly and have been nursing only on one side for weeks now. She is three months old. That may not seem like a long time, but when you count up the hours I have sat in the big black chair nursing her (with a bottle warming in the kitchen), it is. So it was sensible to quit. However, when I see her nervous and fussing, arching her neck and turning her head to one side, pushing away the bottle and sticking her fist in her mouth, hoping for the breast, it hurts more than I can say. The tears have been smarting in my eyes at these moments. She is suffering, and she is too little to suffer. She does not even know how or why she is suffering, and therefore there is no possible way she can understand. That is the worst part of all.

And I feel my own loss, too—bitterly. How was it? Why was it so important? The reasons, the deep sense of satisfaction, are already fading from my memory. Perhaps it was a kind of potency. Early on, if I took a shower before it was time to feed her, the milk, stimulated by the hot water, would come dripping out—big white drops splashing on the bottom of the tub and clouding and mingling with the water drops. When I started to nurse her, when she looked at me with that trusting, expectant look, opening her mouth in anticipation, my breast would tingle and harden and pulsate. I could feel the milk come down as she wrapped her little mouth around my breast. Sometimes the milk came so fast (only on the good side) that she had to stop and pull her head away to keep from choking. Then she would search for the breast, head turning, her cheeks seeking contact with the warm, curved flesh. And so we would sit, her drinking and resting alternately until all the pressure was gone and the milk came very slowly. Then I would switch her to the other side, but the let-down in that breast was weak. I thought it was due to the previous removal of several cysts.

All this took about twenty to thirty minutes, and then she still needed the bottle. Yet, whenever she was very tired, clean, fed but still fussing, it only took a minute on the breast for her to fall asleep, her mouth slightly open, still enfolding my breast, milky but relaxed. Such a blissful, sated look, such a sense of "all's right with the world." I don't know how I could have stopped. Even when she pulled so hard that it hurt, I felt pleasure. I guess I thought I was nursing her more for my need than for hers. But now, too late, I realize that was not true. I knew something only a mother in that position can know. She liked to go to sleep "with her nose in the warm," as my mother-in-law described it, because she still needed that feeling of connection with another being. She was too little to be all alone inside her skin.

Now I can hold her and make her giggle and rock her and talk to her and feed her the bottle or her baby food—but that special contact is lost and it will never be there again. She looks a little frightened to be all on her own, cut off. It is too bad you can't breast feed when you feel like it or just a couple of times a day and not otherwise. But it is all or nothing.

POSTSCRIPT: At nine months of age Alexis was diagnosed as severely disabled. I did not know this when I wrote the above. And I did not understand that there was a reason for the trouble I was having nursing her: her lack of oral motor control. But the sadness I felt, the vulnerability I felt in her, were real.

EMMA PIVATO *has spent most of the last two decades using her skills as a psychologist to improve the situation for Alexis and others like her.*

Mother–Love, Mother–Loss

KAY STEWART

O N THE WALL of this Vancouver hospital room hangs Monet's image of contented motherhood: a blue-gowned woman sits on the grassy verge of a path, her dark head bent over her sewing. Behind her a flowering hedge rises protectively. At her feet sits her young daughter, her legs outstretched as dolls sit, her arms curving loosely to hold a small picture book. Between them stands a wooden horse a few inches high—a token, perhaps, of the generating father.

The reality of this hospital room is different: about to give birth to her second child, my daughter-in-law, a dark-haired woman in blue hospital gowns, paces the floor. Wall, window, bed. Wall, window, pause, bed. Watching her, I am reminded of my quest for ever-elusive lime sherbet the night my son, her husband, was born: supermarket to corner store to drugstore, unaware that walking could—and did—bring on labor, three weeks early. But with luck she won't be wheeled into an operating room, unconscious and alone. She will deliver her child in this birthing room, attended by her husband, a nurse midwife, and (how privileged we feel!) my husband and me.

It is healing for me, being part of this birth. Only the first of my three pregnancies ended in childbirth, and by the time it did, I was separated from the father. The second time, a single mother with no prospects of a secure job or a secure relationship, I had an abortion, and, certain I would never be in a position to have more children, a tubal ligation. The third pregnancy, accomplished with the aid of a tubal reversal and fertility pills, aroused tremendous ambivalence in a partner who both yearned for a child of his own flesh and feared the responsibilities of parenthood. I, too, felt ambivalent, unsure that, with my son grown, I wanted to start over as a mother. That pregnancy ended in blood and pain. Diagnosed initially as a miscarriage, it turned out, ten days later, to be a tubal pregnancy, and I was rushed into surgery. Because we did not fully want this child, we locked away our hurt and anger and sorrow. After this brush with death, no more attempts at birth.

But now we sit holding hands, my husband and I, as my son rubs his wife's back, times contractions, encourages, provides a hand to push against. After hours measured in two- and three-minute chunks, it is suddenly too late for the anesthetist, too late for the family practitioner. My husband offers a second hand for holding; I wipe a brow. The nurse midwife gently guides the young intern through the delivery.

Long, dark hair, brick-red head and shoulders, a cry, eraser-pink trunk and legs slipping out, and then they, too, glow like a banked fire. The cord is snipped. Another daughter enters the spiraling dance of mother–love, mother–loss.

Across the city, our first granddaughter, a blonde, blue-eyed four-year-old, plays with friends, is tucked into bed, sleeps. When Caitlin was born, we were hundreds of miles away. Though I felt blessed to be a grandmother, my shift in roles didn't hit me until two months later. That's when the generations converged in Edmonton: my son and his wife (both only children) and their newborn daughter from Vancouver; my daughter-in-law's grandparents from Pennsylvania; my mother, grandmother, and niece from Texas. There's no photograph of all of us together, but there's one of the five generations of my family and one of the five generations of women. It bowled me over then, the idea of generations stretching forward and back; now it haunts me. Janus-like, I am in the middle.

Being present for the birth of Rowan, this berry-red baby, reawakens the pain and guilt and joy of my own childbearing, childrearing. Over the next few days, as I cook and wash dishes, read to Caitlin, and hold the baby, I become a shapeshifter. Some moments I am my mother, self-effacing, needing to be useful and anxious not to intrude. She is in my voice as I apologize for the dryness of the roast, the too-thick crust on the fish pie, as I stand silent while my son chats with neighbors. She is in my bones as, arms akimbo, I watch Caitlin climb up the slide or bend stiffly to don thick socks and thick-soled walking shoes to protect my back.

But when I put Rowan to my shoulder, I am suddenly the twenty-two-year-old sitting in a small first-floor apartment while the hot Texas sun streams through the kitchen windows. Glad of a son, having grown up with four brothers, but otherwise ignorant of this thing called mothering, I read Dr. Spock and dress my son lightly, if at all. It is only now I wonder, as Rowan, well swaddled, snoozes through warm Vancouver days, whether I should have so cavalierly ignored my mother's comments about baby's cold hands and feet. My son hates the Canadian cold—now exchanged, irony of ironies, for the Texas heat I was so eager to escape. And perhaps in this instance I am creating guilt out of false memories, for another image arises of my son snugly cocooned in a white wicker bassinet beside my bed. I'd forgotten the bassinet, borrowed from the friend whose pregnancy prompted my own.

Listening to my daughter-in-law chat with another young mother about painfully engorged breasts, sore nipples, and breast pumps, I am reminded of how much of the bodily experience of mothering I and many women of my generation missed. Having thankfully passed out from self-administered ether not long after going into labor, I awoke some six hours later just as my son emerged. Intent on ending my marriage and finishing my undergraduate degree, I had neither sought nor been given much information about childbirth—no prenatal classes then—and so was totally unprepared to experience either the pain or the joy of giving birth.

Nor was I planning to breast-feed. Two reasons: 1) my mother was not able to, though she tried with the first two of us, and therefore I probably couldn't either; 2) even if I began by breast-feeding, I would have to quit in three months when I started graduate school. Sound convincing?

Pure rationalization. My daughter-in-law cycled home every two hours to breast-feed her first child. She considered breast-feeding important, and so she did it. In the sixties, bottle feeding was the *deus ex machina* that enabled mothers to have careers. And I wanted a career.

But there was more to it than that. What I didn't want was to face the anxieties about my body that breast-feeding would evoke. Some of these anxieties belonged to the social context in which I grew up: women did not nurse in public and even in their own homes were likely to hide breast and baby under a carefully draped blanket. The deeper anxieties were a legacy of my religious upbringing, which made it hard to separate breast-feeding from the "sins of the flesh" for which I felt sure I was going to hell.

So my son was bottle fed and by his teens allergic to a number of foods, especially soya, the main ingredient of infant formula. A consequence of my decision not to breast-feed? Who knows. All of my family, including my undoubtedly breast-fed grandmother, have multiple allergies.

As I compare my experience of childbirth with that of my daughter-in-law, it becomes clear that the most profound change in motherhood over the last thirty years is not the return to midwives and breast-feeding: it is fathers' active participation in child care. Even when I was not a single mother, I assumed that my son was my responsibility, however much "help" I might be obliged to ask for. Even when I was a full-time student or teacher, I carried my parents' division of labor in my head. Aware of the fathering he missed, my son engages fully in his daughters' lives.

Yet being a mother is still not easy for women with careers (it isn't easy for many women, for other reasons). Especially if, like my daughter-in-law and me, they choose to have their children young. When I was in graduate school and beginning to teach, none of my classmates or colleagues were mothers of young children. My daughter-in-law's experience has not been so different. Several of her widely scattered friends have now had children, but her female colleagues are mostly single. For them, the demands of scientific research are too great, and job prospects too uncertain, for marriage and children. So for her as for me, work and home are still split.

For I am again mothering, long after most of my friends and colleagues have seen their children move out or at least into semi-independent adolescence. My niece, now twelve, has lived with us for five years. After trying out "mommy" and "daddy," she calls us by our first names and refers to us as aunt and uncle. She was not quite four when her father, my brother, died; her mother is living but seemingly incapable of mothering. Sometimes as I face another evening's homework, another request to have a friend over, another weekend without the solitude I crave, with classes to prepare and manuscripts to finish, I, too, feel incapable of summoning up whatever patience I once had. Incapable of creating what Jean Shinoda Bolen calls the psychological space in which others may grow. Incapable of mothering.

And so I contemplate Monet's mother figure. Clothed in the blue of the Madonna, removed from the path of life, hedged in by the fecundity which both surrounds and emanates from her, she seems utterly content, utterly fulfilled. The life she represents is not the one I chose, nor my daughter-in-law. Yet so strong is this image of motherhood that women who work outside the home almost inevitably feel guilty.

But work in itself, I am beginning to realize, is not necessarily the problem, nor the solution. For me the problem is learning how to escape the dichotomies—individual/community, autonomy/relationship, self/others. To become a self in relationship. And this problem began long before I became a mother. As I try to understand what it means for me to be a daughter, a mother, a grandmother, I am reminded of the refrain in Liza Potvin's *White Lies,* an incest narrative in the form of journal entries addressed to her mother. "Maman, maman," she asks over and over again, "why hast thou forsaken me." Mother–love, mother–loss.

This feeling of having been abandoned by our mothers—whatever the circumstances, whatever the reality of the situation, whatever the father's role in the family—seems to me fairly common among women. I see it in the women of my family.

I look back through my mother and her mother to my great-grandmother. When I was a child, two of my great-grandmothers were still alive, but not this one. She exists for me only in the tinted portrait that hangs in my grandmother's bedroom and through my grandmother's stories. The portrait shows a beautiful young woman with delicate features in a high-necked dress, golden-brown hair piled on top of her head. She died still a young woman, leaving three children, my grandmother the eldest. A year later their father married again, this time a stern, critical woman who threw chunks of firewood at her stepchildren.

What has been the effect of mother-loss? After mothering her siblings and half-siblings, my grandmother married at sixteen and gave birth a year later by caesarean, her only child by doctor's orders. After a fairly active adult life—with my mother never far away—she has lived with my parents for almost thirty years. Since she was widowed at seventy-four, her life has become more and more constricted (her younger sister, in contrast, was still square-dancing in her eighties and married for the third time). Having spent the first part of her life in service to others, she has come to rely on others to serve her.

And my mother? She spends much of her day seeing to the needs of my grandmother, my father, and a grandson in his twenties, as earlier she provided for six children, of whom I'm the elder daughter. Only now and then there's an hour's reading or gardening, a hint that she once loved swimming, that she was good at working with people. That there was a self that might have flowered.

And me? With four younger children and a house to help care for, I was also mothering when I should have been developing a sense of self. So it was hardly surprising that I should have seen marriage as the only means of becoming independent and motherhood as the next logical step. And as my mother has aged, I've spent most of my family visits trying to make things easier for her and often losing myself in the process.

When I lose myself, I feel abandoned. And that empty space where self should be gets labeled "mother"—the mother we yearn for, the mother we need to mother, the mother we try to be.

What can I give to myself and my niece, what psychological space can I create that will help us both to grow? What can I, as a grandmother, give to my granddaughters?

Under the pressure of mothering in my fifties, I'm gradually learning that if I don't bring a self to my relationships, I, too, end up sucked dry and draining the life from those around me. So in the midst of mothering, I must take care to mother my self: to write, to walk, to garden, to read, to feed my soul.

And one of these days I will have another go at the piano, take up watercolors, traipse the Tuscan hills. Unlike Monet's mother figure, I can get up off the grass, leave the path, and explore the dark, empty, exciting spaces that lie beyond the hedge.

In memoriam
Alta Jones, December 10, 1900 – August 7, 2000
Jeanette Jones Thornton, November 17, 1918 – July 19, 2000

KAY STEWART, *happily retired from her university teaching position, has published short stories, textbooks, and, with Caterina Edwards, a previous collection of Canadian women's essays. She is currently completing a detective novel written with her husband. She hasn't yet made it to Tuscany.*

Reinventing
Places

My Island Home

LAURIE ABEL

"Courage!" he said, and pointed toward the land,
"This mounting wave will roll us shoreward soon."
In the afternoon they came unto a land
In which it seemed always afternoon.
—Tennyson, "The Lotos-Eaters"

"HOW ARE THINGS IN LOTOS LAND?" my father asked, long-distance. It was the first time I had heard Vancouver Island referred to by this name. I had been told that many people leave wide-eyed from Ontario for the Coast, only to return a few months later, disillusioned and empty-pocketed. But I had never heard about the ones who stayed on the Island. I wanted to tell my father about the phosphorescence in the water and how one scoop could shower down stars, but instead I told him about banana slugs. "About six inches long, they wear a skin that looks like army fatigues."

"I've met someone," I told my father a few months later. I'd met someone who was actually from the Island, a rare breed in Victoria. Over the phone I told him about Trevor's arrest at Clayoquot Sound. My father said that there were a lot of tree huggers on the West Coast and it sounded like I'd found one for myself. His voice was soft, like it didn't matter what he told me, I'd go and do whatever it was I had to do. I liked the term "tree hugger"—the image it created of holding onto trees with all the strength of love.

It was Trevor who set me straight the next afternoon. "What did you call me?" he said. I learned, then, that tree hugger was a term of derision. Trevor showed me his video tape of his arrest and over the next few weeks took me to an old growth forest, took me to a clearcut, took me to a small cafe in Port McNeill with posters on the walls in support of the logging industry. Told me how environmentalists and loggers turned against each other while trees were cut and jobs disappeared.

I fell in love.

I didn't talk to my father much over the months that followed. He refused to visit the West Coast. Once in a while he called from Ontario to ask me if I needed any money. Not that he had any to give, but I should let him know if I ran into trouble. "In Ontario they think a lot about money, don't they?" said Trevor. We were busy packing for a trip to Salt Spring Island, but not so busy that I didn't notice the way he said Ontario, like he was talking about the moon.

"My father's funny that way," I said. "He offers and then unoffers money, just in case I might need it."

Trevor shrugged his shoulders. He did not understand our ways.

"Lunch for tomorrow," he said, holding up a large bag of oatmeal. "With apples and raisins."

I didn't usually eat hot oatmeal for lunch, but I liked his enthusiasm. I was packing a couple of bottles of red wine for later that night. For my first meeting with Maiya, another of Trevor's old girl friends.

It is dark when we step into a house that smells of cedar, with a sweeping staircase to the top floor. Maiya greets us with hugs. She has just taken some bread out of the oven. Would we like some? She is beautiful. One arm all silver bracelets from her elbow to her wrist. Brown eyes that settle on nothing. She pours wine, gives us chunks of bread, and sitting cross-legged on the floor, begins to talk about banana trees.

Banana trees grow, shoot out of the ground, grow into a plant that curves and bushes its way to the sky. Lush, lush, lush. One tree grows one big bunch of bananas. Maiya uses her hands to shape the bunch in the air, and I see it heavy and green, the bananas overlapping like petals.

"Have you tasted avocado fresh from the trees?" she asks. And I realize that somewhere we've switched from one fruit to another. Is it the wine or because I am nervous that I can't concentrate? But I like listening to her stories. It's a bit like time-lapse photography. The shoot of the banana tree breaking the ground, then quick, quick unfolding leaves, and then the clump of bananas, already heavy formed fruit, but still green. They cut them down that way. Slashed from the tree with a big banana knife. Heavy.

That's what her conversation is, rich with talk of mangos, avocados, and bananas. And a quiet Ontario voice says very clearly in my head, "You're not actually swallowing this stuff?" Swallowing stories of houses that grow octagonally shaped from the ground. Not grow from the ground. You heard Maiya say seventeen hours a day. She and her partner, Adam, were working seventeen hours a day to build their new house in Australia. Long days because the wood couldn't be exposed to rain. Because if rain got into it, it would ruin and blacken. I picture blond wood, the color of Maiya's hair. The wood blackening like, like Trevor's hair. Soft-falling around his face.

They talk about their plans to meet in Spain. Maiya will be doing some traveling in November and she will try to meet Trevor in Granada. She says, "Gran-ah-dah," and the name lingers in the air. "Aren't there waterfalls?" she asks.

I picture plunging Tarzan falls. Loins wrapped in leopard spots. First Trevor, then Maiya, diving into waterfalls. Hot, hot, hot in Spain. With ferns and parrots and swinging vines.

Where am I? I wonder.

I am sitting on a pillow on a Gulf Island, listening to talk that sounds strangely like a mating ritual. I have had too much wine. I give up trying to follow the conversation. Feel, instead, the velvet patches of the pillow against my cheek. I am half in love with Maiya, seduced by her imagery. What fairy tale am I in? Red Riding Hood. But then, who is the wolf? West Coast trees are bigger than my Ontario trees, but they are still cedar, and that smell, if not the size, is familiar. But still. Be still. They want to be together in Spain. What will be?

They talk about "Remember when" in high school, about being in the band together, and even they sound bored with their talk now that my eyes are closed. They hold each other before saying goodnight, and I hear Trevor murmur, "It's so good to see you, Maiya," in a voice husky with sex.

It's the same voice he uses to rouse me from my pillow, gently calling my name. He tells me that Maiya has been kind enough to give us her bed. I am tired of their kindness to one another, tired of the attraction between Trevor and the other old girl friends: Tanya, Sage, Autumn. Doesn't anyone have a normal name out here? I hear my name shifting and shrinking on my lover's tongue. Trevor says, "Good-night, Susan." I knew a Susan once, but it wasn't me. He apologizes. Says he's tired and that of course he knows my name is Suzanne. I tell him to get some sleep, and then I lie there thinking about sex.

When he is away in Spain for four months will he have sex with other women? Will I have sex with other men? We've talked about it and decided that we should use our own discretion. That neither of us will go out looking for it, but if by chance we are tempted and it were to just happen, there would be no guilt. Although no one plans to be tempted. Or are we really making plans? Really, really leaving the dance card open in case. In case who? Who knows. In case variety. Difference. Tasting someone else's curves. Yes, I suppose I might want to fall to temptation. Whatever that means.

I feel a loss. I feel that practically speaking we've made the right decision. Not to demand, not to police my lover's body. Our decision to use our own discretion is very mature, adult. Very. But what does it mean? That we can't "commit" to one another for four months. Four is a low number, but what if you think of it in days or hours? Hundreds of hours of not being touched, mentally or physically. If we were married, we'd say, "No sex with anyone else," wouldn't we? But marriage is outdated, unnatural.

Trevor and Maiya have sun bathed in the nude many times together. How do I know this? It must have been one of those details of introduction that Trevor gave me about his friendship. It's okay, okay, okay then that Maiya comes into our bedroom the next morning, really her bedroom, and takes her clothes off. Not that I can see her because I am nearsighted and so is Trevor. Both of us can't really see Maiya, long-limbed, choosing from the clothes in her closet. A shift of rose pulled over her hips. Very, very natural. Naturally, we don't do this in Ontario.

Things are different on the Gulf Islands. But on the first morning? After I've only just met Maiya. Why not? Why should she act any differently with me in the room? She acts as if I am not here. But I am. It doesn't last long. Maiya slips into her rose dress and pulls her tights up from ankle to waist. She's heading to the Vancouver Folk Festival. Says that it was nice to meet me and hopes that we enjoy the rest of our stay on the Island.

Yes, it's been a slice of magic realism, I want to say.

"Good-bye, Maiya," I call, naked beside my lover. I know I should add thank-you, but I don't feel like it.

Trevor and I eat hot oatmeal with apples and raisins, lying nude in the sun on Maiya's porch. He tells me he used to sun bathe on this porch with Maiya all the time. He is repeating himself. I wonder how I will tell him that this world he inhabits is too strange for me. I am somewhere in between his world and the one I've left behind, and still changing. The warm air lulls, and I close my eyes against a conversation I know will come before he leaves for Spain.

"How are things in Lotos land?" my father asked. I went outside under the carport and held out the receiver so that he could hear November rain falling on the Island. He asked me if I needed any money, and I said I would be sure to let him know.

LAURIE ABEL *is a short story writer, poet, and teacher living in Victoria, British Columbia. She studied English at McMaster University (B.A. 1985) and Creative Writing at the University of Windsor (M.A. 1994).*

Why I Live Where I Live

SANDRA BIRDSELL

I LIVE IN THE RED RIVER VALLEY. I grew up in a small prairie town, moved on, and lived in several others. You know the type: one grain elevator, railroad tracks, abandoned train station, general store, and a curling rink with eight sheets of artificial ice. The kind of place about which people say that if you blink when you drive by, you'll miss it. Now I live in Winnipeg, and I suppose some may say the same comment applies. But these are just tourists skimming across the valley in their boats or trolling with empty hooks. Valley, they say. Where are the hills?

True, one must travel far to find them—but they're here. Comforting little brown humps on the shoreline. Why do I continue to live here in Winnipeg in the Red River Valley? It's God in a CBC T-shirt, calling to make me think.

I've contemplated moving to Vancouver, where they tell me that the difference between Vancouver and Toronto is that in Toronto people dress up in bizarre costumes and pretend they're crazy, while in Vancouver they really are crazy. I don't mind the crazy people in Vancouver. They're like wildflowers on the side of a mountain, pretty to look at from a distance but never meant to be picked and taken home. But I find when I'm in Vancouver that after three days I no longer see the mountains. All I want to do is find a quiet place, huddle down in the sand, and stare at the ocean. And the same thing happens to me when I'm on the east coast. Why do I live here?

I ask a friend. Grasshoppers and crickets sing from either side of the dirt road. It's not quite a full moon but bright enough for long shadows. Perfect night to play Dracula. It's my turn to wear the cape. The question eats at me, interferes with the game. On the horizon Winnipeg shimmers pink and still. You live here, he says, because you're short. You're close to the ground and if a big wind should come along you'd be safe. And yet you feel tall. Naw, that's not it, my daughter says.

It's Sunday, and the question rankles as I make my weekly trip through the forest where thick dark trees wrestle the granite boulders for soil. I push the speed limit to get to the lake before all the others, and finally I find my spot, huddle down into the sand, and stare out across the water. I think: Why do I live here? The answer comes to me. It's because when I live in the Red River Valley, I'm living at the bottom of a lake.

When you live at the bottom of a lake you get cracks in your basement walls, especially in River Heights, where they can afford cracks and under-pinning and new basements. I like the cracks. The wind whistles through them, loosens the lids on my peach preserves, makes the syrup ferment, and the mice get tipsy. In the potato bin, sprouts grow on wrinkled skin, translucent, cool sprouts. They climb up the basement walls, push their way through air vents and up the windows in my kitchen. I don't have to bother about hanging curtains.

And time is different here. The days piled on top of lake sediments shift after a good storm so that yesterday slips out from beneath today. Or even last Friday with all its voices will bob up from the bottom and it's possible to lose track of tomorrow. You can just say to hell with tomorrow and go out and play Dracula.

When you live here at the bottom of a lake you can't pin your ancestors down with granite monuments. They slide out of their graves. They work themselves across the underground on their backs using their heels as leverage, they inch their way back into town until they rest beneath the network of dusty roads, and they lie there on their backs and read stories to you from old newspapers.

Now, this is something tourists can never discover as they roar across the valley in their powerboats, churning up the water with their blink-and-you'll-miss-it view of my place. Sometimes a brave one will leap from the boat, come down, and move in next door. I've seen it happen. They become weak and listless, like flies trapped inside a house at the end of summer. And you'll see them walking along the highway in scuba gear muttering to themselves or rowing across the lake in search of a hill. I'll admit, sometimes it's nice to surface, to take off the cape and put on my respectable prairie jacket and boots and do a walking tour of Halifax, sniff a wild mountain flower in Vancouver, get a stiff neck looking up at all those skyscrapers in Toronto, or a three-day party headache in Montreal. But inevitably my eyes grow tired, glazed, and like a sleepwalker I awake to find myself crouched down beside an ocean, a lake, a river, and I know it's time to get back there—to get down in the basement and breathe the wind in the cracks of my walls where, nestled up deep against the foundation of my house, is the pelvic bone of an ancestor.

SANDRA BIRDSELL *is the author of two novels and three short story collections, the most recent entitled* The Two-Headed Calf. *She also has published a children's book. Born in Manitoba, she now lives in Regina, Saskatchewan. This piece first appeared in* Writing Home: A PEN Canada Anthology.

Mexican Disturbance

PAULINE CAREY

B ECAUSE THE SUN SHINES. Because there is shocking color everywhere and soft red earth and pale green stones. Because it's an adventure to discover the past. Because it's exciting to learn another language. Because I like the people.

Why Mexico? people ask. I find new reasons all the time.

I first booked a flight to Mexico City because I wanted to explore something new, by myself. What I found, eventually, was myself.

I started off in Mexico City because I love cities. I feel at home in their dirt and confusion, and I welcome the ease of being among crowds of people who take no notice of me, make no demands. I admit that, as a middle-aged woman, I was not as ignored in Mexico City as in North America, but at least I avoided the embarrassment of being the only stranger in town.

When I moved on to Guanajuato, in the northern mountains where the Mexicans began the revolution that was to establish their modern state, I felt more adrift than in the big city. The central plaza is a perfect place for an idle chat, but its very smallness made me feel conspicuous, and in those early days I was reluctant to strike up a conversation with a stranger whose response I was not going to understand. In Mexico City I had talked with cab drivers. Here I talked to shopkeepers and waiters.

In the stores, I practiced my Spanish as I looked for treasure in this silver-mining town. In the restaurants, I carefully explained that I wanted no meat and no fishermen. I hadn't yet sorted out the difference in Spanish between fishermen and fish. The waiters were kind and listened with a straight face.

When not engaged in commercial transactions, I explored the town. Guanajuato is small enough to walk almost anywhere, but, thrown together on mountain slopes, it's a higgledy-piggledy hike. I met more donkeys than cars as I climbed up and down the many steps and the very narrow cobbled streets and laneways. Flowers of magenta, orange, and purple cascaded over the stone walls and reminded me of my grandmother's villa in the south of France, where I spent summers as a child walking in similar streets and climbing up and down between the beach and the villa up in the mountains. It was in Menton that I first learned what happiness the sun can bring.

On Christmas Day in Guanajuato, I took the steps up to the statue of Pipila and sat on a wall overlooking the town. The sun was warm on my skin, and I thought of my grandmother who had died when I was still a child. I had clear memories of her villa with its stone terrace shaded by vine leaves and its view over the town below. I had less clear memories of her. She died during the war, when she was living at home. I thought of my mother living alone in England and me by myself in Toronto. We all had families, grown-up children and even grandchildren, but at the end of our lives, we lived alone. For none of us was this deliberate, but it seemed to suit our natures.

In Guanajuato I went to Christmas concerts of Spanish music that always ended with a rendition of "White Christmas"; I visited the famous mummies, dead people who had never decayed, only shrank; and I found the silent company that I always look for—the artist. The house where Diego Rivera was born is set up as a museum and holds many of his early drawings. Rivera's few lines breathe magic into empty spaces.

People did not talk to me on the street. I put it down to the fact that mountain people are more reserved than those in the city, but later I thought perhaps it was I who was overly shy in a small town.

I never went back to the cool mountains of the north. For my second Mexican outing I turned to the Yucatán, where in the dark jungle I found elegant Mayan ruins, pyramids uncomfortably high and steep, and signs of human sacrifice that made my skin crawl.

I also found intense and comforting heat. In the plaza of Mérida, large trees offered shade from the hot midday sun. Mimes and musicians entertained all over, and in the warm evening, streets were closed off for performances of traditional dance.

Here people touched me and talked to me. A child stroked my bare arm as I talked to his mother. A woman placed her hand on mine as she told me about her grandchildren. A man explained Mayan hieroglyphics to me while adjusting the strap of my sun-top which had fallen off my shoulder. A policewoman, María, sat next to me on a bus ride and gave me a gold ring off her finger.

A pattern began to emerge. Whenever I visited Mexico, no one spoke to me for the first day or two. It was some time before I realized that it was I who was unapproachable. On arrival I was still prickly with Canadian anxieties. When approached by cab drivers at airports, I suspected their motives. When I saw my hotel room, I wondered why on earth I was there. I stayed in cheap hotels where the room was usually sparsely furnished, the toilets didn't work and the water often ran cold. It took me a few visits before I remembered that in my Toronto house the doors didn't close, cracked windows weren't fixed, ants invaded my kitchen and squirrels made hay in the attic.

After two days I would settle down and people would begin to speak to me. I have never been the kind of person to talk first, but after my Spanish had improved a little, I found that I took most people as they seemed to take me—wanting to have a few words, to pass some time, to put a sunny spin on the day if only for a few minutes.

On a warm evening in Mérida, I wandered into the Government Palace and found upstairs a large room full of paintings of Yucatán history and, in one corner, a beat-up grand piano. It was a Blüthner. The keys were yellow, the ebony surface scratched. Seated in front of it was an old man who seemed when he first spoke to me quite crazed. Then he started to play, and I listened to the lovely, real sound of a good piano.

My father played a Blüthner. His friends told me that he could pick up any instrument and play it by ear, but I only remember him playing his Blüthner. He played with exuberance, unlike my mother, who played as if a metronome was ticking in her head. My father laughed as he played.

I talked to the pianist in Mérida about my father, who had died thirty years earlier. I hadn't thought about my father for a long time, and it made me happy to have him re-enter my life in the sunny white city of Mérida. I thought I was returning to Mexico year after year to uncover its past, but now I found I was disturbing my own. In Mexico I found myself tripping over memories of childhood.

Finally, I sat for three months in a Oaxaca apartment and wrote about my father. I had left Toronto on a cold and damp December day, and stepped off the plane in Oaxaca into the warmth of bright sunshine in a clear blue sky. The airport was unexpectedly small, with roses blooming in front of the building and people hanging over the balcony above the entrance to welcome those coming off the plane. I think it was as I looked around at the distant mountains that I began to feel the tears in my throat.

I felt that I belonged in Oaxaca.

I've never lived in a place that tugged at my heartstrings. My family moved constantly when I was a child, and I went to many different schools in many parts of England. I was happiest in Cumberland, in the north, where I liked nothing better than to climb to the top of a mountain and look out over what was below. But Oaxaca nestles in a valley, and I never climbed its mountains.

I have read of people who arrive in a strange place and feel that they have come home, but I don't know what that feeling is. I call Toronto home, but I don't cry when I return to it.

I have heard of people who feel they have been in a place before, in another life, and my head accepts this idea quite readily. Yet this is not how I felt about Oaxaca when I first saw it. I knew I had not been there before. At the time, I accepted the emotion that made me want to weep, and in the Mexican way, I let it lie. Only now, several years later, do I see it as the sadness of some kind of recognition, the appearance of something that was lost from my life.

In Christmas of '91, the city of Oaxaca was a shabby town with paint peeling off the walls, a river that had run dry, and great holes in the sidewalk with no warning barriers to prevent a careless pedestrian from falling several feet underground. The city was built by the Spanish, but Indians have lived around the site for thousands of years, and their presence is everywhere. The city's quiet mystery draws in every visitor who walks its streets.

In Oaxaca, I became a different person.

The change started when an American architect came over to my table in a restaurant and asked what I was eating. She had just sailed across the Atlantic as part of a small crew and had come to Oaxaca to do some painting before heading back home. I loved her immediately, as sometimes happens, and we went to dance concerts and drank chocolate together in the evenings.

I met other travelers on other adventures. I met a Canadian builder who had given up his business to walk from Toronto to Brazil to protest the destruction of the rain forests. I met an American playwright who had just had a play performed in Hungary. When I sat next to a young man at a breakfast counter who spoke English to the cook, I astonished myself by turning to him. "Can we talk?" I said, and we did. For the first time, I spoke first.

I also began to meet the people who were born in Oaxaca. I had a lot of questions, and I needed to know the answers. I wanted to know about the pre-Hispanic clay figures of laughing children in the Rufino Tamayo museum, about the local artist Francesco Toledo, about the seventeenth-century feminist and writer known as Sor Juana Inés de la Cruz who became a nun and was told to give up her books and her music. Deprived of her art, she died two years later.

When I asked questions, people responded. Mexican men talked with me and walked with me. A Mexican woman who had lived in the States explained some of the subtleties of social behavior in Oaxaca. Most of what she said was contradicted by a lively and exciting man who spoke to me about the workers in Oaxaca who couldn't find work and about the children who didn't eat, about the rich North Americans who wanted to haggle over prices in the plaza and about his fears that free trade would send all the money out of the country. He drove me around the city and showed me places that did not turn up in the guidebooks and he made me laugh.

On the first evening we met, he took me to the local basilica and told me a story that I have not forgotten. I heard other versions from other people, but I like his the best.

Many years ago, two donkeys were carrying a beautiful statue of the Virgin. I am not sure whether they were pulling the statue on a cart or carrying it on their backs. Details often elude me when I listen to a rapidly spoken Spanish tale. The donkeys came to a spot where they stopped and refused to go on. Nothing the people could do would make the donkeys take one more step. So the people listened to the animals and in that place built the basilica for the Virgin of Solitude, who is the patron saint of the city of Oaxaca.

Serendipity is a word I have never used. But Mexico opens up new understandings of many things. I was charmed by the discovery that the city which captured my heart is a city whose patron saint is the Virgin of Solitude.

PAULINE CAREY *was born and educated in England, came to Canada in 1957, and grew into an actor, playwright, and fiction writer who lives in Toronto. She is currently working on a novel about an artist in search of her father. The story ends in Mexico.*

Where They Have to Take You In

CATERINA EDWARDS

Everyone has been there, and everyone has
brought back a collection of photographs.
–Henry James on Venice

FOR YEARS I HAD A RECURRING DREAM. I was about to arrive in Venice. I could see the city shimmering before me. I was almost there. But at the moment of arrival, it vanished and I found myself instead on an empty, windswept street. I could never arrive, never return. Sometimes I had made a mistake: taken the wrong direction or miscalculated the distance. But usually there was no reason. At the moment of arrival, the city vanished. And I was suspended in a cycle of longing and loss.

To arrive was to be safe, to reach refuge, to be home.

As James said, everyone has been to Venice. The number of tourists who visit annually is in the millions. On a summer day, they are a horde, a swarm that invades the city, clogging the narrow streets, overloading the *vaporetti*, funneling into St. Mark's Square as if it were a football stadium. Push, push, must be room for one more, though they stand practically shoulder to shoulder. They have come to see the palaces of marble, the streets of water. And too often, they find Venice reduced to a painted backdrop, assembled for their viewing. "Amazing," they say to one another. "But I wouldn't want to live here."

The city becomes a packed raft about to capsize, to sink under the weight of bodies and the volume of human wastes. In the evening, the tourists retreat to the mainland, abandoning their debris: plastic bottles and bags, sandwich wrappers, papers scattered over the ancient stones. At night the cleaners sweep up the mountains of garbage and carry it off in barges. Morning, and again, tour buses pour over the causeway, disgorging French school children, American seniors, German honeymooners, the entire first world, it seems. Most eastern Europeans arrive dazed; they have traveled a day or more on their buses to arrive in this fabled city, this wonder of the world, once beyond their reach. It seems they cannot afford even the coffee and shade of a cafe. But the sights are free, and they are free to gaze upon them and litter.

The last time I visited Venice, we (my husband, two daughters and I) avoided the tourists, renting an apartment in Castello, a working-class neighborhood. The stone stairs to the attic apartment were cracked or tilted alarmingly. The air was heavy with humidity and heat. We sweated at each step. At night, since we didn't have a fan, we closed the shutters, but not the windows. There was a *pizzeria* a few doors down, the equivalent of a neighborhood pub. The patrons' laughter, the buzz of their conversations, the sudden shouts of a fight, crockery smashing, chairs splintering, kept us awake late into the night. At dawn the neighbors began hailing each other in the street, calling from window to window; the woman opposite screeched at her three-year-old son. In Edmonton we were buffered by trees and lawns, protected by space. Here, everything and everyone was closer, louder, brighter.

I was happy, comfortable, connected to the city by history and family. Two elderly aunts, a multitude of first and second cousins lived here: the conductor on the *vaporetto,* the girl behind the bar, the manager of a leather store, the seamstress, the fish farmer, the bank clerk, sprinkled from one end of the lagoon to the other. I knew the city, not as a tourist does, as a series of "sights"; I knew its daily rhythms, its hidden life. In those labyrinthian streets, I was at home.

Yet—I am not Venetian.

Despite the many summers I spent there, despite my affectionate extended family, despite everything I know and feel about the city, I am an outsider. Although my mother has spoken Venetian to me since I was born, when I open my mouth to speak *Venexiane* I expose myself as a foreigner. My words are correct, but my intonation lacks melody. I can hear, but not reproduce, the local rhythm. Likewise, although I look stereotypically Venetian with my red hair, long face, and heavy-lidded eyes, the way I dress and move (hesitantly, unobtrusively) is Canadian.

At home and not at home.

Another year, we rented a *capanna,* a hut on the Lido beach. At first, the Venetian families, who had rented their *capanne* for three generations, ignored us, branding us tourists. But after a visit from a cousin, our position changed. "So you're related to Michele," one mother said, taking us up. The Venetians offered food, advice, and conviviality. They also observed and criticized. We were expected to dress with a certain taste; to perform ritual courtesies, including shaking hands on arrival and departure each day; to eat three course lunches on proper dishes, not sandwiches cupped in napkins; to rest quietly for two hours after lunch: in general, to follow all the unwritten rules. *"Signora,"* a voice would intrude. "Haven't your daughters been in the sea far too long?" Or, "Shouldn't the girls change out of those wet bathing suits?"

At home and not at home.

The Venetian lagoon was first settled in the fifth century by Roman citizens of nearby towns seeking refuge from Attila and his Huns. With each new barbarian invasion, more refugees fled to this delta of three rivers, this swamp of shifting sands. Searching for the safest, most protected spot, the settlers moved from island to island. Heraclea, Mazzorbo, and Torcello took their turns as the major center. In 810, when Pepin and his army invaded the lagoon, the inhabitants retreated to Rivalto, or Rialto, the core of the present city. And for a thousand years, until Napoleon, Venice was unconquerable. A thousand years of a great Republic. The series of sights the tourists come to see exist because the city was never assailed. Venice needed no thick walls, no fortifications; she could flaunt her splendors.

Venice remains a contradiction: a city built on water, stone that floats in air. Ambiguous, Venice has long inspired its visitors to fantasize, rhapsodize, create bloated metaphors. Centuries pass, yet both the Romantic poet and the latest tourist off the *vaporetto* call Venice a ship, a haven, a museum, a backdrop, the bride of the sea. Venice is compared to a seraglio, a freak, a fairy tale, a mausoleum. Since Venice's decline in the eighteenth century, the city has been a symbol of decadence, death, and dissolution. *Dust and ashes, dead and done with,* Napoleon said as he handed the city to the Austrians. *Venice spent what Venice earned.*

It is the strangeness, the sheer otherness, of this slippery city that classifies it as a place of reversals, of transgressions. I played with the notion in my first novel. The wicked carnival city, where nothing and no one is what it seems. But with age and experience I am more skeptical of received ideas and literary conceits. Visiting Venice is such a sensual delight that I wonder if her reputation for wickedness sprang from an Anglo or Nordic puritanism. A place so dedicated to pleasure must be evil.

If Venice is sinking, her doom is recent and comes from ignoring ecological rather than moral truths. Her survival is threatened by a loss of the delicate balance between sea and city, by pollution and tourists, and by her transformation into not the city of the dead, but the city of the near dead, the old. The younger generation is exiled to *terra ferma* or solid land. "Very few of my old classmates live in the city anymore," says Tony, a younger cousin who has managed to stay by buying a tiny wreck of a place and, doing all the work himself, rebuilding from the foundation up. "None of the boys I played basketball with at the parish hall. All gone." They cannot afford the price of apartments in the city, driven up by the international rich, who can pay an exorbitant sum for a second home. Venice has been reduced to a holiday resort, the majority of houses (especially in the better neighborhoods) uninhabited for most of the year.

I bemoan the trend, loudly and sincerely. But if I had the chance—I would buy an apartment in a minute. On the last visit, we contacted a real estate agent and toured various renovated flats. All four of us found ourselves fantasizing yearly visits, then a home. Having breakfast on that terrace, setting a computer up in front of that window. *Isn't that all it takes? Cash? You buy a home, and it is yours.*

You wish. Home is not simply the place where you live. Home is a feeling, a haven, a cage, a heaven, a trap, a direction, an end, and the generator of more metaphors than Venice. If I claim that I am both not at home and at home in Venice, it is longing that keeps the contradictory states from canceling each other out.

On Via Garibaldi, where we went to buy sweet peaches and melons, arugula and tomatoes from an open stall, and yogurt, mineral water, and toilet paper from what was called the supermarket but was not much more than a hole in the wall, goods piled to the ceiling, aisles where you had to turn sideways to pass; on Via Garibaldi, the widest and some said the ugliest street in Venice, though the buildings were deep red, sand, and buff, and geraniums bloomed at the window; on Via Garibaldi, where we sat out in the early evening and sipped aperitifs and watched the parade of young and old; on Via Garibaldi, where each time I passed the last house, the one that faced out to the lagoon, I paused and read the plaque: *In this house lived Giovanni Caboto, explorer and discoverer of Newfoundland;* on Via Garibaldi, almost superstitiously, I paused and felt the glimmer of that other place, where I live and which I should call home.

Edmonton in Venice and Venice in Edmonton: in each place, I feel the presence of the other. Nostalgia is always double, double presence and double absence.

Who belongs? And where?

When I was growing up in Alberta, going to twelve schools in seven years, when I was at university, I felt out of place. I thought I would never belong. Like the dream, I would never arrive. With the years, my attitude has changed, partly because most of the people in my life do not have a specific place they call home. They are hybrids—different in complicated and interesting ways.

My husband grew up in California and though he feels an affection for dry, fierce heat and the fecundity of that inner valley land, he insists he never felt American. Or rather, he never felt *only* American. It is entirely appropriate, he thinks, that he has three nationalities (Italian, American, and Canadian). My adopted sister was born in Yugoslavia, spent her childhood in a refugee camp in Genova, her adolescence in Calgary, her working girl years in New York City, and the last twenty-five years in Puerto Rico, married to an ex-Cuban, who also spent his early years journeying from country to country. These are the lives we lead now—in transit and flux.

Since the beginning, for century after century, Venice was a haven for refugees: Byzantine Greeks, Sephardic Jews, Armenians, Slavs. They were not given citizenship; they had their own neighborhoods and churches or synagogues, but the cultures they brought influenced and altered Venice.

The aesthetic principles seem more eastern than western—gold mosaics and onion domes.

To arrive was to be safe.

In the last few years, new migrants have come looking for refuge. In the Mercerie, between Piazza San Marco and the Rialto, the Somalis and Sengalese alight on vacant squares of pavement and spread out their wares: fake designer bags and sunglasses. The newspaper complains of the Albanians squatting in an empty palace while I notice more beggars planted at the feet of bridges. A gypsy woman stretches her hand out to me. "Need," I think she says. "The war." Others have their cardboard signs: BOSNIAN REFUGEE written in pencil. They look wretched, hungry, desperate. Yet there is a system of refugee aid with offices in the neighborhood police stations, jobs and housing provided by the city council. *Extra communitari,* the Italians call them, those from outside the community, and despite Venice's traditional role, now the citizens debate their responsibility to these outsiders. Many of the Venetians complain: what about us, what about that homeless family camping in the middle of Campo Santa Margherita, what about our sons and daughters who are forced to move away.

Venice for the Venetians.

(France for the French. Germany for the Germans. And so it goes.)

My grandfather, Renato Pagan, was born in a house on the Calle delle Rasse, a narrow street that runs behind St. Mark's Basilica. According to family lore, the Pagans, like the rest of the Venetian upper class, had lost their fortune years before to the gaming tables.

Renato went to sea to win a new fortune or, at least, a more comfortable living. He found land and a wife in Dalmatia, for centuries a part of the Venetian empire. And he prospered, with a pretty house and eight healthy children, he prospered until the first World War. Although Dalmatia was a part of the Austro-Hungarian empire, he could not imagine himself fighting on the side of the Austrians. He was a Venetian and an Italian. Like many men in the towns of Dalmatia, he joined the Italian navy, sailing under the command of Nazario Sauro.

The family and the historical stories divide when explaining how he died. My mother claimed that he drowned in a submarine; one cousin insisted he died of hunger, of want. "That's our history," he says. The history book states that Sauro did command a submarine that ran aground. The patriots were captured by the Austrians and tried for treason. Your ethnic background makes no difference, they were told. You live under our empire. *You owe your allegiance to us.* They were executed.

My grandmother, Caterina Letich (a Croatian), and her children were forced out of their house. Soldiers confiscated their belongings, transported them to Fiume, and loaded them onto cattle cars. (With other wives and other children of Sauro's troops.) *Go back to where you came from.* Although she and all the children were born in VeliLosinj. Still, they were not sorry to be going to Italy. They thought that in Venice, with Grandfather's family, they would be safe. Instead, when the train reached the Italian border, the Italians declared them foreigners. The doors of the cattle cars were closed, and they were shunted from place to place. In the dark, without food and with little water. They were all ill; one aunt, Antonietta, nine years old, died. They were locked in with their body wastes and her corpse. And when finally the doors were opened, when they were let out, my grandmother and her children found themselves in a camp in Sicily, a camp for *enemy aliens.* I know little of their experience there. My Aunt Maricci, who was the oldest, told me that they were given nothing to eat. Since my grandmother spoke Italian with an accent, it was she, Maricci, who had to beg the guards to be allowed to take potato peels from the garbage.

Who belongs? (And where?)

At the end of the war, they were allowed to settle in Venice. Twenty-five years later, my grandmother was dead; the seven siblings had dispersed to jobs in the greater Veneto area. One aunt married a fisherman and lived in Chioggia, a fishing village on the southwest end of the lagoon. By 1944 the Veneto had become one of the focal points of the war. A German soldier warned my aunt, *Take your children to Venice. They'll be safe there.* And she did, leaving just before part of her street was destroyed.

My mother, working for a bakery in Padova, was in a bomb shelter when it was hit. Since she was claustrophobic, she found the crowded shelter almost unbearable. She stayed by the entrance, and her position saved her. In the center, everyone was killed. Body parts, she told me, shattered flesh. Nothing else, she said. My mother moved back to Venice. She knew neither side would ever bomb that city. It meant too much to both sides, beloved as it was of Goethe and Wagner, of Byron and Ruskin. Venice was not touched.

A safe haven.

My father was a royal engineer in the British army. My parents met in Venice when my father's company requisitioned the house where my mother and two aunts were living. (Which is why I am Welsh/English/Italian and Croatian.)

Who belongs? And where?

My sister, the Yugoslavian/Italian/Canadian/Puerto Rican, visited Venice as a child. Thirty years later, arriving again at St. Mark's Square, she burst into tears. "I felt like I had come home," she said, "though it didn't make sense." She reminds me that my longing for the city is commonplace rather than unique. The city is both strange and familiar to all its visitors, for its image is everywhere. As James said, "It is the easiest city to visit without going there." The world claims Venice as its own, and as its home, calling it, in the words of a UNESCO document, "a vital common asset." An international movement argues that the city is too precious for the Italians to continue to mismanage. Venice can be saved, the group argues, only if it does not remain a part of Italy but is made a world city. *It belongs to the world.*

This spring a group calling itself Armata Veneta Serenissima and calling for the separation of the Veneto from Italy unloaded a tank on St. Mark's Square and seized the campanile. In a survey conducted by the city's newspaper, a majority of Venetians named these separatists not terrorists but patriots. *Venice for the Venetians.*

Extra communitaria: one who is outside the community, yet comfortable, at home. When I wrote my first novel, I thought I would be able to exorcise my dream of Venice. But the dream repeats itself. I find myself writing this essay.

Venice again.

In explaining the origin of the name Venezia, Ruskin quotes Sansorvino, who claimed that Venezia came from the Latin *VENIETIAM,* come again, for no matter how often you come, you will always see new things, new beauties.

Return.

CATERINA EDWARDS *is an editor and author. She has published a novel, a book of novellas, a play, and a collection of stories,* Island of the Nightingales.

Discovering the World of Art—Utica 1948

HELEN McLEAN

MOTHER USED TO CALL ME her "little artist." She'd take her women friends out to the pantry to show them the stick figure with a round belly I'd drawn on the underside of the wooden ironing board when I was three. She didn't mention the figure she'd had to scrub off, the one with legs spread and a pile of poop underneath. Now, more than six decades later, the human figure is still my favorite subject, not necessarily singled out for a starring role like the man on the ironing board, but represented as an object among others, part of the composition. A vase of flowers, a window, a chair, a figure—the model often my own daughter, whose features I know by heart, as indeed by now I ought. My upcoming exhibition will be entirely of figures in interiors, even though the gallery owner has muttered uncomfortably that a few of my landscapes might attract the occasional drop-in buyer. These days I paint and exhibit what I choose.

As a child I spent all my spare time drawing and coloring, copying pictures of animals from the *National Geographic,* designing wardrobes for a collection of Jane Arden cutout dolls. I got a set of little tubes of oil paints for my eleventh or twelfth birthday and painted landscapes on tiny canvas boards. At school I made posters and painted scenery for plays, and spent all my spare time in the art room. But when I finished high school and told my parents I wanted to go on to the art college they said no, I was to go to university and study literature and history, things that mattered. I could paint on my own. I'd always have art as a hobby. They didn't want me ending up just another uneducated artist. As far as I knew they weren't acquainted with any artists, educated or otherwise, but I did as they said.

In my final year at college I won a small scholarship to do graduate work in any field I wanted, and saw my chance to study art before I'd have to start supporting myself. I dreamed of Paris or New York, where all the great European artists had flocked after the war, but Paris was out of the question and my parents thought it was too dangerous for a girl to be on her own in a city like New York. One of my professors told me about a school in Utica in upper New York State, a city a mere tenth the size of Toronto, but in those days I thought even the smallest city in the U.S. was more modern and worldly than any Canadian town, and even if Utica was only a few hours' train ride from Toronto, I'd be away and living on my own. It seemed like a wonderful adventure.

I loved Utica from the moment I arrived. The city was set among rolling hills in a landscape very much more beautiful than the flat featureless countryside around Toronto. In the center of town, giant elms arched over a broad main street that was lined with handsome white clapboard houses. I'd arranged to have a room in a YWCA residence, a few minutes walk from the art school, and I could get breakfast and dinner there, too, for a modest weekly rate.

At twenty-one I'd never been away by myself for as much as a single night, and I woke up those first few mornings in Utica with such a stifling sense of apprehension and grief that I actually considered getting on the train and going home before the classes at the art school had even begun. It seems strange today, when young people travel around the globe with such insouciance, to remember how even in that carefully supervised women's residence and in that straight-laced little city, I felt besieged by what seemed like a series of assaults on my naiveté and innocence.

Most of the girls were younger than I, students at a nearby hairdressing school or enrolled in secretarial courses. They talked about nothing but their boyfriends. One of them gave me a sheaf of crude little pornographic stories graphically describing the activities of young couples in the backs of cars and on blankets in the woods, and I read them alone in my room with a flaming face. If I was stunned by what those girls talked about so freely and no doubt actually did, they in turn were in awe of a person who'd graduated from university, and they couldn't understand why I was living in a dump like the Y and still going to some kind of school.

A girl in the room across the hall limped and walked with a cane, and after we got to know each other she stripped to her bra and pants and showed me the pronounced curvature in her spine. She told me she was living on her own because her brother had got her pregnant the year before. The family doctor had performed an abortion, which was still completely illegal, and after that she'd been sent to live away from home. In my psychology courses at university I'd read about incest among depraved mad clans, but I'd never imagined it occurring among people I might ever know. I'd made some sketches of the girl as she sat awkwardly cross-legged on her bed playing a guitar, but after she told me about her past, the drawings were spoiled for me. I associated the word abortion, to say nothing of incest, with criminality and vileness, and I couldn't separate my prejudice even from the drawings.

One Sunday afternoon soon after I arrived I took myself to see the film *Rope,* expecting it to be a western. It turned out to be the grisly true story of the infamous Leopold and Loeb, who murdered a fellow university student as a sort of intellectual exercise. I staggered out of the theater nauseated. The world was much more complex and full of suffering and horror than I'd ever imagined.

Utica had a large population of Italian immigrants. I often went with other students for lunch at one of the cheap Italian bar–restaurants where I ate wonderful things I'd never tasted before—hot-sausage sandwiches or lasagna—and I sometimes joined a group after school for a glass of weak American beer. One of the students, a Utica girl, said her parents wouldn't allow her to go into those bars, which made those outings even more enjoyable. I had coffee a few times with a young Italian man who came to night classes, and after he walked me back to the Y one evening, the housemother, who had seen him in the vestibule, took it upon herself to tell me it wasn't done, mixing with those people. It pleased me that I was free to ignore her advice.

The art classes turned out to be everything I'd hoped for, nothing like what I'd encountered before, where everyone was obliged to undertake the same project and follow instructions. We drew and painted from the model two mornings a week, and the rest of the time developed ideas of our own, getting instruction or criticism only after something was well under way. In the afternoons I took sculpture classes, and worked in clay and wood and even a block of recalcitrant stone. The days came and went, weeks flew by, the seasons changed. I'd never been happier.

The sculpture teacher was a short, cheerful, fair-haired young man only a few years older than I was myself. One day as we were leaving the studio at lunch time, he asked if I'd like to come and share a lettuce-and-tomato salad with him and his wife. When we got to the old house where he lived, he punched the doorbell a couple of times before putting his key in the lock— a code, they told me later, to let Faye know he had someone in tow—and I was surprised that she seemed to be expecting me when she met us at the top of two long flights of stairs. He'd told her about his Canadian student. Faye and Winslow became my closest friends in Utica.

Their apartment consisted of one room with sloping eaves and low windows. There was a studio couch covered with a Mexican blanket that doubled as a sofa, and a basket chair, and a painted wooden table and a few hard chairs, and little else but pieces of Winslow's sculpture, and paintings and drawings on every piece of flat wall. Everything about that couple's life seemed simple and sane—their frugal household, his job that paid little but left him time for his own work, their plans for the future. They were completely optimistic about Winslow's work and believed that critical acclaim and public appreciation were inevitable. That winter he was preparing for his first one-man show in Manhattan, and he'd applied for a scholarship to study in Europe. They planned to have children later, when he was established.

In February they told me they were going to spend a few days in New York

City and said I was welcome to come along if I could find a place to stay. By coincidence my mother had just written that she was making her annual trip to New York, and I invited myself to join her in her hotel room. I went to galleries and she went to shops, and we met in the evening and had dinner together. Winslow called on the last evening to say Faye was visiting relatives in New Jersey, but he was going over to Brooklyn to visit his old mentor, the sculptor William Zorach, whose work could be seen then in several public places in New York. Winslow said if we wanted to come along, he knew Mother and I would be welcome.

I didn't know how my mother would feel about meeting these "arty" people, as she would have thought of them. She seldom strayed from what was safely predictable, and I watched her with interest when we stepped down into a tiny basement restaurant in Brooklyn, which had been an old student hangout of Winslow's, for a bite of dinner before going on to the Zorachs' place. The few tables in the restaurant were filled with groups of young people, many of whom were black. In Toronto in those days, we never would have seen a black man sitting with a white girl or the reverse, and in fact in Toronto, we seldom saw a black person at all. Mother was unusually silent through our dinner of fried chicken and black-eyed peas, and I could see that she was mulling over this phenomenon of mixed races. When black artists like Paul Robeson and Marian Anderson came to perform in Toronto, they stayed in private homes because the hotels wouldn't accommodate them, and everyone said it was terrible, but nobody did anything.

The Zorachs lived in rooms above what had once been a firehall. The enormous garage that had housed the fire engines was the sculpture studio, with the brass pole still running down through it from above, and Winslow said he'd used the pole in the mornings for quick descent when he'd lived there and worked as Zorach's assistant. The apartment looked exotic and sumptuous with its heavy dark furniture and velvet curtains and fringed lamp shades, a tall painted screen, everything foreign and rich and old. Mrs. Zorach served us tiny glasses of purplish wine, and Mother and I sat sipping it, looking around more or less mute, while Winslow and the Zorachs talked about their work and Winslow's upcoming show and mutual friends. They discussed exhibitions and concerts and new plays, this actor, that musician or artist, as though they knew them all well.

I had imagined that there were people like this, who regarded music and painting and theater not just as pleasant adjuncts to their lives but as the essence of them. I felt ignorant and gauche, an outsider in a world I longed to be part of. I didn't condemn my parents for the way they lived, but I felt our values were skewed. It seemed to me, as I sat there listening, that none of us had any idea why my father worked so hard to keep us in our neat little semi-suburban house, trying to look smartly dressed, acquiring up-to-date gadgets and appliances and observing all the little social proprieties. Our goal seemed to be not the nourishment of our inner selves but the approbation of people we thought were a notch above us on the social scale. The Zorachs, and Faye and Winslow, appeared to be fully aware of everything they did and why they were doing it, living according to no criteria but their own.

Back in our hotel room, when we were getting ready for bed, Mother said, "Would you want to live like that?"

"Yes," I said, "I think I would."

She stopped creaming her face and looked at me in the mirror. "In a FIRE HALL?"

Mother's ideal life, I knew, would have been to live in a penthouse on Park Avenue and to dine at chic restaurants where doormen and waiters would know her by name. The trips she made to New York every year were excursions into make-believe in which she did her best to imitate what she considered a New Yorker's blasé manner in shops and restaurants, discussing the menu with the waiter, and over tipping at the end of the meal. The encounter with real urbanity and sophistication in a firehall in Brooklyn had unsettled her.

"Well if I know you," she said later, as she reached over to switch off the lamp between our beds, "you'd find that kind of life would soon wear pretty thin."

Back in Utica I knew for certain she was wrong. I'd discovered a world I wanted to be a part of. As spring came I went for long walks on the weekends in the pale sunshine, intoxicated with the feeling of being wholly awake, my senses sharp, my way forward clear. I finally knew exactly who I was and what

I wanted to do, and although I had no idea of how I might manage to accomplish it, I decided I would spend my life living and working as an artist.

And then my time away was over. In May I reluctantly packed up and went home. My parents looked at the work I brought back with me, but they didn't understand what I'd been trying to do and really preferred the little things I'd done in high school. I was aware they weren't informed critics, weren't knowledgeable about art, but for reasons I couldn't explain to myself, their lack of enthusiasm hurt me and undermined my self-confidence. They were glad my time away had been enjoyable, but took for granted that that phase of my life was over, and my first priority would be to find a job. My parents were comfortable but not wealthy, and both they and I believed their responsibilities had been fulfilled when they'd seen their two children through university. It was their turn for a little ease.

In our narrow social milieu, young unmarried women lived under the parental roof unless there was some good reason for them to do otherwise, and the idea of my moving to a place of my own would have been deeply offensive to my mother and father. In any case I was poorly equipped to earn a living—a pass B.A. and a year at an art school didn't open many doors. I looked for work in window display in the two big department stores and in the art departments of a few advertising agencies, but got turned away because I lacked professional training. I wound up with a job as a poorly paid assistant at the university library, where, because I was an artist, I was given, among other duties, the job of lettering the backs of books with white ink and a tiny brush. My salary wouldn't have been nearly enough to support me even if I had decided to try living on my own, so I stayed on at home, a daughter in the house, helping Mother, going to work, trying to fit in time for my painting.

I hadn't given up on myself as an artist, and I worked at it whenever I could. I filled sketchbooks with drawings. I bought a small fold-up easel to set up in my bedroom, and commandeered an old card table for my paints and brushes. I stretched and sized my canvases in the basement. Then one day I came home to find Mother looking secretive and mischievous. "Go and have a look at your room," she said. I went upstairs. She'd refurbished my bedroom with a new rug and chintz curtains and a matching bedspread. The easel was stowed away in the closet, and the card table was folded up behind the door and my paints put away in their box, so everything would look nice.

"Now where am I supposed to paint?" I wailed, hurting Mother to the quick.

As the year wore on, my time in Utica began to feel like a dream, like one of my mother's excursions into playing at being a New Yorker. I exchanged letters with Faye and Winslow during the summer, but in the fall they went to Paris on a Fulbright scholarship and our correspondence dwindled. All my friends from school and university were getting married or were already married and having babies. I met a man I loved and wanted to marry. He was interested in my painting, but in those days a man's career came first. If we had children, as we hoped to do, I would unquestionably be staying home with them. Perhaps I'd be able to fit in some time at my easel, but since I'd left Utica I'd produced very little work that satisfied me, and I seriously wondered whether my talents were even worth the time I spent trying to develop them. Maybe art was just going to be a hobby after all.

When we told them we were engaged, our families descended on us. My mother-in-law-to-be marched me down to the laundry room in her house to show me the right way, the one and only way, to iron a man's shirt.

"The first thing anyone notices about a man is his shirt collar," she said as she commenced her demonstration, touching the iron with moistened fingertip. "It has to be perfect."

My own mother began buying linens and having them monogrammed. Plans snowballed for a wedding about which I was scarcely consulted. My habit of deferring to my parents took up where it had left off, and I began to give way just as obediently to my in-laws.

The pernicious fifties were upon us. Like other women who grew up during the forties, I had been shown the tantalizing possibilities of a life to which a higher education could give entrée, glimpses of the wider professional world that had been closed to previous generations of women. Now, the day we got married, we found ourselves pressed back into lives as restricted and narrow as our mothers' had been. I was invited to housewarmings in newly done up apartments, to bridal showers, kitchenware parties, baby showers, christenings. Married women with one or more university degrees turned up at hen parties with workbaskets full of their husband's socks to darn or pattern books and wool for baby clothes.

There was something masochistic and neurotic in the prideful way we immersed ourselves in domesticity and servitude, like nuns taking the veil and going into a cloister, as though self-abnegation were in itself praiseworthy. One of my friends set aside her doctoral studies when she married a professor. She became a housewife while he continued to do what she'd wanted to do. Another friend wrote from the western city where she'd moved with her new husband that she was sitting in her tiny apartment dying of loneliness and boredom and depression. She was a trained nurse and the hospitals were crying out for staff, but her husband forbade her to take paying work because it was socially unacceptable for the wives of professional men to have careers outside their homes. Even women with medical degrees quit their practice when they married or were pregnant with the first child, and they never went back to it. Young women of my generation all embarked on the career called "homemaker" no matter what their interests were or their training had been, and the strange thing is that there seemed to be no doubt in anyone's mind but that we were doing what was right, what we'd been born to do, and that the setting aside of our own ambitions and interests was not only inevitable but somehow virtuous.

I was not strong enough, not sure enough of my abilities, too fearful of failing, too much in need of approbation, to try to diverge from the normal and acceptable, and I proceeded to live my life very much the way my mother had led hers. Over the next twenty-odd years I cooked thousands of meals for my family, played hostess to my husband's colleagues, sewed clothes for myself and my children, painted and wallpapered rooms in the houses we lived in, gardened, escorted my children to music lessons they didn't want, and ironed my husband's shirts, perfectly. I did a little painting and drawing after family matters had been attended to, but it wasn't until my children were almost as old as I'd been then that I finally went back in search of the person I'd been that spring in Utica.

HELEN MCLEAN *was born in Toronto in 1927. An artist, writer, art critic, and teacher, she continues to exhibit her paintings across Canada. Recent writing has appeared in the* Globe and Mail *and* Brick. *A memoir,* Sketching From Memory, *was published in 1994, and a novel,* Of All the Summers, *in 1999.*

My Father's Top Hat

BARBARA CURRY MULCAHY

HOW I LOVED MY FATHER'S TOP HAT. It was taut and made a pleasant rich thrum when I tapped it. It was smooth inside and out. The lining was a soft tanned yellow with a green label inside which announced the manufacturer's name in ridiculously undemocratic terms—something like:

George Brown Bros.

Hatters

By Appointment To The Queen

Since 1774

I could place this hat on my head and leave behind my life as a child of American parentage born in Trinidad, raised in India and Greece, and now, because of my father's job, exiled to Fairfax, Virginia. I could place this hat on my head and traitorously enter a world of royalty, subservience, ceremony, and—of course—arsenic and mad hatters. A world so scandalously un-American, so pompous, so impractical and unfair—and yet—so comforting.

When I stroked the hat, it was like petting a dog. The fibers were smooth, so utterly smooth and soft, but if you stroked them backward, they rose like hackles. I could run my finger around the rim and make glossy tracks in the blackness. However, this made me feel guilty, and afterward, I always smoothed down the fibers with the palm of my hand.

The hat had its own box, a big stiff cream-colored box, like a wedding

cake—except that it was oval. The oval lid fit snugly over the box. It was wonderful to tug it open, especially when I was lonely. After we had moved "back"
to the country I had never lived in, after we had moved, as my parents said,
"home," and I could not understand the heavy southern accents of the people speaking "my" language, it was comforting to hold the hat and smooth
the fibers with the palm of my hand, sometimes putting the hat on and letting it slide down over my eyes and settle on the end of my nose. How stiff
it was around my ears. How enclosed in it I felt, the way it must feel when it
was tucked inside its box.

In Virginia, everything was different. No bottle man came to the door to
buy our old bottles and put them in a sack which he carried over his shoulder. In Virginia, we piled our bottles with the garbage at the edge of the lawn.
In the center of the lawn, a crabapple sapling bloomed wisps of flowers. We
drove out of our development, past the cheery "Apple Tree Village" sign, to
go to the liquor store in the city. The taxes on alcohol were lower there,
where, on streets under overhanging boughs, the Negroes lived. My father
emerged from their store, its barred windows behind him. He carried two
paper bags. The store owner followed him. The man was cuffing a boy about
my age. He roared at the child, "Naa, Ah told you to doo thet raaaat naa.
R.A.T.T. N.A.W.: raaaat naa!" My father opened the trunk and laid the bags
inside. We drove away, and my father said to my mother, "Betteh, put this
here change in your puss." My mother was looking at the map. "Betteh," my
father said, "Ah said ta doo thet raaaat naa—R.A.T.T. N.A.W.: raaaat naa!" My
mother said, "S-sh, Jack," but she put the map down and opened her purse.

Everything in Virginia was incomprehensible, and no one except my
father thought it was funny. When my teacher, an Alabaman, drawled out her
gibberish, none of my classmates laughed. Instead, like a school of fish flashing in some new direction, they turned at an instant to start some new activity. When I worked away at the wrong exercise, my teacher singled me out
and, in the most patient manner, repeated her gibberish slowly and carefully,
over and over, while my classmates put down their pencils and stared, and I
smiled and nodded my head.

How I did not like the kindness of my people as they waited for me to "adjust." How I did not like the way my teacher was so good to me, as if I had grown up among heathens and she must be patient. How I raged, finally roaring at her in Greek.

The top hat reminded me of happier times, times with our Greek maid, my co-conspirator. One night, after my parents had gone to a party, our maid awakened me, telling me she had a wonderful surprise. She guided me into her narrow pink room with its unevenly plastered walls splayed with cracks, her room with its bare light bulb and narrow iron bed. She sat me up on her windowsill (oh, that was a wonderful, dangerous place to be perched, her smell like safety all around me, her pungent body odor mixed with the smell of her harsh Greek soap), and here she taught me to jeer and hoot at the teenage couple kissing in our garden. It was fun to make such a racket, and I felt so successful when the couple glared up at us and left, and yet, also so disappointed that they were gone.

My mother said our maid was half-witted. My mother fired our maid for incompetence almost every week. But at the start of the next day, our maid returned and both she and my mother pretended that whatever had happened yesterday had happened in a language neither of them could comprehend.

My mother did not understand Greek, and now, in Virginia, it was no longer necessary for me to translate for her when we went to do errands. No one understood Greek in this world of laundromats and dishwashers. My mother was quite capable here, but I was useless.

On a humid Virginia day, I could go down into our cool basement, open the hatbox, and troll for memories. How I had cut my thigh on my metal doll house, and the wound was not stitched but closed with a metal clamp because the doctor said I might grow up to be a cancan dancer and need perfect legs. And how, when I dressed up in my brother's rough jeans, the clamp pulled out, and the scar that formed on my thigh had saved me from any possibility of a life of enticement.

The hat was too big for me. I had to wear it at an angle if I did not want it to slide down to my nose. With my head tipped back to hold the hat aloft, I could remember the bright sea and the boatyard with the brave fisherman with his missing fingers. How I loved the great boatyard with its smell of caulking tar and salt. How I loved the huge steel plates and the ribs of the ships being welded together, and how I tried not to look, even out of the corner of my eye, at the beautiful flare of the welder's torch. In one corner, the fishermen repaired their small wooden boats. Their nets were hung out to dry and repair, and the smell of seaweed and salt was fresh and strong on the breeze blowing in from the sea. This fisherman, the one with the missing fingers, was friendly, yelling out, "Come over here if you want to see something." The fisherman showed me how he was fixing his boat, but all I could see were his three missing fingers.

In Virginia, there was no one to laugh at my horror of his stubs, no one to laugh at my concern, no one to tell me the story of how each missing finger was lost: this one when he was pulling up the nets, that one—*Tzing!*—in a saw, this one again at sea in the tackle. The brave fisherman laughed when I said I thought he should do a different kind of work.

In Virginia, everything was untouchable, unmentionable. The bread was soft and tasteless. People bought it in plastic bags at the store. They did not carry the towel-covered dough on platters down to the bakery to rise there and then be put, loaf by loaf, on a long-handled wooden paddle and pushed deep into the vault of the oven. There was no fire to see in Virginia, no crust on the bread, no stone oven. Before I ate in the school lunchroom in Virginia, I mashed my sandwiches down to give them substance.

I grew up, but even so, the top hat remained too big for me. It didn't fit anywhere at all. The age into which I had grown outgrew top hats. They were useless. The proletariats had won; grand occasions had lost their grandeur. And, of course, I had grown up. I had, in fact, become a woman. Women don't wear top hats. Unless they are can-can dancers—and I had been saved from that. I grew up, but still I liked to go home to wherever my parents' house was, and I liked to put the top hat on, wear it at a jaunty angle to keep it from falling over my eyes, and, in its loose embrace, be encompassed by what once truly was.

BARBARA CURRY MULCAHY *was born in Trinidad and raised in India, Greece, the United States, and Israel. "My Father's Top Hat" was previously published in the* Foreign Service Journal. *A collection of poems,* The Man with the Dancing Monkey, *was published in 1997.*

Never the Same River

ANN PEARSON

BOVE ENTRAYGUES THE ROAD IS BEING WIDENED, a deep gouge along the side of the hill where trucks and machinery are shifting gravel. If it's changed too much we'll just keep going, I tell myself. There are two or three small towns along the valley, each with its medieval bridge, its church and chateau, its market. I've chosen Entraygues because it lies at a natural crossroads where two river valleys meet, but also because I think it is the town J and I *didn't* stay in twenty-nine years ago. Entraygues, Estaing, Espalion: they have all melded in my head and neither the postcards in the scrapbook nor the descriptions in the guide could help me locate my memories precisely. J might have remembered, but I didn't want to ask him.

The car bumps off the gravel back onto smooth pavement, we round a bend, and Entraygues lies below like an illustration to a fairy story, its houses strung out along the river, the steep, slate-tiled roofs glittering like fish scales in the late afternoon sun. I feel like a magician, producing this vision for Allan. The single-lane stone bridge across the river is the entry to another world. We drive slowly down the main street and back again, checking the hotels. I recognize the farthest as the one that had been too expensive in 1967 and the second as the one where J and I stayed. So it was Entraygues after all, where on market day we'd watched the town crier with his drum informing a crowd of peasant farmers that it was time to pay taxes at the mayor's office and where the local newspaper, a one-sheet spread, announced the presentation of medals to mothers of large families, gold for ten or more children, bronze for four and silver for some intermediate production. It made me angrier than I knew how to explain in those prefeminist days. Was I already on the pill or still fumbling with a diaphragm? Both were then illegal in France.

We settle into a third hotel. Our room has a view over vegetable gardens and rooftops to the steep wooded hills that enclose the valley. Every night the Big Dipper hangs suspended above the roar of the invisible river surging over the weir; in the mornings the valley is filled with mist and the hills vanish until the sun burns through. We set off in a different direction each day, alternating between the river valleys and the high plateau of the southwestern Auvergne with its summer pastures and immense views ringed by the cones of ancient volcanoes.

Surprisingly little of it stirs recollection, though the physical shape of the place hasn't altered substantially in spite of the obvious social changes. Yet only occasionally do I have the sense that I've passed this way before. Nothing in Espalion triggers a memory, nor in St Côme d'Olt, though a postcard of each in the scrapbook proves I was once there. A mental image of waiting for a bus outside a hotel where they charged a supplement for the bath I took seems to be connected with Estaing but doesn't correspond to any of its streets and buildings, and the one hotel is too grand for J and me to have stayed in. I've come back apprehensive of memory and instead I'm confronted with its inadequacy. The past vanishes; days, weeks, months evaporate without trace. The fragments that remain are inconsequential and disappointing. A stretch of road in bright sunlight, the discomfort of blocked sinuses and itchy eyes. It was haymaking season, and my pollen allergy was a torment, forcing us to return to Paris, where in the fug of car exhaust and cigarettes I could finally breathe freely again. Perhaps the antihistamine dopiness contributed to my present lack of recall. But it's the nature of ordinary experience to fade, each holiday eclipsed by the next in the long succession of summers. Now I record obsessively, photographing details, writing up the day's smallest impressions every night before I sleep. I refuse to let time slip away. I want to bite each day to the core.

I find I'm not even sure which year it was that J and I were here or whether we made two separate trips. In 1967 I was still thinking of doing a thesis on the concept of love in the writings of Jean-Paul Sartre. Somewhere on our travels, in a bookstore window I saw a newly published book entitled *Sartre et l'amour* and was crushed because it seemed to make my own project redundant. When I think now how little I understood of Sartre or love at twenty-five, it seems just as well I moved on to something else. One evening coming back along the valley at that hour when the sun has just vanished behind the hills and the approach of night induces a momentary loneliness and longing for home, I am visited by an acute sense of those first years of my life with J when we were still uncomplicatedly happy together and I hadn't yet acknowledged the deep contradictions within me that were to be so destructive to our relationship. I no longer feel the needs that impelled me then, which makes it harder to forgive the imperious emotions of my younger self.

What's most cruel about memory is that while it retains only a faded image of joy or pride or pleasure it seems to preserve feelings of guilt and shame almost intact in their original strength. And it's in that consciousness of responsibility for past acts, omissions, and betrayals that I locate the core of identity, for if it weren't for this sharp remorse, I would feel radically disconnected from the selves of my twenties and thirties. Ghosts in sack dress and teased hair, in mini-skirt and Sassoon cut, in Laura Ashley smock and pageboy—their inner life seems as much a product of the times as their clothing. Is it because they were false selves whose masks and costumes I have shed, or is this just the inevitable detachment from one's younger self that comes with aging? At thirty-three I ripped up a boxful of once cherished school-days memorabilia—school reports, prize certificates, class pictures, poems, diaries—every relic of the convent schoolgirl I had been. But that urge to obliterate a former self isn't the same as this feeling of remoteness from the young woman I once was.

The past is another country, someone wrote. In my case literally. The immigrant's dislocation, even when tempered by regular visits to the old country, exacerbates the sense of amputation from the past. As does the end of a marriage, the breaking of a thousand invisible threads that tie you to another, create a common identity. Like a spider whose web has been torn from its anchorings, I have spun new connections to moor me securely above the void. But the sensation of disconnectedness pervades everything. I feel it in what I have just written. In writing I become another, the observed self and the observer equally distant from the self that reads them. I start out with the aim of transparency, writing through which experience can be seen direct without the distortion of personal style, but the words, the sentence structure, the rhythm of paragraphs seem to be produced by someone else, a somewhat sententious persona who takes over. It/she repels me. We struggle for control. I eliminate stylistic mannerisms, I delete sections top-heavy with analysis, I cut out adjectives. But her imprint is inescapable even in the most stripped down prose I can manage. Verbalization objectifies, solidifies the fluid and elusive into fixed shape, an 'I' not me and yet mine, like all my past selves.

In 1967 J and I were limited to places we could reach by hitchhiking or on the few local bus routes. Now, in the rented car, Allan and I can get to previously inaccessible villages, though we're uneasily aware of the car's threat to the remoteness that has preserved them from development. But our presence is a symptom of the times. We walk through woods of sweet chestnut, the dominant native tree in this region to which it has given its name—La Châtaigneraie. The ground is thick with fallen chestnuts; the prickly outer casings spiny as sea urchins split open to reveal the bright brown nuts. Once the peasants would have gathered them for the soup pot or to fatten the pig, but now, like the apples and plums in the abandoned orchards, they lie untouched and will germinate in the rich litter of the undergrowth till the chestnut forest has entirely reclaimed the hills. Everywhere we walk we see traces of a vanishing world—dry stone walls overgrown with brambles and waist-high bracken where once there were grapevines. The steep hillsides and narrow valleys laboriously cleared and terraced by generations of peasant farmers are no longer worth cultivation in an era when agriculture is practiced on an industrial scale. But the stone walls that mark field boundaries and the foundations of tumbledown barns will persist in the undergrowth for future archaeologists to trace long after folk memory has lost the location of the farms.

On the edge of a clearing, I photograph a rusting piece of machinery through which a young birch sapling has threaded itself. I have no idea what it is or what it was used for, though my grandfather was a farmer, and my father and stepfather grew up on farms. It's the fashion, we've noticed, for renovated farmhouses to have a plough on the front lawn. The lawn itself is a novelty that reveals the presence of outsiders. Real farms have barnyards churned up by tractor wheels and manure heaps where ducks and chickens forage. What do the old-timers make of ploughs transformed into lawn sculpture? Soon the villages will be taken over by newcomers for whom the past is a picturesque weekend decor. Already some of them are transformed into showpieces, gaudy with marigolds, competing for nomination as "village fleuri." They look like film sets where nothing real happens anymore. It disturbs me to think that soon people won't be able to tell the difference, that this artificially constructed version of rural life will become reality.

I would not want to restore the old world with the ignorance and isolation that made the town crier necessary or the society which rewarded with hypocritical official honors a fertility that had not been chosen but endured, like those heartbreakingly numerous "sacrifices for God and the Fatherland" inscribed on every village war memorial. Yet I have to acknowledge that what attracted me to Entraygues then and now is precisely the degree to which it's not yet entirely part of the modern world. I collect its oddities, I'm delighted by its survivals.

The hotelkeeper is one of them. He tells us his history. An illegitimate child, abandoned by his mother and raised by relatives, he was set to work minding the cows at six. School, in his intermittent attendance in the winter months, when he wasn't needed on the farm, was bewildering because he spoke patois. Getting his driver's license was the passport to a larger world. He became a truck driver, met his wife on his regular stopovers in Entraygues and married into the hotel business. When he's not busy with customers in the bar or restaurant, his face in repose has the withdrawn and uncomprehending look of the deprived child. He has little grasp of contemporary Europe, and we suspect he supports the far-right National Front. But he's a kindly man with a childlike pleasure in small things.

The hotelkeeper's childhood must be set against my pleasure in old stones.

Every night after dinner I lie on the bed surrounded by maps writing the day in my journal. Routes and places, picnics, plants, graffiti, encounters, the collie dog who escorts us round the village of Muret-le-Château, the regulations for mole killing on the bulletin board of the mayor's office in Vieillevie, the hole-in-the-floor cafe toilets I still cannot bring myself to use.

If my younger self had kept a journal, would she have noticed and recorded the same things? In the natural world, no doubt, though then it was high summer and haymaking season, and now it's fall, that threshold between the ripeness of late summer and autumn's decay. But she would have written without questioning the nature of the act, without the skepticism that now accompanies every attempt to represent experience. Walking alone one evening on the island in the river, where tall, close-planted poplars rise like the columns and high-branching vault of a gothic cathedral, I'm aware even as it comes to me that the image is a cultural cliché, where once, a fifteen-year-old writing a poem, I thought it my own unique perception. But while I see her through more knowing eyes, I also see myself as she would see me: wandering round this island of poplars—a Romantic space, I tell Allan later with gratitude that he understands the allusion, that we share a set of references—is the unromantic figure of a middle-aged woman in a raincoat and sensible shoes of a kind that younger self would not have been seen dead in. For the first time, it hits me that now the future number of these journeys can be calculated. They are limited in a way that wasn't apparent when the whole world and the time to explore it lay ahead of me. With luck perhaps another twenty summers of travel lie ahead (twenty-five, Allan says optimistically). Will that unimaginable older self feel as disconnected from her middle-aged predecessor, in a world perhaps even more radically transformed?

I press a poplar leaf in my passport. A week later its gold has already turned to sepia. If I try to recall a particular place, I get a visual memory of one of my own photographs. Will the daily accounts I have written come to replace certain details, privileged over the myriad impressions I might have noted, constituting a version of experience that will block spontaneous recall? If I keep no record, this journey will soon be as vague as the one I took with

J so long ago. But to record is to give form to experience and thereby run the risk of deforming it. If there is a way out of this dilemma, I have not found it.

ANN PEARSON *was born in England in 1942, came to Canada in 1966, has taught French and women's literature, worked as a professional gardener, and now teaches in the Arts One programme at the University of British Columbia.*

there's no such thing as repetition

GAIL SCOTT

She's in Paris!

Paris, where writers for generations have gone for nourishment. She sets to work immediately. Walking. Or in her studio, takes down notes, writes down quotes, to pin down how aspects of ideology, attitudes toward language, memory, affect narrations (her project). Also, to soak up ambiance as, earlier in the century, Stein & Hemingway.

She walks down curved white streets with a delicious sense of déjà-vu. Smiling because Gertrude Stein said (writing in the neighborhood) there's no such thing as repetition. "No matter how you say it you say it differently."

Surprised to see so many beggars.

Evicted squatters, from Africa, huddle near a métro.

"I listened to people." (Stein's voice again). "I condensed IT in about three words . . . " (speaking of her portraits).

What about the context? the current writer admonishes. Meaning Paris's contradictory layers: wars, revolutions. But also, art, beauty: extraordinary detail. She surveys the elegantly curved walls of her studio; outside, signs saying *Onglerie, Maître Parfumeur, Fromagerie* (three hundred cheeses, twenty kinds of butter). Feeling slightly guilty.

Still, in bed at night, dreams of autumn light shining on la Seine. So romantic. One's heart skips a beat. Bittersweet. The literature of happy exiles, *poètes maudits,* postcards. Getting up to close the window to keep out the din of traffic.

On the boulevard, two men of North African origin in the bright green overalls of city cleaners vacuum up the dog shit.

"I wasn't situated outside of time, but subject to its laws, like characters in a novel," Marcel Proust complains.

She also wanted to escape.

To read, to write, to dream.

She buys a suit of black.

Reads nineteenth-century novels.

Haunts cafés with names like *La Coupole,* once haunted by "exiled" writers of the thirties (rich Americans). Who enjoyed the way Paris offers space for thinking, the sense of dignity created by the graciousness of buildings, of people in their clothes and perfume, the excellence of food and wine and books.

Strolls on le Pont Neuf.

Standing straighter to avoid a scraggly North American look. Reflecting on why this improves one's sense of self. Which in turn seems to serve clarity of thinking. Smiling wanly at her dream last night that she'd become "The President," she leans over the bridge to take in the sun setting on the iron-and-glass roof of the magnificent Grand Palais at the curve of the river.

A man of African origin, soon to pause there, taking in the view, will be accosted by some cops and asked for his papers. Possessing (she reads later in the paper) only a photocopy, he panics, jumps into the river and drowns.

"If I wanted to make a picture of you as you sit there, I would wait until I got a picture of you as individuals and then I'd change them until I got a picture of you as a whole," Gertrude Stein says louder.

She speeds up various streets in the hallucinating light. Past a fading slogan, *Socialisme = immigration,* from a rightist party of the ruling Balladur coalition. Fights through crowds of tourists. Rushes up rue de Rennes, full of people (many homeless) from every possible nation. Having expected, it's true, a Paris more . . . traditional nineteenth century? More surrealist? More *nouvelle vague* film? More . . . "integrated" culturally?

". . . renaming by the European," injects an African-Canadian voice (M. Nourbese Philip), "was one of the most devastating and successful acts of aggression carried out by one people against another."

The name Anthony Griffin scores across her mind. Black man shot dead in a Montreal parking lot by a policeman. The policeman was twice acquitted of manslaughter by an all-white jury.

Entering cafés, she orders coffee, water, wine.

At night, lies down between intensely patterned sheets under a single shelf of books (only two in English—she's proud of this). The television flickering with some old Canadian documentary called *La vie des esquimaux*. A child in an igloo. Learning how to sew. Looking up wondrously at her mother, also sitting, sewing in a cotton housedress. The whole somehow framed like an ideal family scene from a fifties *Chatelaine* magazine.

She may have something to cover up.

Dresses, paying strict attention to the shine of her shoes.

Gets a better haircut.

Strolls out past shop windows advertising the fashions of the season: designer clothes in uneven burlap (made of silk), safety pins of silver, miming poverty. In another window, two headless male mannequins wearing one-thousand-dollar suits make violent gestures toward each other.

"What I am trying to make you understand is that every contemporary writer has to find out what is the inner-sense of his contemporariness," Stein pipes up again.

But *she* wanted to escape. Maybe be a narrator. Muffled in the white skies, the gray-white streets, time-curved walls, of Paris. Richly treed courtyards. Squares with fountains. Buildings like the exuberant Second Empire Opéra, with its wings, domes, statues, *oeils-de-boeuf,* ceiling illustrated by Chagall. Walking, breathing, tasting: all the senses feasting.

Focused on this completely, she strolls through an art nouveau entrance to *le métro*. Sitting on a bench. *"Vos papiers, s'il vous plaît,"* says a cop to two men of African origin on her left, a veiled woman with a baby on her right. She is asked for nothing (although she lacks a visa).

"Superstition expresses infrastructure," she says (trying to improve).

Misquoting Marx. Who said super*structure* expresses infrastructure. The word "structure" conjuring up the iron-glass-work on roofs of museums, stations, ornate nineteenth-century commercial "passages." Also, blooming like petals over métro entrances. Signs of economic ebullience under thriving capitalism. Which economics, for Marx, sustained individualist ideology.

She scurries through the traffic. Wondering if the African family in the art deco flat above her also gets harassed. Entering le Palais Royal, where Colette used to live. Silent, delicious, like so many Paris gardens hidden from the street. Trees in rows, squares of flowers, arcades that served to shelter aristocratic children, then commerce, gamblers, hookers, before becoming genteel again. She turns toward a café on the left with curtained windows, with pastries only the French can make. A young man stepping from behind a column asks for a handout. His pale eyes bright with hunger. She looks around, then grumpily refuses, afraid he'll grab her change purse if she takes it out. Noting he is neater than she; also, she believes he is sincere.

Walking home she leans over le Pont des Arts and looks into la Seine.

It blinks back at her ironically.

Proust resentfully attributed to his father the notion that he was subject to time's laws (consciousness).

She buys Wittgenstein's conversations (to think of something else; he makes her think of consciousness).

Strolls up St. Michel, watching her reflection in shop windows.

Past a snowy ad for Canada (irked at the repetitive images of snow, toques, "funny accents" in Paris, referring to back home).

Feeling morally superior, the way tourists do when they detect faults in their host.

Heads toward the domed, columned Panthéon, dedicated *Aux Grands Hommes.* Eye taking in shoe styles, pheasants (complete with feathers) in a butcher's, cheeses wafting all their myriad smells through a transom window. Past a baker (remembering not to nasalize *à la québécoise* when she says *pain,* bread). Past the iron fence of Le Panthéon where France's great men are buried. Where feminists annually put flowers, a reminder there were women, too, in the French revolutions. It's October 26. On a terrasse next to l'Hotel des Grands Hommes, where the surrealist movement started, she opens up her paper. It says

A rightist party (anti-immigration) has swept the Canadian west.

"(I shall) . . . attempt to analyze and understand the role of language and the word from the perspective of a writer resident in a society which is still very colonial—Canada," injects M. Nourbese Philip.

The cars whiz round the square.

She gets up and walks.

"The twentieth century created the automobile as a whole, so to speak, and then . . . built it up out of its parts," Stein pipes up again. "The United States . . . created the twentieth century. . . . The nineteenth century was roughly that of the Englishman. . . . And their method . . . is that of 'muddling through.'"

But—in creating the whole, what of the parts remain?

She walks by a bookstore. Her coattails juxtaposed, in reflection, on a display of Balzac novels. Whose critics said he created bankers out of Mohicans in redingotes. Reminder to her, in Canada they pushed through a railway allegedly for the *creation of a country*. Destroying Métis culture.

Turns towards St. Sulpice (her favorite square in Paris). Of which Henry Miller wrote, "St. Sulpice! The fat belfries, the garish posters over the door, the candles flaming inside. The square so beloved of Anatole France with that drone and buzz from the altar, the splash of the fountain, pigeons cooing . . ."

Thinking (offended by his words): "Realism is the view of One, of pseudo-synthesis."

This she both hates and envies.

Continues towards Montparnasse. Where Hemingway wrote: "Paris belongs to me."

Turns towards a nice café with green-striped awnings. White cups inscribed Café de la Place. Excellent espresso. With a square of good, dark chocolate by the sugar lumps in the saucer. On the terrasse, face turned toward the sun, she tries to change the subject. *Que faire* (today). Writing in her agenda, "Definitely la Louvre. Maybe Les Folies Bergère (new socially conscious version, complete with a great Tunisian singer 'found' in the métro), and old Hepburn movie. The fine Arab Institute library. Balzac's house, where he hid from his debtors." In Paris they have everything. Again she opens up the paper. It says a famous Kenyan athlete has jumped into la Seine to save an elderly Frenchman trying to kill himself. Shortly after, the Kenyan received two letters from the préfecture: one, a citation of merit; the other, an invitation to leave the country.

Proust later tried to catch up with lost time.

Strolling over le Pont Neuf, she looks into the river, into the white light of Paris gathered on its surface.

"The United States . . . instead of having the feeling of beginning at one end and ending at another . . . had the conception of assembling the whole thing out of its parts," Gertrude Stein persists.

She climbs back into bed. A ray of light shines through the gauze curtains. Gray with soot, from the cards on the boulevard outside the art deco design of her balcony. The traffic sounds are deadening (as in a Godard film). In her dream she strolls past Joyce's former home, boulevard Raspail, and Stein's, rue de Fleurus, trying to lose herself in the curves of streets, pockets of courtyards, fearing all the time the nineteenth-century buildings are about to dissolve in a pile of white dust. Behind her flows la Seine, breathing forth, some poet said, the very air of Paris. "The air of Paris is a republican notion," her dream-speak says, "a synthesis."

"The other thing which I accomplished was getting rid of nouns," trumpets Gertrude Stein again.

Was Stein's whole, then, about synthesis in movement?

In her dream she's walking. Not a noun but (possibly unfortunately) not a verb either. La rue de Rennes so thick with pedestrians, it's difficult to move. Now and then a beggar, with a child, sometimes very large, lying on his or her knee for hours, as if asleep. She goes into *La Coupole,* "Bar Américain," very air-conditioned, frequented by well-dressed elderly women from Montparnasse going through their afternoon tea rituals, the odd anti-Soviet Russian who could go back now but naturally doesn't want to, some lesbians.

She strolls, knowing she's ridiculous. Thinking the narrator can no longer be a single notion. Thinking the "synthesis" required for a work of art involves absorbing the reader into the vortex of the author's vision. To seduce excludes breakage. Thereby, excluding others or only partially, caricaturally absorbing them. But how to keep in a state of listening? All these interceptions. At the same time, maintaining faith in one's way of doing, one's mark as an artist. She strolls past her reflection in the mirror of a wine store: dark eyes, very short lashes.

Also slightly sloppy.

She strolls under the white sky of Paris.

It looks down on her ironically.

Quotations in this piece come from Gertrude Stein, *How Writing Is Written* (Los Angeles: Black Sparrow Press, 1974); Marcel Proust, *A la recherche du temps perdu, II* (Paris: Gallimard, 1988); M. Nourbese Philip, *She Tries Her Tongue, Her Silence Softly Breaks* (Charlottetown: Ragweed Press, 1989); Henry Miller, *Tropic of Cancer*; Ernest Hemingway, *A Moveable Feast* (New York: Macmillan, 1987); *Le Monde; Libération*.

GAIL SCOTT *lives and works in Montreal, Quebec. Her publications include the novels* Spare Parts *(1981),* Heroine *(1987),* Main Brides *(1993), and* My Paris *(1999), as well as a collection of essays,* Spaces Like Chairs *(1989). This essay first appeared in* Books in Canada.

Reclaiming
Our Bodies

Measuring Out My Life

COLLEEN ADDISON

"YOU SHOULD LOSE SOME WEIGHT," Dad agrees and i nod back at him, my resolution reinforced and so i start the next day

> Breakfast: ½ cup corn flakes/1 cup skim milk/½ banana
> Lunch: 3 crackers/10 slices of 10% milk fat mozzarella/1
> apple/1 carrot
> Supper: 1 slice bread/1 piece meat

i sit in class, the vectors flying unnoticed on and off the blackboard beside me and i add up the calories i am eating and i read all of my mother's Weight Watchers pamphlets and Dad smiles at me and 118 pounds says the scale and i am happy

and the Hunger is not really hunger but strength and my feet hit the pavement hard as i walk to school, i am tough, i am in control, the Hunger giving me new power as it eats away at the fat

i'll walk on water with no weight to hold me down and make me drown, and it's a silly metaphor but i still believe it

i listen as Cindy Crawford, goddess of glossy magazines, laughs at me and i laugh louder

i am thinner than she is

Breakfast: ½ cup corn flakes
Lunch: ¾ cup 1% milk fat cottage cheese/¾ cup yogurt/1
  apple
Supper: ½ piece meat/1 carrot

cereal without milk! it's a miracle! the bowl is the same size but i know it has 100 less calories sitting in it.

there's a Wall between me and the food and i am safe on the right side of it and the article i read about dieting is silly, how you will gain more weight if you jump back and forth, diet to regular eating. why don't all these women just stay on their diets?

the path is strewn with thorns but i'll get the primroses at the end and my feet are the better ones the bleeding tells me that

but bleeding every month has stopped. there is a special word for that: dysmenorrhea. i look it up but the dictionary says only: dynamic, dynamism, dynamite

Breakfast: 1 apple
Lunch: 1 apple
Supper: 1 carrot

and it all adds up to 143 calories and is it wonderful?

92 pounds says the scale, not my scale, not the everyday black numbers at my feet but a big Gray Thing and the doctor uses her pencil to push the scientific knob back from 100, and back and back and she can't hide the line in her forehead

i am finally losing some weight and i am glad

but the mirror in the pristine office makes my eyes look sunken and my cheekbones sharp jutting mountains above the sudden valleys of my cheeks

at home there are friendlier enemies, showing the familiar fat, telling me all i have to do is lose weight, at home there aren't any hollows filled with dark shadows

i am so cold, the long underwear scratching my body, the red arm of the thermometer gleefully threatening to slide down from −5°c my hair is falling out, dull red clumps lie on my bathroom floor when i am done combing

The Hunger is coming, i don't try to run i almost welcome It because It chases away The Weakness

what is hunger? i can't really feel anything anymore, there is only tired and cold

sometimes i hear a roaring in my ears and i know the blackness will come and swallow me up

i want be able to walk without being tired but i don't know isn't everybody tired when they walk?

it doesn't matter i am almost thin

how much does hair weigh?

my mother is crying and i stop looking at Dad because he's not smiling he just looks scared

i'm scared too

i read a book about anorexia—i can almost say the word my lips can shape it but the five syllables stick in my throat

the book calls it a disease i have a disease

like the lepers in the movie i watch who nobody wants to touch

and i can't take it anymore i can't take the cold and the food and the never being thin and the doctor who lies and tells me i am thin i see the disgust in her eyes and the fat on my body and it isn't ever coming off ever and i want to be strong again but i'm weak and my mother keeps crying when she looks at me and sometimes when i look in the mirror i see someone different i see someone too thin and i cry too

i want someone to help me

Theresa the nutritionist says

i have to eat more food. i will die if i don't eat.

her voice is calm and she smiles at me and i hang on to that smile and she says i am thin enough even too thin and almost

i believe

but i go home and there aren't any more of her smiles and there isn't anything left but the eating and the not-eating.

The eating:

it's more than i've eaten in a very long time i can't eat this much i can't i can't

and my teacher frowns at me when he sees me eating in his class

and that guy who sits across from me says that i am always eating whenever he sees me and i don't know what to say and so

The not-eating: i break the crackers into crumbs so it will seem like i've eaten them all but the crumbs form a mountain

and the blackness keeps coming and i can't keep it away

there's a program on t.v. about a singer Karen Carpenter

it shows her getting thinner and thinner and then she is in and out of hospitals and at the end she dies

i am not going to be like her

but she took diet pills and i didn't take diet pills and maybe i should and maybe i shouldn't and maybe i don't want to

Theresa says

i will die if i don't eat

and maybe she is right and the girl on the other side of me says that my crackers look yummy and she gets her peanut butter sandwich out of her bag and takes a big bite. she's eating a big sandwich and i just have three crackers maybe it doesn't matter so much maybe i can eat this

i don't want to die

the tears are still in my mother's eyes they look like stars

and she is smiling it's not the same smile as Theresa's

but the stars push the blackness away a little

and i eat another cracker

my mother has hidden my scale and so there aren't any more black numbers to tell me what to do and i have to hang on to smiles instead

i am almost glad

every week i hang on when i see Theresa's scale, it's like the doctor's scale Big and Gray and the numbers keep climbing and maybe the smiles are false maybe everyone is trying to make me more fat and the pencil pushes the knob forward and forward and i don't know if i should look or not

my hair has stopped falling out it's a brighter red and i can walk without
feeling so tired and i've taken off the long underwear and i am almost happy

Theresa keeps smiling she says she knows it is hard

like when a man tells me i am voluptuous, and i know he means it as a
compliment but my mind is filled with the dimpled thighs and triple chins
of Roman Venuses and i cringe

but i will make it

i am not going to die

i listen to a friend tell me her story, it is the same story as mine but

locked away in a hospital she rips the tubes from her veins

she perms her hair to hide the bald spots

she wears a heavy woolen sweater in March when the classroom is a sea of
white T-shirts

she is winning says the voice in my head but i ignore it

I am not jealous.

> Breakfast: 2 pieces of bread/2 tablespoons of peanut butter/1
>   piece of fruit
> Lunch: 2 oz cheese (10 slices)/2 pieces of bread/1 piece of
>   fruit/1 cup of yogurt
> Snack: 2 pieces of bread
> Supper: 3 oz of meat/2 pieces of bread/1 piece of fruit/1 cup
>   of yogurt

COLLEEN ADDISON *is a recent graduate of the University of
Alberta English Department. Her work has been published in* blue
buffalo. *This piece was first published as "Walking with Karen Carpenter" in* Fireweed *Summer 1995.*

Re-Covering

DIANNE LINDEN

SEVERAL TIMES IN MY LIFE I have been thin: thin as a knife blade or the sweep hand on my grandfather's gold watch. Thin enough to snag an eyeball should someone glance at me from a ninety-degree angle. That's the point of being thin, of course. Catching the eye. Also fitting into a particular scheme of decoration.

Once or twice I've been so thin I've been able to sit in straight-backed, wooden chairs with my arms and legs wrapped around the chair's arms and legs, so that only a trained observer could tell where I ended and the furniture began. From so doing, I became, at times in my life, chairlike. Gothic, to be specific, although I have had thin friends and acquaintances who were more Shaker or Chippendale. One friend amazed me by managing to be thin and also have breasts, thereby achieving a very high *objet-d'art* rating. Sadly, she was also bowlegged, which made her Louis xv when she really wanted to be Heppelwhite. With an exaggerated wheel-back.

I'm grateful in retrospect. Chairs are unable to initiate action and therefore aren't required to make decisions. Careers, marriages, sex, personal identity are not matters of concern for them. The wooden chair, all her bones and breeding exposed, does not anguish over hormone replacement therapy or the lack of a spiritual life. No chair of Jacobean or Restoration inclination (no chair of any inclination, in fact) has need of a voice.

I've implied that thinness was a gift to me at several difficult times in my life. It allowed me to be passive and yielding (except in holding up the burdens that were placed upon me). It aided me in becoming nonreactive and mute. These were qualities much admired in the circles of my acquaintanceship.

It's true that even as a thin woman I managed some mobility. How else could I have worked my way toward and almost through middle age? Of course I moved in my thin life, but only from position to position, and then, posefully. In between moves I held my breath and waited for someone to tell me where to move next. It was the best I could do at those times.

Now I can do better. Now I'm willing to admit that in between thin periods I have been—large. Sometimes very. Overstuffed, as we call things we sit on that don't show their limbs. Whereas during thin periods I externalized my body, during large times in my life I abandoned my body altogether. Didn't relate to it. I was the lumpy daybed my brothers leapt from. I was the humpbacked horsehair sofa, abandoned in our alley one winter night.

In the eyes of people I met I saw that I was no longer decorative, and in defense I ridiculed myself. I joked about buying clothes at the Fat Lady's Store. At recess I rushed to be the first into the staff room of the school where I taught. There I overindulged in sweets parents had baked, concoctions my thin self would have despised: shortbread made with margarine, coconut and maraschino cherry clusters that were mouth-burningly sweet.

"I'm eating for two," I used to say when the custodian looked at me askance. "Me and My Body."

Now I admit that I have been entirely disrespectful of myself at such times in my life, and I see the fact that I am becoming large again as an opportunity to improve on something I've done badly before. This time I will be more accepting of my body's size. I will regard myself as a unique resting place in progress.

Cocooning is, after all, the byword of this decade. The economy may be downsizing, but in our homes, more than ever we want coziness. *Gemütlichkeit.* Why should I be barren, when I can more comfortably be surface- and texture-augmented? Great, sumptuous couches are attractive, give us support when we need it. Sofas of generous proportions allow us to sit easily with a friend while still maintaining personal boundaries. Weight is not an issue in the living rooms of the nation. Harmony between space and shape are. So let it be with me and my body.

I'm surprised it's taken me so long to come to my present awareness. Any furniture magazine I open up informs me I can grow larger without becoming the lumpy daybed in my parents' backstairs sunroom. I can be a chaise longue if I desire to be, curvaceous and exotic. I can be ample and well-nourished and still familiar with sexuality.

I will evolve my own style of movement in time. I pledge that. My feet will leave their impression on many astonished Berber carpets when I'm accustomed to my body's new size and shape. And, out of charity, I will find ways to use my voice.

It occurs to me that this minimalist furniture phase I have gone through off and on since I was an adolescent is over. I want to be large again, to move largely. I want to think largish, generous thoughts of rickety, bentwood rockers made whole again through care and cushions and the right fabric. I will seek out and refurbish the discarded furniture of my dreams. And if good intentions can make it so, I will become the most generous reupholsterer my body has ever known.

DIANNE LINDEN'S *poetry, essays, and short stories have been published in a number of Canadian literary magazines and have been anthologized in Canada, England, and the United States. Dianne is also a fiber artist, currently at work on a collection, "Precious Small," involving the dialogue between symbol, color, texture, and text.*

Swimming the Gaps

Janet Lundman

BODIES ARE A BOTHERSOME ARRANGEMENT OF PARTS. Mine has been bothering me for as far back as I can remember. Even before the serious trouble began at puberty, I can dimly recall my physical being making demands for food, for warmth, for comfort of one sort or another. Just as one comfort level was satisfactorily established, mysterious currents flooded my parts and flushed away familiar anchors. Settling into a cozy harbor was always just around the next landmark of physical change and upset.

Girls' bodies are particularly bothersome, I think, because they come equipped with the unequivocal power for procreation, a force without which the world could not go on. And men know it. Boys are drawn by it. And girls are distracted by all the attention their bodies evoke.

I watch the transformation of young girls in the locker room of my local pool. Up to the age of six, they are boisterous and curious sprites challenging their world. By the time they're eight, most of them have become languid wraiths withdrawing into self-absorption. They stop running and start gazing into mirrors. They arrange hair, apply lipstick, check suits, and pat thighs. They have become aware of their body parts. From now on, comparing and assessing the value of particular parts for manipulating male approval becomes a devout preoccupation.

The realization of my quirky power jolted me like a slap with a wet towel.

I was twelve when some pimple-faced cad in the neighborhood swimming pool squeezed my left breast. My indignant howls only elicited more leers and hoots from the lifeguard.

Suddenly, my body was no longer entirely my own. Swinging through the world using my body as I pleased had, in an instant, become a perilous activity.

The astonishing inconvenience of acquiring substantial breasts had already unsettled my confidence. Moving in the world with these new acquisitions was tricky. Despite some niggling doubts about my mother's taste, I had gamely strode poolside in the two-piece suit she'd sewn for me. (It was blue and scattered with a shower of white flowers.) Then, under cover of water churned by a hundred hot kids on a steaming prairie day, this red-faced pimple attacks.

WHAP! A sting like a wet towel! I become a sexual thing.

The slow apprehension of injustice and betrayal scalds my brain. Suspicions of the world and my mother's motives scatter my beliefs. Some hard questions won't go away.

What was all the yammer I heard at home about "making something of myself" if Mother parcels me up in a blue bathing suit to display my wares to the world? Where's the advantage in having what my older sisters call "a good pair" if what you get is pawed? How come this little turd can humiliate me and get approval from a lifeguard? What do you make of yourself when what you see is beleaguered mothers gritting their teeth and young girls competing for diamonds? Where do you put your body while you try to make other things of yourself?

Bodies were valuable assets. No doubt about that message. It continued to burn into my bones as I stumbled through my life. It was the other part of the message that kept tripping me up: bad girls use their bodies, but good girls pretend they don't have one.

Over the years the mixed messages can cause brain slack. Focus and energy for "making something of yourself" become muzzy.

When we were both twenty-eight, a colleague of mine said to me, "What the hell. I didn't get rich or famous, and I'm not young anymore. I might as well end it all and get married."

And she did. Traded her capital at the eleventh hour, you might say.

Her disappearance slowed me down, got me thinking about mixed messages, who I was, where I was drifting. I'd figured out a few things by this time. Like, bodies are not what they seem. And what we know is not what we tell. And dousing knowing parts of ourselves becomes automatic. And if we're careful, relying on our body parts becomes a survival skill. And always the social fiction beckons, lures us into traps, closes down our options, keeps us safe from risking our own desires. Because, the fiction goes, if you're a good girl you'll be looked after.

I, like gazillions of women before and after me, have fallen for the social fiction; smile, don't make a fuss, lie ever so still in the bed you've made.

On the other hand, trading body parts for knowing parts can win a well-endowed woman a choice spot in the social hierarchy. She may need luck at that, and certainly she needs to complete her negotiations before the age of fifty when her visibility fades.

I well remember the evening I became invisible. My experienced wit and intelligence were utterly stonewalled by a pair of outrageous breasts sitting next to me at a dinner conference. The young woman had little else to recommend her, but all the men at the table, including my husband, hung on her every breath, perhaps wondering which breast would wrest free from its confines first.

Even then I did my best to eradicate knowledge of my declining allure. It's been a slow grind. At age thirty I was alarmed to discover erumpent capillaries on my too large thighs. By age fifty-two, when the irrefutable evidence of my invisibility hit me, the loose drape of my upper arms could no longer be disguised, but I still hoped nobody would notice. To my horror nobody noticed—period!

Not fair! some entrapped part of me wailed. Other parts reeled and gasped. Images of my mother's aged body splashed behind my eyes. Would my belly become a cushion? My breasts elongated nuisances? My underbite witchy?

Not fair! I wailed some more. Maddened. Bereft. Swamped by the injustice of it all. After all those years of angst trying to minimize bodily flaws, I was finally creeping up on self-acceptance. Armed with some life experience and an uneasy truce with my body, I felt cautiously optimistic about my place in the world.

Then *WHAP!* I disappear! Breasts, bum, mind, spirit, life experience. All of me wiped!

A stunning blow. My disappearance as a sexual being dies hard. Resurrection in a new form seems improbable. Definitely I need to make easier peace with my mother's image. Biographies of women help. I scrabble at the library. I lock eyeballs with fierce-looking old women I pass on the street. I clasp feminism and alienate friends. I don't care. My family history unravels before my eyes. I unravel. I look for heroes. Dream of Gloria. I devour women's stories and marvel at their ability for survival.

I begin to see I'm surviving, alone and aging.

And slowly, very slowly, I'm beginning to get it. I've discovered the joker in the pack, the snake in the trap.

I see women do it to themselves everyday. I keep telling them, don't should on yourself. If you're angry, tell some one. It's not your fault. You did the best you knew. Nobody's perfect. All the antidotes against self-blame, self-betrayal.

Finally, I'm beginning to hear them myself. There's a space opening up inside, and it doesn't feel empty or frightening. It feels like mine. It keeps filling up. Getting richer. Sixty-five years is a lot of living, and I'm reclaiming them year by year. Getting a different take. Dumping blame. Getting in touch. Springing traps. Making friends with the snake.

I'm almost there, I think.

Some of my best thinking is done swimming. Or call it unthinking. Moving meditation is more like it. Swimming has soothed many rough stretches. I still swim a mile three times a week. It's like brushing my teeth.

So here I am walking poolside in my full-support bathing suit, tucking a last gray hair under my cap. Once more preparing for the deep dive.

A fellow my age or better sits in his loosening expanse of skin watching the varied shapes of senior swimmers. I've seen him before, checking the action.

As I approach, he says, "How're ya' doin', young lady?" and throws me a loaded wink.

WHAP! I'm resurrected! Or no, I'm insulted! Or am I flattered? Dumbfounded? Confounded? Definitely flustered. For sure.

My parts implode. Voices collide. Forgotten parts rattle their traps. Familiar parts scatter like guppies. Voices shatter the murky stillness. One voice wants to stamp and shout, *I'm not young! I'm no lady!* Another is willing to wink back and respond with, *Just fine, me bucko. How's yours doin'?* The rebel wants to hiss, *Piss off, you old fool!* And another is insisting, *Get real, the both of youse!*

But basic training prevails. I'm not finished yet. I smile wanly, collude in the pretense. Jump in.

It seems an impossible gulf. I swim hard. Feel the power. Think of ways to bridge it, this gap in understanding.

What would it take, I wonder as I cut through the water, for this man to comprehend even a small part of what it's cost me to play in somebody else's script? For him to see what it's costing him to stay in the same old act? For him to appreciate the urge in me to be me and not some wonky fiction to keep me from myself? For me to act as though I believe it myself? For both of us to drop the disguise and say yea to baldness and flaccid flesh? For him to hear me say, this is the last act, old man, we can be who we are?

I swim and ponder how I could fit all this into one pithy but friendly retort.

And should I then presume? And how should I begin? I swim like hell. I stretch toward the murky swell, catch a shaft of light, dive for the traps, see how they work. I spring some, loosen others. Buried bits of me float free. Rise to the surface. Come up for air.

I want to call out to the man watching on shore. It's not too late! Plunge in! There's still time for learning how to swim in the elemental murk. Time to catch a mermaid's song.

I lift my arms and breathe. Over, breathe, under, and out. Over, breathe, under, and out.

JANET LUNDMAN *continues to swim the gaps in Victoria, British Columbia. And while the West Coast sustains her spirit, sporadic visits to her prairie roots keep her soul nourished.*

Tracing Elements

LINDY McINTYRE

The Letter

To whom it may concern:

I am the next-of-kin of my mother, the late Greta Geraldine Allan, born October 31, 1912, died January 2, 1992, and formerly of 2815 Hill Avenue, Regina.

My mother was a patient in your clinic in the late 1970s, and I understand you still possess her medical records. My daughter is presently participating in a breast cancer study, and believes that these medical records will be of significance in this regard. I hereby authorize you to give my daughter access to my mother's medical records and to provide her with such copies as she may request.

The Record

Mrs. Allan has been referred because of a breast mass on suspicion of malignant disease. The patient reports that at about the first week of May while retiring, she became aware of a sudden, "sharp stabbing" pain in her left breast. She took an aspirin and slept without difficulty. The following night, the same thing happened and she decided to massage the left breast, and when she did so, she encountered a large mass which she judged [to] be about the size of a 25 cent piece. As time passed, she felt that it remained unchanged for a time but over the past week, she is convinced that it has gradually reduced in size and is almost "gone."

The Study

By signing up to do this breast cancer study, you are consenting to have your data used for study purposes. In addition, the consent form asks for your permission to access other records, both now and in the future. While it is not a pleasant thought, the reality is that during the course of the study some women will develop breast cancer. Some may even die.

The History

Here's Gran, coming to pick us up, coming to take us home to make cookies at Easter, crafts at Christmas. We are wearing the pretty dresses with matching hats that she has sewn for us, wearing them with satisfaction as we accompany her to the drugstore, the supermarket, the salon. Everywhere she is greeted with friendly smiles and kind words. "Why hello, Mrs. Allan! How are you today?" Very well, she answers, before inquiring after that brother and his wife in Ontario or the progress of the children who (can it be?) have just begun high school. And, oh, it is a beautiful day for this time of year. When we recall these childhood moments, we know that all days with her were beautiful. She was beautiful, with her funny laugh and bright face. Like Bette Davis, don't you think? Or Lucille Ball? Oh, yes, I thought that, too.

The Consent

I voluntarily consent to truthfully and thoroughly answer the questions in this study and understand that I may withdraw at any time. I know that participation in this study has no known risk of harm and that it will, in fact, be of great benefit to me and others.

The Record

On inquiry there has been no injury, direct or indirect, of either breast. Mrs. Allan normally wears a brassiere or garment which is supporting, comfortable and has never distressed her. There has never been any previous history of breast masses or other significant features. Menarche age 14, her periods every 28 days lasting 6 or 7 days. Normal flow. Abdomen is soft and flat. Appendectomy scar noted. Patient is a healthy woman of 66. No distress. She is slight but well nourished.

The Study

How often do you give yourself breast exams?

Have you ever found any abnormalities?

What is your bra size?

Do you have regular pap examinations?

Have any of the examination results ever reported an abnormality?

Have you ever smoked cigarettes? Your mother? Your father? Your husband/partner?

How many alcoholic beverages do you consume in an average week?

Have you ever been uncomfortable or embarrassed about your alcohol consumption?

Has anyone ever told you that they have a concern about your alcohol consumption?

How many cups of coffee do you drink in a day? Does this differ from season to season (for example, some people may drink more iced coffee in the summer months)? How often do you have intercourse? What type of contraception do you currently use? How many sexual partners do you have now? How many in the past? What kind of deodorant do you use? How often? Do you shave under your arms? How often and since when? Are you an apple or a pear? An apple tends to gain weight in the abdomen area, while the pear gains in the buttocks and thighs. Are you an apple or a pear? Apple or pear?

The History

And now I am older and we take a trip, she and I, to the place where she grew up, to the house with the big, screened porch where she would sit with her hands pressed together. She didn't have a mother, or at least she did for a while. She was only ten, though, when her mother fell from a ladder and died, not immediately, of course, but later, of complications. We go to the cemetery and find the grave, alone. Her father is somewhere among the rows of white crosses, a veteran of the great war. We walk and she tells me the growing up stories, how her father pushed her into a deep pool to teach her to swim, and how she couldn't swim, couldn't even float. How suddenly her older brother appeared to lift her up and pull her out. She adored her older brother. He worked after school and on weekends, and bought her things when she needed them. There was a younger one, too. He was crippled with polio and complained all the time. He grew to be a bitter man, and she rarely saw him then, lost touch. When he was forty-two he killed himself in some place far away, and she felt sad and tried to remember him in other ways. But look, she tells me, and points to a spot under the bridge. Here is where he proposed. She remembers it was a beautiful day, a warm, sunny day, and they had come for a picnic. They ate ham sandwiches and drank lemonade and then he proposed and then she said yes. She said yes to the serious young man who would go to McGill, who would be a doctor, the polite young man who had good manners and who would provide and care for her, forever. She looks back with fondness, but I know it wasn't easy for her, being a doctor's wife at the dinner parties with the interrupting phone calls. She tells me how he often made stops on their way home, stops to the house of the sick when he'd say he would only be ten minutes. How he was usually two hours: ten minutes with the measled children, the rest spent playing hearts and sipping nightcaps. How he would return to the car and be surprised to find her there, sleeping.

The Record

On inspection, both breasts *are* moderate in size and equal and symmetrical. With the arms raised above the head, however, in the left breast, above the nipple at about 12 o'clock, there is a slight dimpling of the skin and puckering of the skin visible. The mass itself is well-defined, *and* is best felt with the patient recumbent and with the flat of the hand. It is movable. It is unattached to the deeper structures such as fascia or muscle or chest wall and it is not particularly sensitive on examination.

The Study

How often do you use a hair dryer? An electric mixer? A food processor? A microwave? A computer? Are you concerned about exposure to electromagnetic fields? How many glasses of water do you drink in a day? Is the water direct from the kitchen tap? A well? A special filter system? A bottle? Do you have children? How many? Natural birth or cesarean section?

Did you breast feed and for how long? How often do you menstruate? How long does each menstrual period last? Do you have swelling or general soreness of the breasts before, during, or after menstruation?

Have you or any member of your family ever been diagnosed with a carcinoma? A cyst? A tumor? A teratoma? A teratoma is a tumor made up of living tissue, bone, teeth, and hair (tera, from the Greek word teras, meaning monster). Have you ever had a teratoma? Do you consider your life right now to be stressful? How often do you get angry? Feel dissatisfied? Fearful? Anxious? Rarely? Often? Seldom? None of the above? All of the above?

The History

She has many good friends, girl friends who come for coffee and a game of cards. I see them admiring her style, her taste, her passion for green. Furnishings in mint, avocado, chartreuse. The outfit in aquamarine ultrasuede, Vogue pattern #6128. Her eyeglasses, too, tinted a soft olive, but that's to ease the headaches and blinding bouts of dizziness that have begun to plague her. More and more she must excuse herself from her company and hurry to the bedroom to lie down. When she feels better I bring tea and a magazine, and we look through the pages to determine what fashions would be simple to sew for a fraction of the cost charged in the stores. And I am older still and must move away to Vancouver to work, to live, and here she is, coming to me where I sit in the avocado velvet chair with her arms stretched out, her eyes moist. She seems so little as she squeezes my arm, leans her lips to my ear, and whispers "I'll miss you." I realize I've never seen her cry before, and it makes me sting. Don't be sad, I'll be back some day, and you shall come to visit me, too, as soon as you can. We'll have tea and take long, long walks and talk and talk, just as always.

The Record

Blood work has been ordered, and Mrs. Allan goes to surgery tomorrow morning for quick section examination and probable radical mastectomy if malignant disease should be confirmed.

The Consent

No, wait. I don't know. I'm not sure anymore. I want to think about it first because I'm not comfortable with this. I mean, no, I don't consent, if that's all right. I don't consent. I don't.

The Letter

Hello, my dear—

Not a day goes by that I don't think of you and hope that you're happy living in Vancouver. Everything is relatively quiet here. We've hired a lovely woman to come in during the day to help with cleaning and cooking and such—it's a real relief, you can imagine. Actually, I'm pleased to say, I've been feeling much better lately. My treatments are nearly complete and I've been a little less tired, and so we've been talking about coming to visit in the spring. It's been ages since I've seen the ocean, and it would be wonderful to have a break from the business of sickness.

Yes, sweetheart, I think we will be there by spring.

LINDY McINTYRE *is a freelance writer living in Regina, Saskatchewan. She has a degree in English and is currently studying the art of fiction writing through a series of workshops offered by the Saskatchewan Writers Guild.*

The Wall

JAN SEMEER

"Yuk! Pea soup again," I sigh, the heavy smell hitting me with full force when I enter the scullery.

My mother, stirring a thick, green, bubbling mass in the large soup kettle, begins, "Finally! What kept you so long? You could've been home ages ago. It's no more than a ten-minute walk from your school. The stop at the butcher's shouldn't take you longer than five minutes, so you could easily be here by a quarter to twelve. If you wouldn't dawdle, we could eat punctually at twelve. You know how upset your father gets if the food is not ready." Snatching a package from my hands and shoving the soup off the heat, she adds, "That steak has to be in the pan before your father gets back. He was already looking for it. Now hurry, wash your hands and get to the table." She grabs a frying pan, adds a dab of butter, and slams it on the hot element. As the butter foams and changes color, she adds the steak and with a fork turns it quickly, deftly browning it on both sides. The aroma of the frying steak overpowers the unpleasant smell of the pea soup, and I sniff appreciatively. I wash my hands at the tiny sink, careful not to splash water on the floor.

As my sister Lisa and I skipped home from school for lunch, a voice behind challenged me. "Bet I can beat you getting over the wall." It was

Albert, one of the boys from my class. I let him catch up, grinned and said, "You're on," then took off to the high-school grounds, the wind whistling in my ears and my feet barely touching the pavement. While I measured how high I should jump to grab the iron railing on top of the big brick wall, more boys arrived, howling that this time they will do it. The truth was that none of us had ever made it over the wall; it was just too high. But we kept trying. My left side still hurt from running so fast, but I wasn't going to let that interfere. I jumped to grab the iron railing but missed, my knees scraping the rough brick all the way down. Ouch.

Just as I was ready to take another jump, Lisa finally caught up. "Jan, you've got to get father's steak," she gasped. "And look at your knees. They're all bloody."

"Go on home. Tell mother that I'll be there soon; tell her . . . that it was busy at the butcher's," I shouted impatiently. None of the boys had made it on the wall yet. This time I was determined. Taking a running leap, I snared the railing with one hand. Hanging on for dear life, I managed to grasp the railing with the other hand as well. I pulled myself up, my stomach on the railing, then I forced my knees on top of the wall with my feet following naturally. For a moment I stood tall, looking down on the boys. Albert took another jump, hoping to get a hold on the rail this time, but he grabbed my shoe instead, nearly upsetting me. Quickly, I let myself down into the high school grounds. I had done it!

"Well, where are you?" I scoffed.

I heard him laugh. Another boy taunted, "How do you get back then, eh?"

I had already figured that out. A little farther on stood a huge cedar with a branch trailing over the top of the wall. I would climb the tree and slide across the branch onto the wall. That way I wouldn't need to worry about climbing it once more. As I was halfway along the branch, the boys whispered loudly, "Stay where you are. There comes our teacher."

I stopped, hardly breathing, embracing the swaying branch tightly, hoping that the teacher would not notice me. Mr. Hulst jumped off his bike and asked crossly, "What are you still doing here? Your mothers are waiting for you. Get going!" Then he spotted me. A look of astonishment crossed his face and, as if addressing only the boys, he added, "I don't want you to get caught in the high-school grounds. If you are, your parents will have to be told." He re-mounted his bike and cycled on. With a sigh of relief, I made it from the branch onto the wall, but not without badly tearing my dress. "Were you ever lucky the teacher did not see you; he would really have given it to you," the boys said. "He can be so mean." I didn't tell them that Mr. Hulst had seen me but had not said anything. They would have said that I was the teacher's pet. And I was. Mr. Hulst liked me—he had said so himself—because I worked hard in school. I tried not to let my teacher down, ever. But I had now.

As I hear my father coming down the stairs, I dash into the kitchen and slide into my chair. I've just made it. My siblings are already in their places. Ann, our daily help, comes in with the big pot of pea soup, and Mother carries in a plate on which lies my father's fried steak.

"Everything's on the table, Calvin," my mother calls.

"Yes, yes, I'm here. Come on, let's say grace quickly. I don't want the steak to get cold."

After grace is said, my mother ladles the soup while our father cuts into his steak. The red blood oozes from the meat and runs all over his plate, collecting in a red puddle. I watch, fascinated, as the knife carves through the beef again.

"That was done just the way I like it," he says, "crisp and brown on the outside and tender and red on the inside; nice job, Mom." Handing Ann his dirty plate, he holds out a clean one for my mother to ladle full of soup.

Checking around, my mother notices that I am not eating. "Eat your soup, Jan," she says sharply. "Stop playing with it. It's no wonder you are so skinny. You never finish what's on your plate."

"I just do not like the color green," I say. "Red is my favorite."

"Not true," pipes up Lisa. "You like green. You told me so yourself because it's the color of grass and the leaves on the trees and you said you could not imagine them any other color."

"Yea, but that's different. That's not food," I retort.

"What about lettuce and spinach?" my brother taunts. "They're green."

Blast! He's right. I like those vegetables and he knows it. I throw him a dirty look and say under my breath, "Green soup is different; it looks ugly, it looks sick."

My father is too busy eating his soup, but my mother, having finished hers, responds furiously. "How dare you say that, you awful child. You should be grateful to have food on your plate at all. Have you already forgotten the war? During those days anyone would have given their eye tooth for a plate of this lovely soup. Get away from this table before I lay my hands on you—"

I TRY TO RUN, but my foot gets caught behind the table leg. A stinging blow on the side of my head and a vicious kick send me sprawling to the floor. I scramble to my feet, run to the washroom, and slam the door shut behind me. I'm shaking but realize that I've been lucky to get off so easily. Usually when Mother loses her temper, she keeps on hitting and kicking until her rage is spent. Today, however, there are too many people in the way. She is still angry, though. I can hear her raised voice through the closed door. What is she saying? Cautiously, I open the door slightly and listen.

"You know that the health nurse at school said that Jan is much too thin and needs to be fed properly with good solid farm food. Guess what reason Jan gave why she can't go? That we can't afford it because her father needs a steak every day. But that is none of their business. Not everyone needs to know that we have a difficult time on your salary. I was so embarrassed. Stupid child. I don't think she'll ever learn to be discreet. I harp on it all the time, but she never seems to learn. And anyway, what does this nurse know about our children? Jan is as strong as a horse—"

"Yes," my father interrupts, "that's true. One of the church elders came up to me this morning and told me that he saw her fighting yesterday with a boy at least half a head taller than herself."

"PICK ON SOMEONE YOUR OWN SIZE, YOU COWARD! I told you if you touched my sister once more, I would give it to you," I shouted furiously and jumped at him. Never expecting the onslaught, he was taken by surprise and stumbled, falling backward in the gutter. Falling on top of him, I lifted my hand to hit him. Suddenly, I felt myself being raised into the air. "Let me go," I screamed, kicking backward, hitting something, someone.

"Will you stop that, you wildcat? Do I make myself clear? Or do I need to slap some manners into you," a voice growled into my ear. "How would your father like to see you in this state? As a minister's daughter you have to set an example and look at you—disgusting!" Mr. Mulder, looking at me distastefully, pushed me away and rubbed his shin.

Looking around for the boy, I said, "But every day he hurts Lisa. I warned him."

"Quiet! Fighting is always wrong for a girl. Now go home, and if you say that you are sorry, I might not tell your father."

I mumbled an apology, grabbed Lisa by the hand, and ran.

"I just don't know what to do with her," I hear my mother sigh, her voice calmer now. "She is forever tearing her clothes and ends up in all sorts of mischief. If she were a boy this would be bad enough, but for a girl, and a ten-year-old at that, it is inexcusable. She is just too wild. I've got to think of something."

"Ah," my mother says brightly when she lets me out of the washroom some time later, "I've thought of something which will make you into a proper girl. Remember that vest you started knitting some months ago? Well, it is about time that it got finished. Every day after school I want you to knit twenty rows. That way you'll learn to sit still and do something worthwhile at the same time. I'm also going to teach you how to darn socks. A girl should know how to do that. On Wednesday afternoons there is no school. You can darn all the worn-through socks of the family. I'll also enroll you in a sewing class where they'll teach you how to sew. That should be a lovely challenge for you."

I resent my chores bitterly and do them sullenly.

My mother says, "You're a good girl after all."

The boys try scaling the wall again, but they fail.

JAN SEMEER, *a Dutch-Canadian now living in New Zealand, began writing at age fifty and has not stopped since. She does not make pea soup or darn her family's socks.*

Through the Looking Glass

ROSE MARIE THOMPSON

"**G**ET YOUR FINGERS OUT OF THERE!" Mother called. She was peeling potatoes in the kitchen, a mound of netted gems growing higher in a great copper-bottomed pot filled to the brim with cold well water. Then she added for good measure, "You two better stop that if you don't want a spanking."

We two.

My brother and I sat on the living room floor, dipping our fingers into an enormous tin of peanut butter. We had been licking our fingers clean, then plunging them once again through the film of oil, into the resistant layer beneath.

Removing partly licked fingers from mouths, we looked at each other with questioning stares. We couldn't see her. How did she know what we were doing?

Could our mother see around corners?

Had it happened once, we might have attributed it to luck, but it happened over and over and over again.

There we were, struggling to stuff Fluffy into a bonnet and doll's dress. The clothes were obviously several sizes too small even though Fluffy was one-quarter cat and three-quarters fur.

The little feline seemed to be submitting when with a brilliant squirm she twisted from my brother's grasp, gave me a vicious swipe, and shot through the verandah door. Immediately, four crimson lines appeared on my inner left arm, running from elbow to wrist.

Before I had time to cry out, a voice came from the kitchen. "See what happens when you two misbehave? Serves you right for pestering that poor cat half-to-death!"

Or how about the wintry afternoon, shadows everywhere, mere moments from that magical time when Mother lit the lamps.

She, in the kitchen, sweeping hot strokes across starched gingham aprons and calico frocks. Suddenly, through the gloom came the voice.

"You two better put that chewing gum back in your mouths or it will be the last treat you get for a long, long time!"

We stopped, fingers connected to mouths by several inches of pink Dentyne strands. Sheepishly, we gathered together the strings and balled them back between our lips.

We could scarcely see the noses before our faces, and she could *see through solid walls.*

And on it went—whether we were sneaking peeks at Uncle's Daring Detective magazines with their sketches of bosomy ladies in scant dresses rent by violent rips and tears or clenching the stem of Dad's pipe between our teeth, pretending to smoke.

That smoking trick really needed no warning shout from the other side of the kitchen wall. The repulsive taste of tar and nicotine was enough to dissuade us from further attempts for several weeks. We were so thoroughly dissuaded that, left on our own one morning, we scraped one offensive pipe with Mother's good paring knife. All traces of tar removed, we treated Dad's pipe to some brisk strokes from the scrub brush, having first liberally lathered it from a cake of Fels Naptha laundry soap. I can still see the look on Dad's face when he picked up that pipe after supper. Closest thing I've ever seen to a human being not knowing whether to laugh or cry and one of the few examples of us children actually getting away with some adventure without Mother having seen us around the corner.

Guess she must have been outside.

It was many years before Mother's secret was revealed to me, although I learned that she took delight in telling everyone else about her method of keeping tabs on the youngest family members. With us tucked into our beds under the eaves, Mother would regale guests with the latest tale of how she had uncovered some of our mischief by "glancing into the looking glass that hangs on the kitchen wall." Sixteen inches square with a scalloped border, it hung in such a way that a perfect reflection of the living room was mirrored within the confines of the glass if you were an adult. Children were too small to line up the necessary reflection.

And on the day I learned Mother's secret, it solved another mystery, one that had haunted me since I was three. For the looking glass that held Mother's secrets for protecting her children and monitoring their behavior reflected a different image for me. A darker image. One of fright, shame, and whispered warnings, an image which I would hold close to myself for fifty-six years, an image which I could reveal only after the death of my mother. For, after all, how could I have possibly told this loving, dedicated Mother that the mirror had two faces?

It was the summer of '39 that Johnny came to visit his cousins, the next door neighbors we considered family. Johnny was what Daddy called a "big boy" with an unruly mop of dark hair and an intriguing way of screwing up the left side of his face when he winked at me. I suppose he was about twenty. I liked him the first time I saw him. Country life was lonesome, so when this handsome visitor from Edmonton fussed over me, I lapped it up like Fluffy licking warm cow's milk.

Johnny and his cousins would arrive around eight those summer evenings. Everyone would talk for a while until someone invariably said, "How about a game of whist?" Then, it was into the living room, where chairs were drawn round the table and an evening of cardplaying, smoking, and visiting would ensue.

"Good, clean fun," was how my folks always described it.

I would maneuver myself next to Johnny to take advantage of winks, and tickles, pokes, and squeezes. All the attention I craved.

Paying attention.

That should have been the name of the game.

Johnny paid attention.

Attention to Mother's story about the looking glass.

Attention to my hunger for attention.

Attention to every detail.

No one else paid attention.

Attention to the fact that the rest of the cardplayers always said, "Sure!" to the invitation of "Want a beer?" or "Care for a glass of fresh-made lemonade?" Johnny would always say, "No, thanks." And no one paid attention when part way through the evening Johnny would say, "I'm sure thirsty. Could use a nice, cold drink of well water." And someone would say, "Rose Marie will show you where the water pail is in the kitchen." And Johnny said, "Yeah! That will be great! Just count me out on the next hand." And no one paid attention to how long it took Johnny to get a drink of water.

No one could see into the kitchen where Johnny drew a chair into the center of the room, lined up the cardplayers in the scallop-edged looking glass, and drew me into his lap.

No one could see around corners as Johnny slipped nicotine-stained fingers under the elastic of my panty legs.

No one paid any attention, and no one called, "Get your fingers out of there!"

Rose Marie Thompson's *work has appeared in scores of North American magazines and daily newspapers as well as the anthologies* Crocuses and Buffalo Beans *and* Eating Apples: Knowing Women's Lives. *From her loft high above the Cowichan Valley on Vancouver Island, this wife, mother, and grandmother surveys a world of eagle-streaked mists and old-growth forests.*

Symptoms

MARGUERITE WATSON

THE TUMOR CAME WITH ME WHEN I WAS BORN, a free attachment tucked neatly inside my throat, a rare cancer of the nerve endings. It grew hidden there, wrapping its mass of tissue around tender carotid vessels and cranial nerves, working itself into my right inner ear. On the outside I was like any other cowlicked child in Maryville, Tennessee, making mud pies in the backyard sandbox, vying for rides on Neil Griffen's monster tricycle, singing in the Cherub Choir at New Providence Presbyterian. It was not until I was four that the tumor became visible, bulging at my neck as if I had swallowed a golf ball. The doctors at Blount County Hospital had never seen such a growth, and suppressing it proved a challenge. They cleared away my tonsils to get at the hard-to-reach sections. They cut out other portions through an incision in my neck. In one of those surgeries, I lost the nerve that dilated the pupil in my right eye. A minor facial nerve was also taken. In the end the surgeons had to leave the bulk of the lesion for fear of disturbing more essential nerves and vessels. They treated it with radiation—one quick burn and the cancer was gone. Later, at the bright age of twelve, I was the only kid on my block to go to the famous Mayo Clinic for a third operation, "tumor trimming." Still, a big lump remained in my throat, wedged against my right ear drum like an indigestible vegetable, obstructing my hearing. It has not moved in twenty-two years.

For eight long weeks this summer, I have been feeling sickly. Almost every day I suffer a bout of low-grade nausea, an ambiguous churning in my stomach that refuses either to stop or accelerate. My forehead grows warm but not enough to register a temperature. What is worse, I am bothered by disequilibrium, the queasy sensation that rooms, trees, buildings are turning in the slowest of motion while I am standing stationary. Some days I have to lie down after bending over to make my bed. Some days I am not able to work at my desk. Two times I almost faint. I enlist friends and neighbors to drive me to meetings and appointments. Eventually, I go to my family doctor, who diagnoses my symptoms as "vague." He sends me home after one, then two visits to "wait and see what happens." On the third visit he predicts I have an inner ear virus. I fear I have something else. I feel weak, pukey, awful, bad. I cannot find appropriate words to describe my "condition." By the sixth week, I begin to think I have passed through an invisible door to another existence and will never sound in my body again. My imagination, already prone to story-making, pitches melodramatic scenes of lying in a hospital. In bed at night, I worry that I will not wake up in the morning. I cry myself to sleep.

Toward the end of the summer, I decide to fight my "illness," however serious, to heal myself with my mind. I check out a stack of books from the library. *Psychoneuroimmunology: The New Mind/Body Healing Program. The Power Within: True Stories of Exceptional Patients Who Fought Back with Hope. Visualization: Directing the Movies of Your Mind. You Can Heal Your Life.* Twice a day, I listen to a meditation tape. "Imagine yourself involved in the healthful activities of life," Dr. Carl Simonton's soothing voice says. I visualize a stream of gold and white energy flowing into my bones and veins, tanking them up like wells with strength. The meditation leaves my body quiet and loose. "Thinking positive," I force myself to walk turtle slowly, zigzagging, two kilometers to the university a few days a week. Those I call "good" days. "Bad" days I spend on my back.

I did not know I had had cancer when I was growing up. I did not discover that fact until I was twenty-one. I knew I had a "tumor" and it was the source of pain. Screeching sinus headaches in the dead hours of night, nearly forty-five decibel hearing loss in both ears, trouble swallowing, regular vomiting, inability to gain weight. I see myself at eight years old throwing up macaroni in the hallway of our house in Wichita, Kansas, on the way to the bathroom, an almost nightly flight. Further back, I hear my Grade Two teacher screaming at me for not telling her that I cannot hear instructions, making me push my awkward metal desk to the front of the room. I am timid and shy, and weigh no more than forty pounds. In other memories, I am being taunted by kids at school because the pupils in my eyes do not match, because I have skinny legs, because I am small. I can not go swimming with my classmates because I have hearing tubes implanted in my ears that fall out under water. The kids ask me, "Why?"

So I learned to compensate for the legacy cancer left me: how to respond to questions I did not really hear because I was embarrassed to ask "What?" or "Huh?" too many times; how to look strangers in the face without letting them see my eyes. Yet I did not identify with cancer. Cancer affected other people, other children, not me. Mary Esther Campbell, a little girl I knew in Maryville, died of leukemia, and I pitied her. She had had cancer, but I only had a "tumor." With a tumor I did not fear the future. As I grew older and the tumor's "side effects" receded, I even managed to forget it. It was a phantom lump that had life in my throat strictly in the past, where I was determined to leave it.

Now this fall and winter, despite my attempts at self-healing, anxiety sets me on a course from doctor to doctor, test to test in search of a definitive diagnosis. For each appointment, I trot out my symptoms like poor, tired wooden horses from a merry-go-round.

It begins with my family doctor, who schedules a blood sugar test for hypoglycemia. Six hours of sacrificing a vial of blood every hour on the hour. "You can lie down at the back if you get woozy," the nurse at the clinic says. I wait for it to hit—a tornado of disequilibrium—but nothing happens. Even so, I hope for positive results. I retrace my steps to the library. The self-help books prescribe too much food and work, but I psyche myself up to handle it. When the sugar test comes back negative, I stop telling people how badly I feel.

My spirits rejuvenate when my family doctor again suspects an inner ear virus. He dispatches me and my symptoms to an ear, nose, and throat specialist, not the one who knows my history—he is at a medical conference—but Dr. D., a stranger. I tell him my story. He looks down my throat, nodding at the lump there, and in my ears. He notices the bulge in my right ear drum and mistakenly deduces that it is caused by a polyp or cyst. "Cysts are a common occurrence for people who suffered ear infections as children," he says. "That could be what is disrupting your balance."

"Of course," I say, not thinking of my tumor's reach into my inner ear. "I do remember having bad ear infections."

To investigate further, Dr. D. orders a CT-scan. It is a surreal, almost out-of-body experience—lying immutably still on a padded lounge with my head and neck dropped inside the hole of a massive revolving doughnut, radioactive iodine injected in my arm (to make internal structures show up in purple), the scanner humming. For five infinite minutes, I am not allowed to swallow. Saliva builds, dries on my palate. My skin flushes warm from the iodine. I feel it running through my insides like an uncontrollable flame, as if not only my muscles and bones have ceased functioning but also my autonomic nervous system. I wonder if my breathing will stop, too.

A few days before Christmas, Dr. D. calls me at home to relay the results. His pleasant, near retirement voice says the radiologist who analyzed my CT-scan was concerned to find a tumor mass in my throat. "Is this the lesion you've had since you were young?" he asks.

"I think it's called a neuroganglioma," I say. "Or something like that."

"A ganglioneuroma?"

I laugh at my mistake. I explain that the tumor was cancerous at first, but I underwent two or three operations. "It's been benign since I was four."

"Were you given any radiation treatments?" he says.

"Just one," I say. "But I don't remember it." I assure him, too, that the tumor has always been large. "I can understand how it might have shocked the radiologist," I say. "He probably thought, '*What* is this woman walking around with in her throat?'" This time we both chuckle.

Even so, Dr. D. advises me to follow up the scan results with Dr. K., my longtime ear, nose, and throat physician. He offers to call Dr. K.'s office and request a special appointment. "We can't tell from the CT-scan whether the tumor has grown," he says. "Dr. K. might have more background."

I hang up the phone not worried. I believe I know my tumor.

My tumor made me a star at the Mayo Clinic—it was so rare. That is why I came to be there: perched on top of an examining table, spindly legs dangling, twelve years old, and weighing 49 ½ pounds. The pediatrician team was fascinated. I remember my jaws being cracked open like a baby rhinoceros while two doctors examined me. One of them was holding the back of my tongue with a tongue depressor as he peered down my throat with a small lighted beam. "Jim," he said to a colleague entering the room, "come look at this."

The third doctor eagerly took the depressor and beam.

"Have you ever seen one of these before?"

"What is it?" the third doctor said, looking.

"A ganglioneuroblastoma. Or it could be a ganglioneuroma . . ."

My jaws hurt, and I needed to swallow. Involuntarily, I started to gag on the tongue depressor—gag and cry.

That was the time the specialists at the Mayo Clinic discovered my tumor was encroaching on a vital artery. I could have died if a section of it was not removed. I was sitting in the consulting room when Dr. Devine told my parents. He passed his prognosis over my head to them, and they passed their questions back like objects from a cupboard I was too small to reach. "With any surgery there is also always the risk of not recovering from the anaesthetic," Dr. Devine said. Frightened, I looked up at my mother. Her face, normally bright and vivacious, appeared ashen and numb. For the first time in my memory, I saw tears well in her eyes.

Shortly after Christmas, I continue my circuit to Dr. K. As usual, he remembers me as "the girl who has been to the Mayo Clinic," although that was twenty-two years ago, two years before I became his patient. Dr. K. talks loudly, at breakneck speed, as if working with hearing problems has adapted his vocal chords. "HOW'STHEFOLKS?" he says.

He ushers me into his private office, which is almost big enough to absorb his voice, and shows me the report of the scan. In small, tight letters it describes "a huge mass lesion . . . causing considerable erosion of the base of the temporal bone . . . and markedly eroding [and destroying] an enlarging area [of the skull] around the jugular foramen. . . ." "A glomus tumor . . . should . . . be considered," the report says. "A nasopharyngeal carcinoma would also seem a likely possibility." Further on I read that the "lesion is definitely aggressive and is invading the sphenoid sinus and . . . may well be growing into the very bottom of the middle ear . . . the mastoid air cells on the right side are completely opaque. . . ."

Immediately, my mind fixes on the words "eroding," "destroying," "invading," "aggressive"—so dark, so ominous, like deadweight falling. Old responses I thought I had left in the office of some other doctor, there with the Curious George books and *Children's Stories from the Bible,* catch me up, off guard. I feel my face coloring with pain, my eyes shining too brightly.

"Don't be put off by the strong language," Dr. K. says. "These folks are just alarmed by the pictures. There may not be any change in the tumor. The problem is we have no way of comparing its size now to when you were younger. Even if we still had the X-rays we took twenty years ago, you were smaller then."

I love Dr. K. at this moment. To further reassure me, he digs out a copy of a report written in 1975, the last time my tumor was "photographed." It describes a "large soft tissue mass" and "distorted anatomy" in less startling terms but the same areas, the "bulging right drum," too. I feel strangely relieved.

"We need to do an MRI to get a more precise picture," Dr. K. says. "Then I want you to see the ear, nose, and throat people at the university hospital. There's a Dr. O. there. Depending on the results of the MRI, he may want to do a biopsy to find out if anything is happening with the tumor cells. Part of the tumor may have become cancerous. It sometimes happens after radiation treatments."

"Even after only one treatment?" I ask. I hear my voice faltering, small and squeaky.

"It's possible," he says. "If it's cancerous they may decide to treat it with chemotherapy or maybe try to remove it."

My throat stiffens. Cancerous. Chemotherapy. In my ears these words are still alien, inadmissible. Yet Dr. K. says them with ease, as if he's talking about run-of-the-mill doctoring like treating strep throat or taking out tonsils. I know it is his way of sparing me grief.

"Dr. D. and I didn't tell you this before Christmas because we didn't want to spoil your holidays," he says as he walks me back to the lobby.

I manage to nod, fighting to present an even front.

"Now just sit tight," he says. "No need to worry. Let's wait and see what the MRI shows."

I cry in my car on the way home.

The Magnetic Resonance Imaging test turns out to be another venture into near science fiction. This time I lie like a mummy inside a narrow "tube" with my head tilted backward into a shallow depression, strapped down at the temples. Without warning, the curved walls of the apparatus shrink in, centimeters above my forehead and nose. A disembodied female voice, melodious and smooth, announces the length of each section of imaging like calling out train departures—two minutes, three minutes, three minutes, three minutes. I quickly lose track of the total. For the first few rounds, the laser quietly purrs. I imagine it drawing bands of light and dark, shadings of my skull and neck, like the invisible wand of an enormous Magic Etch-O-Sketch. Then the machine begins to knock and grind, first like rusty metal gears, then *GRRR, GRRR, KNOCK, KNOCK, KNOCK, GRRR* like a not-too-distant jackhammer. I visualize, count, concentrate on keeping still. The noise speeds up, slows down. I cannot escape it.

The voice over the intercom apologizes. "Just a few more minutes."

At last the grinding stops. "All done," the voice says. "You did very well."

When my tomb is opened up, I lie numb on the table.

A week later I proceed to Dr. O., the specialist at the university hospital, to claim the results, but first I must get past an intern. While we wait in Dr. O.'s consulting room, she practices her bedside manner. "What is the problem?" she asks. From her questions I suspect she has no knowledge of my history, and I can see that her case report sheets are blank. For once I hear myself answering calmly, with confidence, the familiar doctor's office responses at bay. She studiously records every tidbit. When I report that I had a ganglioneuroma, I make my eyes meet hers. Her interest is spurred. She leans toward me with her clipboard. Out of habit I list the surgeries, display the scar down my neck. Suddenly, she is peering at my eyes, her focus flitting from the right to the left. I am not alarmed. I have experienced this moment of discovery before—the veiled pause in conversation over afternoon tea in a restaurant, the titillated, stolen gaze.

"One of your eyelids is retracted," she says, "and the pupil is not fully dilated." She unclasps the examining light from her lab-coat pocket and shines it in each eye. "That's interesting," she says.

What a wonderful specimen I am, what a marvelous learning tool. "Yes," I say. "The tumor was wrapped around the nerve that controlled dilation of the right pupil. When they removed that part of it, they took the nerve, too. I also had a Horner's Syndrome," a droopy eyelid, but I use the medical term. I explain that I have undergone three surgeries to correct the eyelid, but it is still not quite "right." I even tell her how the ophthalmologist for the first operation botched the job so badly that my eye came out looking permanently astonished, the eyelid raised too high above the iris exposing the milky white. It took a second surgeon two tries to lower it. I do not tell her how I grieved for four years before I found the second surgeon. How I thought I would not be able to live looking like that.

The intern jots the details in my file. By the time Dr. O. arrives, I am working to maintain an edge—in control but pleasant. He skims the intern's notes, and we discuss my symptoms. After all this time and testing, they have not become less vague.

"I just feel out of balance," I say.

When we turn to the tumor, I again rehearse the surgeries, radiation, nerve damage, residual effects. My voice trembles ever so slightly.

"Let's look at your pictures," Dr. O. says. He clips the results of my MRI test to a lighted viewing screen.

Immediately, I blanch and pull back. It is the first time I have seen it—the tumor, the inside of my throat. The mass is huge, gleaming white against the viewer like a knobby, peeled potato. It stretches from the base of my skull behind my right ear to the base of my neck. A good six centimeters long, three to four centimeters wide. That is me, a voice in my head wails. All at once I am the helpless girl sitting in Dr. Devine's office at the Mayo Clinic, twenty-two years of struggling to grow up, gain weight, be healthy obliterated by this singular image on the X-ray screen. What will become of me with that in my throat? I blink quickly to keep from crying.

Dr. O. and the intern do not notice my emotion. They analyze the tumor with their backs to me, like the other doctors zeroing in on its size.

"It's always been big," I say, hoping to sound convincing.

Dr. O. turns around. He must see the trouble on my face: his manner is gentle and kind. He speaks to me as if he respects my knowledge of my history.

"It's still not clear if the tumor is growing," he says, "but it doesn't seem to be causing problems. Removing it would be risky. We don't know what nerves and vessels would be affected. You could lose the ability to speak, facial sensation, blood flow to your brain, any number of functions."

These words prick and sting, but Dr. O. does not use the term cancer. He does not mention biopsies. I swallow a knot of phlegm at the back of my mouth and try to remain calm.

Dr. O. continues. "My preference is to treat cases like this conservatively. I suggest we leave the tumor alone for now and monitor it closely for changes. You've gotten along fine with it for the last twenty years, you could go twenty more without any trouble."

While absorbing this appraisal, in the fluorescent light of a dreaded doctor's office, it occurs to me that I need my tumor. This swollen mass of tissue, which the medical books say possesses no physiologic function, holds me together. The "thing" I have tried to ignore all my life is part of my body, and whatever misery it has given me, acknowledging it will keep me whole.

I breathe in Dr. O.'s good news like purified air, but I am still concerned about my symptoms. "Could they be related to something else?" I ask.

Dr. O. replies vaguely: they could indicate an inner ear virus. "We'll run a test to check your balance."

My wooden horses have come full circle.

MARGUERITE WATSON *was born in Indiana and lived in four other states before moving to Alberta in 1974. She graduated from the University of Alberta in 1982 and makes her living as a writer and editor. Her work has appeared in* The Gaspereau Review.

Reconstructing Experience

Around the Corner

NORA ABERCROMBIE

THERE'S A SNAPSHOT OF ME AND LAURA on the bank of the river. She grins, gesturing at the buckets of food and water-proofed gear we are about to load into the canoe while I slump cross-legged and morose on the tawny spring grass.

I agreed to the trip at Laura's urging. We dissected maps, absorbed how-to books, frequented whitewater paddling courses and assembled supply lists. Laura's parents fronted the money to buy a Kevlar canoe customized to our specifications. We named it Igorth, smashed one bottle of beer on the bow and drank the rest of the case. That summer we taught ourselves how to canoe, dumping, crashing, and smashing Igorth until his red hull was gouged to pink. Friday afternoons after work Laura and I would lash Igorth on top of her Mazda, cram our gear into the tiny back seat, and sprint to a river for a weekend run. My feet on the dashboard to make room for the sleeping bags stuffed on the floor in front of me, Laura scanning the rearview mirror for cops looking to ticket us for overloading, paddles rattling with every bump in the road. We liked ourselves: two young women embracing adventure, star-tling our friends, alarming our parents. It was fine.

I don't know how Laura tolerated me that summer. I was slow moving and evil-tempered. While I hung back, Laura's hand shot up whenever a course instructor needed a volunteer; Laura chirped enthusiasm at every turn in the river. I didn't. Perhaps Laura was used to me by then. Perhaps she even enjoyed the negative contrast to her own relentless effervescence. Certainly by then we were an established oddball couple—Laura was a likable, exuberant honors student and athlete; I was a reckless brooder ambling listlessly to academic and social dereliction. We would never have chosen to know one another had we not been assigned to share a room at college. Yet we were drawn to one another. Laura's happiness proved that everything was not always thoroughly hopeless, and I clung to the fact of her. I suspect Laura's affection for me rose from her romantic, sensitive soul. She was a great fan of the dismal short stories of Katherine Mansfield and was drawn to things mildly dreadful.

I will always be sorry that Laura's magnificent adventure was tainted by such a deplorable companion. But I must recognize—and honor—the expression on my face in that snapshot. It's the same one I saw many years later on the girl who sat defiantly at the back of a class I taught, blowing bubble gum, refusing assignments in favor of writing poetry calculated to insult me. It's the same one that marked the boy with his forearms disfigured with slash scars, scurrying along the hallways like a roach ambushed in sunlight. It sat camouflaged behind flawless makeup on the face of the pretty overachiever in the first row.

I remember an exceptionally upset student who brought her poetry to me. She had inked words onto seedpods, the kind that spiral from the branch on the way to the ground. It was a wet summer day, but we sat outside on the step regardless of the drizzle and she tossed the pods into the air. The result was alarming not because of the accidental arrangement of words as much their bleak meaning. We bent together, silent over the fallen poetry, while I wondered whether to continue the interview or alert child welfare services about a potential suicide. While I dither she comments on a bug struggling in a puddle on the sidewalk.

"If that bug was born today," she says, "all it would ever know is rain."

"So all it has to do," I venture stupidly, "is hang in until the sun comes out."

"The sun won't come out."

"The sun always comes out sooner or later."

"Not for this bug." And she steps on it.

I want to tell this girl to smarten up, stay alive, *try*. But I know it will do no good. Far better to just shut up and keep her company. Like Laura did for me.

THE FIRST LEG OF THE TRIP with Laura is tricky. At low water, rocks lurking under the surface of the Little Smoky can open a canoe like a tin can. But it is spring now, and the water is high, so we should be okay so long as we keep an eye out. There will be standing waves at the confluence of the Little Smoky and the Smoky but nothing we cannot handle. The high cliff banks on the Smoky River present danger only because there's nowhere to get out if we tip the boat. After that we can lie back, quite literally, while the mighty Peace River delivers us north to the Slave River. We'll hire a guide to help us traverse the famous Slave River rapids and finish in the fall at Great Slave Lake, tanned and triumphant, four months later.

My dad lends us a rifle and a shotgun and delivers an admonition: "I've dragged a river for corpses before, you know."

I nod, remembering his drowned friend.

"I don't want to do it again," he says. "Phone when you can."

On the banks of the Little Smoky: force a smile for the snapshot, tie the buckets and bags into the canoe, grab a paddle, and wave good-bye. The first week is good; we canoe well. I shoot a duck, illegally, and we eat it. It's early May, and there are still small hunks of ice in the water. Put your bare foot in the river for more than twenty seconds and you get a killer headache. But the sun glares hot and the sky is blue. We heard later that the snow in the mountains melted at an astonishing rate, causing severe flooding throughout the province. Eight paddlers died that week. All we knew then is that the river suddenly got very high and very fast. The seventh day we hit the most serious rapids we had ever paddled.

When too much water is forced down a narrow channel, there's nowhere for the extra water to go but up. Waves erupt like volcanoes, pressurized water squeezed into a peak. The trick to surviving these is to back paddle, climb them slowly, ease the bow over the top, and ease your way back down. Climb one too fast and your boat cuts it open, shattering the integrity of the wave, and the broken water bursts into your boat. Slip down into the trough too fast, and your boat torpedoes toward the riverbed.

The waves come seconds apart. We can't think to shout strategy. Screw which route to take, anyway. Keeping the bow pointed downriver demands every bit of our concentration and strength. Laura grabs whatever water she can reach. If she misses a stroke, we're lost. It's all I can do to keep the boat parallel to the current. If we go broadside, we're sunk.

There's nowhere safe to stop, not even one eddy. In two hours we are spent. Finally, we see a low spot on shore, and, bellowing our intentions, we perform a deft eddy turn and bump gently against the bank. We crawl out of the boat.

I sit on a rock and look at the river, feeling sick. Laura sits on another rock, not smiling for once. It's a long time before we can talk.

"What do you think?" asks Laura.

"Well," I say, "we can always walk to the road and hitch a ride home. But I don't want to do that." It is a revelation, as I say it, that I speak the truth.

The next day we heat water on the fire, wash our hair and our clothes. In the afternoon, Laura scouts the next mile while I sit on a boulder and smoke.

"It's not so bad," reports Laura. "There's one really bad sweeper, but if we keep left we'll miss it."

Okay, then. We're not going home.

I lie in my sleeping bag in a silent panic, watching the tent walls fade from green to black as dusk becomes night. Laura breathes steadily, already asleep. I envy her oblivion. Just as I lose consciousness, I feel the sand hollow beneath my weight as if to cradle me. I am startled and strangely comforted.

We pack the canoe in silence. Jittery and giggling, we perform our ridiculous pre-paddle ritual: two sticks of gum crossed like swords before a fencing match, and we yell, "All for one and one for all!" I fear I may puke as I push the boat from shore.

We don't make it past the first turn. A fast current propels us too close to the bank, and a small sapling obscured in the glare of the sun catches the boat and tips it. I would like to think that I did a slapping brace, as hard as I could, to keep us upright. But I didn't.

It's cold! I float in shock, grasping the floating stern rope. We are carried through standing waves so powerful they squeeze my chest like a vice. The air evacuating my lungs sounds like a deflating balloon. We shout encouragement to one another as we try to swim the boat to shore but the current sweeps us along like twigs. Laura is suddenly, eerily silent. I yell, "Leave the boat!"

Laura lets go of the rope and swims for an eddy. I see her stand up as her feet touch bottom. She screams and screams at me to swim harder. I am farther out in the current and know that I can't possibly reach her eddy. I'll try for shore around the corner. Sort of. I don't seem to be working very hard at it. But Laura shouts from shore, and, bloody hell, I don't want her to worry.

"I can't make it," I holler, stupidly neglecting to add the crucial end of the sentence: that I mean to try for shore around the corner.

The eddy I end up in is just large enough for my legs. There is white water behind me and a twenty-foot mud bank inches from my nose. I stand, thigh-high, in freezing brown water, blowing my whistle for Laura. She doesn't come. And then I forget about Laura because I realize I am freezing to death.

A few feet down river a branch hangs over the cliff. It is beyond my reach, so I dig holes with my fingers to put my feet in so I can climb up and grab the branch. The first try, I manage to grab the branch, but it breaks and I crash back into the water. I try again, and again, and each time I fall. Then I can't feel my legs, and my hands are so cold that my fingers won't go straight. I dig into the bank with my fists. I keep falling. I turn and look at the river, wonder if I can make it to the other bank. But I remember the sweeper Laura described yesterday and I know there is no way I can cross the river before the sweeper catches and drowns me.

Panic rises in my throat and I sob.

A small beaver pokes his head up in my eddy, sees me and dives beneath the surface. I stare at the ripples it leaves behind, and I am suddenly, overwhelmingly enraged. I am dying. For sure I am dying. Defiance cascades through me like lava. Suddenly, I feel almost hot. I try one last time. This time, the branch holds. I drag myself up the bank until my head touches the overhanging sod shelf. I can't go farther. I look down and I am sure as hell not going back down there. Fuck it! Fuck this, and fuck that, fuck everything. I do a bent one-arm hang, grabbing for bushes. I grasp a handful of prickles and scrabble wildly. One foot catches a loop of roots. I lunge forward and am over the top.

For a while I let my legs dangle over the side. Then I get scared that the overhang will collapse so I wriggle further back. I let out a barking laugh; I look around. Nothing is different. The sun still shines; the river roars. I cover my ears, laughing.

I am suddenly very hot and stand to strip off my wet sweater. I blow my whistle and holler for Laura. I start walking back to where I saw her get out. No sign. I walk, calling and whistling. Half an hour later I start to plan how I'll tell her parents she's dead, but I can't stop chuckling.

Suddenly, I hear her voice. She appears out of the bush and rushes to me. She took my last words to her—"I can't make it"—to mean that I felt myself drowning. She started to run as soon as I disappeared around the corner, ripping her legs to ribbons on the underbrush, never thinking I'd retain the strength to make it to shore so soon. After an hour of fruitless searching downriver, she was sure I had drowned. Seeing me alive, she surrenders to hypothermia and tears. I am bemused to see that she never lost her paddle. I give her the handle, grasp the blade, and lead her out of the bush. The least I can do. The very least.

Laura says that the unchanging brightness of the sun, the quiet of the river, the supreme indifference of nature as it was killing us is what struck her. It is true that, had things gone differently, we would have succumbed to hypothermia and slipped under the waves. There would have been a police report, a dragging of the river, news reports for a day. A couple of funerals. That would have been that.

But we didn't die. And I came close enough to realize I'd really like to have a life. Hell, after snuggling up to my mortality for a half hour or so, I felt lucky just to be breathing. Breathing is good; a sunny day is a bonus. Reading the paper in bed, playing checkers with my kids, washing dishes, all the ordinary stuff of life. Excellent! I try to tell my dad what happened, how nearly dying gave me my life back, how I am not afraid anymore. I try to explain what it means to me to fish and eat and paddle and sleep, and feel welcome and easy in the world. His eyes soften, I assume he's remembering some expedition of his own, and he says, "I guess that's why they call it re-creation." Then he tells me not to worry about the guns we lost.

Two summers later Laura and I go on another trip. We have to sit on the shore and eat potato chips for a long time before we screw up the nerve to get in the canoe, even though it was an easy river. But we go, and we float down that easy river, and we often say to each other, "It doesn't get any better than this." And we are right.

Laura eventually married my brother. They live twenty minutes down the road with my two nephews. We see each other all the time.

She read this essay the other night when my husband and I, and our two kids, went over to their place. She laughed and nodded, leaning against her washing machine and sipping a beer as she flipped the pages. Then she let me off the hook, once and for all, for not swinging that slapping low brace. She said it didn't matter that we never made it to Great Slave Lake, never saw the world's northernmost rook of pelicans, or that she spent the rest of that summer on a shitty job instead of on the river. She let me know that the twenty-two years we've spent together are what matter. And that I haven't let her down.

I love Laura, and we will canoe again. That's all there is to say about that.

I like to share what happened to me at the base of that mud cliff, especially with the one or two desperate students that always seem to find their way into my classes. I wish I could communicate the core truth of my canoeing experience: that some rivers, like some people, will try to hurt you. But not *all* of them. I want them to believe that misery, like most things, is circumstantial. And that they're miserable not because misery is the standard existential state but because they're stuck in a puddle or up against a wall. But in the end I have to admit that I was lucky. The branch might not have held. My lifespan might not have been long enough for me to see the sun come out. Nature may have looked upon me like a bug in a puddle and snuffed me out on a whim.

The snapshots of me and Laura are tacked to the wall beside my bathroom door. Most of them are from our second long trip, most of them silly, flirty poses on the banks of the easy river. But there is another from that first summer. I am wearing sunglasses, holding the duck I shot, not smiling. The expression on my face is alien, and no wonder. I haven't yet sliced through its skin to retrieve its breasts for the frying pan. And I haven't seen the black bear chase her three cubs up a tree and turn to challenge us, snorting on the bank. Or the herd of elk that crashed across the river in front of the canoe. Or the branch, the beaver, and the friend who saved my life.

NORA ABERCROMBIE's *literary nonfiction pieces have appeared in a number of periodicals and anthologies. Nora is a former editor of several periodicals, including* The Edmonton Bullet, The Visual Art Newsletter, Prairie Bookworld *and* Arts Bridge. *She also writes fiction and screenplays. "Around the Corner" won first prize in the 1999 Jon Whyte Memorial Essay Contest.*

A Stone's Throw Away

MICHELLE ALFANO

I often feel as if I am trapped within this skin, with a face formed by a history, culture, and race which is not of my own making. At times, if I could, I would discard this too pale, too dark shell, neither white nor brown, which peels away, not so gently with a touch. We Sicilians are an anomaly, in many ways, closer to Africa than to Rome. We tolerate no breech of the unwritten codes that reach back thousands of years. Our blood, which mingled so freely with a plethora of races and cultures, blindly adheres to the conception that we are "pure" that we, and we alone, remain inviolate.

To escape this legacy I have often assumed the mask of another. I turn my face from my roots. Much to my mother's displeasure, I don't strive to retain the first language that I learned from her lips. I did not marry an Italian, do not move in circles made up of Italians. I don't go back to Sicily to pay homage to the village where my parents were born. I have never seen Sicily. My name is Michela, which is my grandmother's name and the name given to the eldest daughter of each her children, but I am known as Michelle. As if a name could change who I was, what I still am.

Hamilton, the city where I was born, is known as a "lunch-bucket town" dominated by steel mills, blue collar workers, and, allegedly, Mafia, although I did not realize this until I moved away.

Italians made up the largest minority in the city when I was growing up there twenty years ago. Within that enclave there are a large number of Sicilians. Not just Sicilians, but thousands and thousands of persons born in, or descended from, a small village outside of Palermo called Racalmuto in western Sicily.

Racalmuto is a stone's throw away from Montelepre where the famous Sicilian bandit Giuliano lived and loved and died at the hands of assassins led to him by his cousin. Sicily is an island that has been terrorized by the Mafia for centuries. It is an island that has been colonized, bled, and isolated for more than a millennium. And the blood that flowed on that island also flows through my veins and the veins of my child. My child, named for that bandit, my child with a birthmark imprinted on her right side, the shape of the three-cornered island of Sicily. And now I live a stone's throw away from the city my mother emigrated to. I am close enough to remain connected to her but far enough to escape her and the family. Or am I?

I remember the small murders of my teenage years in a large extended family. The situation that stayed with me the most involved a man closely connected to my family. Even now I can't repeat his name because I fear what it would do to our family, to the people who still care for him. He tried to kill his wife with a gun. He was a close friend of my father's, like family, like an uncle. When did I realize that we as women meant so little in this family? When did I know that some men are forgiven much and may do much that remains unchallenged? I still hear the words that were uttered when we first learned that he tried to kill her: "Maybe she did something to make him do it."

Did I actually hear those words, or was there something that suggested this? The lack of recrimination. The lack of specifics. The fact that he was still welcomed into our home as my father's friend? But what of that woman whose name now escapes me? I can't remember ever seeing her again after that startling revelation, almost as if she had gone into hiding from shame or remorse.

What could she have done to provoke this? Adultery? Lack of care for her almost grown children? An improperly cleaned house? The thing that frightened me the most was not even the attempt on her life but that the people in my family could somehow rationalize what he tried to do.

I resisted inculcation into the ways of womanhood, against the restrictions. I refused to cook unless compelled, refused to learn how to sew (even a button!) and took but one typing course in order to type essays but never memos for a boss. I chafed against tasks assigned to me and not my brother, making beds, his and mine, washing dishes and clothes. There were gifts: a bicycle for him, yet none for me. Freedom and mobility were dangerous for young girls, even in small cities under the watchful eyes of many relatives. He inherited a parcel of land from my grandmother Michelina; I didn't.

"You see," my mother murmured complacently, "she's forgotten about you." This was said matter of factly. The anger and disappointment were left to me.

These were not injustices. But they were clear demarcations of what I was expected to be, and do and, collectively, they represented far less than what I was. Women's lives were expected to be small, to fit in the palm of a hand, to be diminished in the larger scheme of things. To shine was to overstep one's place. I wanted to be lawyer, but my mother told me that being a bank clerk was more appropriate for a girl. She meant this kindly. She meant it with love. She did not want me to have a difficult life.

One uncle prophesied, "She'll never become a lawyer," and the prophecy came true but not for the reasons he ventured. Fear and lack of confidence slowly became lethargy and a lack of focus. He and many others tried to destroy my will in a thousand ways. *Destroy* is not too strong a word. Sometimes it was innocent; sometimes it wasn't. But always it was with the intent of molding me into a certain image of young womanhood which had more relevance to Sicilian village life in the 1930s than life here in Canada in the 1970s.

When I was sixteen my father died of cancer. I started plotting my freedom. I had simple goals. For me freedom meant space, the languor of emotional and physical space, where a locked door would not be perceived as hostility toward the family and where reading was not seen as an idle luxury, where an interest in the other sex was not seen as an opportunity by which to ruin or shame the family. Freedom meant a place where difference did not pose a threat.

Why, I once asked, does independence for Italian women always suggest sexual promiscuity and emotional distance from the family? We say, "I want to be on my own, to be independent." *You want your own place so you can do what you like with whomever you like.* We say, "I want to meet other people, experience other cultures, other lives." *You hate your own kind; you despise your own people.* "I want to sustain myself financially, emotionally." *Why won't you let us help you? Why do you hate us so much?* The questions linger, remain. And I am a stone's throw away from their approbation still.

When my father died I receded into emotional infancy, either consciously or unconsciously. This only accelerated as I grew older. I made myself useless, lazy, and nonproductive by my family's rigorous standards. Although I was the eldest, I was the least hard-working, least responsible member of the family. I was the emotional one, the difficult one, the childish one. Gradually, the responsibilities of the small family business shifted to my younger brother and sister. It was physically hard work and gut wrenchingly important as the only means of our livelihood. But I selfishly decided that I didn't want to devote my life to it. And I knew that if I stayed at home it would destroy any independence or courage I had. I loved myself better than I loved them. That was my first crime.

How I escaped: I left for the bigger, more glamorous city of Toronto forty miles away. It would be cruel to say my father's death represented a sort of liberation for me. But it would be true.

And yet I love the myth of Sicily, the myth that Sicilians weave around themselves. Perhaps because I have never been there my vision of it is potent, vivid, drenched in the red blood of my family, in the blue of Sicilian skies, in the rock-colored dreams of crumbling Grecian temples, in the ebony of Sicilian eyes borne of some Arabic ancestor.

Café au lait skin burnt brown by a Mediterranean sun. My grandmother's lullaby like an muezzin's call to prayer. The piazza of the small village bereft of women who dutifully remain home so that their husbands and fathers will not be shamed. My father riding with pride on a horse ornamented in the colors of the flag in a religious parade. So beautiful, so pure, it pains me to look at his photograph. The houses which appear carved from stone. My father calling out to my mother as she passed the field where he tilled the earth with his brothers. Perhaps she gently exaggerated the swing of her hips for her future husband. Long, black braids tossed back suggestively. My grandfather gunned down over a small dispute by a young boy who was duped into believing he would not be charged. My father, a nine-year-old boy, the only witness, forced to go into hiding. The bandit Giuliano's mother licking the earth where her son's blood pooled after his betrayal and murder.

I slip into these memories, these dreams and myths like a pool of warm water and think of my family's life there. Somehow more alive, more real than this endless struggle for the acquisition of more and more which has become North American life.

My tribe, my blood. When I was younger the intensity of my conflicting emotions—love, fear, anger, shame, pride—threatened to engulf me. Now I am more at peace with myself, at peace with my culture, which has both threatened to choke the life from me and provided me with great moments of pride and beauty. Perhaps having had a child, I am less disposed to think of my own unhappiness first. Juliana is not the answer, but I have found that she is more important than all the endless questions and self-recrimination.

My father's portrait sits above the plastic-covered couch in the never-used living room. His half smile hides a strong and sometimes cruel nature. Don't slander the dead, and above all don't slander the family, it says. I am warned by his and a hundred other voices within and without. Yet the truth, my truth, spills out of me like water from an overfilled glass with nowhere to else to travel but up and out.

MICHELLE ALFANO *is a freelance writer living in Toronto. Her short fiction has been published in numerous literary anthologies and journals including the* 1995 *Journey Prize Anthology. Her reviews and nonfiction have been published in* Paragraph, Canadian Forum, eyetalian *and* VIA.

Sargent Sundae

ANN ATKEY

Winnipeg, Friday, May 6, 1994

OUTSIDE SARGENT SUNDAE'S ICE CREAM PARLOUR, children, parents, cyclists, and seniors crowd the sidewalk with their treats. A cartoon Mountie eating ice cream smiles down from the sign. Soaking up early evening sun, a man licks his Heavenly Hash cone and languidly watches the street scene. Something is vaguely out of place. As an old brown Dodge Dart rounds the bend at Portage and Overdale, the passenger door swings open, and a young blonde woman jumps from the moving car. Stunned, he watches her stumble, then run toward the median. Cars jam on their brakes as the woman dodges through the four westbound lanes.

The car jumps the curb, just missing the latte-sipping women outside the Sunstone Cafe, and stops two feet from the floor-to-ceiling glass of the Sargent Sundae window. The driver's door opens. A dark-haired man jumps out and chases the woman, screaming at her to stop.

The woman reaches the median before he catches up. Most cars have stopped, but some eastbound drivers are still unaware. Motorists and pedestrians watch amazed as he starts to thump her on the back. Blood starts to stream: he has a knife. Many stand slack-jawed on the sidewalk. Others yell for him to stop. Some run to her defense with improvised weapons from their cars: a jack, a golf club. Two men pull him away; he turns and cuts them with the knife. He bellows that she is getting what she deserves.

He turns and runs east down the sidewalk, several pursuers just behind. Onlookers rush to help the woman, who lies half on the brick median, half on the asphalt, her green T-shirt and denim shorts blood-soaked. Others call for help from the ice cream parlor and on their cell phones.

Still pursued at Linwood Street two blocks away, the attacker bolts left, then circles back down the lane running parallel to Portage Avenue, and returns to the scene of the knifing. Terrified parents grab their children and run.

Officers from District 2 Police Station arrive as the crazed man stands over the woman's body, yelling and gesticulating with the knife in his bloody hands. The officers point their guns and give him instructions. Some in the crowd shout at them to shoot. He screams that he doesn't care if he dies, she got what she deserved. He drops his knife. The officers handcuff him and shove him into the squad car.

An ambulance jerks to a stop. Frightened paramedics hurriedly grab the stricken woman from the dark red pool of blood, hoist her onto the stretcher, and take off.

Six more police cars arrive. Officers redirect the four lanes of westbound traffic. With bright yellow police ribbons they create a police investigation zone three blocks long and four lanes wide. Others take statements from witnesses:

Margaret Black, who operates Black's Vintage Books and Antiques on Portage Avenue . . . said by the time onlookers realized what was happening . . . it was too late.

"Two people were with her—one was doing CPR and the other was trying to get the breathing going, but she was dead on the road," said Black. "You could tell she was dead. Her eyes were open, staring, and her skin was a pale, yellowy color. It was horrible. . . . Nobody was sure what he was doing at first, whether he was hitting her, pounding her on the back or stabbing her. But then the blood came."

–Brad Oswald, Winnipeg Free Press

At 7:00 P.M. my eleven-year-old son Sean and I drove down Portage on our way to spend the evening with my friend Susan and her son. It was the kind of gorgeous summer evening that is such a relief to Winnipeggers after a long winter, and so we drove with the windows open. The sun warmed our skin; the breeze cooled it.

From blocks away we saw the red and blue flash atop an eastbound cruiser car at Overdale. Yellow streamers formed a crooked rectangle in the landscape, reminding me of Christo, the artist who wraps public buildings in swaths of cloth. Sean thought the police ribbons were "cool." An old car rested on its belly by Sargent Sundae, where subdued onlookers milled with police. I felt uneasy, because the car didn't look like it had been hit.

When we returned at 10:30, the ribbon markers were still up, and a curved line of intense pink flares led us off Portage onto Linwood. I wondered, but was careful not to turn on the radio or TV news. Part of me didn't want to know what had happened.

So many people were screaming for him to stop. And then people started to go back to their cars and get two-by-fours. . . . I was just kind of locked in place. One guy had even got a hatchet out of a car.

He was standing right over top of her. People kind of backed away again. By that time police started arriving, and they all drew their guns and were pointing them at him, and then the crowd went, like, crazy. They were screaming . . . 'Shoot him. . . . Shoot the bastard.' They were mad at a man for killing someone. But they wanted the same thing by having him killed.

It was as if he was taking over their souls—like he went into all of their bodies.
—Fourteen-year-old boy interviewed by Gordon Sinclair, Winnipeg Free Press

Saturday, May 7

ALL MORNING I WAS RESTLESS AND CRABBY despite my usually pleasurable Saturday morning routine of fresh coffee and the *Globe and Mail* on the back deck. I didn't listen to the news, but yellow streamers kept appearing in my mind. At noon Sean and I biked to the corner of Overdale and

Portage, across from Assiniboine Park. As a tiny ten-year-old, I rode my blue CCM bike here to the Overdale Coffee Shop, now Sargent Sundae, for an orange Popsicle or blueberry Mr. Freezie. Today before crossing the bridge to the park, we stopped off at Sargent Sundae for a peanut crunch waffle cone. But this usually familiar visit to my childhood corner felt other-worldly.

I asked the server about the yellow markers the night before. Looking sick, he told me. After a moment's silence, I asked if she survived. Tears hung in his eyes as he mumbled apologetically, "I don't think she made it." I asked Sean if he'd mind if we skipped the park today. He agreed, looking unsettled.

On the way home I bought a *Winnipeg Free Press*. "Woman year's seventh homicide victim" appeared under Police/courts, with very little information other than she was twenty-three years old and had been stabbed several times, allegedly by a man she knew.

I turned on the six o'clock TV news. The murdered woman had a name, Kelly Lynn Stewner. The reporter was interviewing witnesses. A paunchy middle-aged man: "I can't believe it happened again, and this time in St. James, such a safe neighborhood. A peaceful summer evening and—*boom!*—a man goes crazy and knifes his wife to death right in front of us. And kids saw it, too. We tried to save her but couldn't. Well, at least it's not like New York, where people step aside. Everything hasn't gone berserk; we're still looking out for each other in Winnipeg."

An athletic twenty-year-old woman: "All my life I've never seen actual violence—only on TV. My parents warned me to keep my eyes open, stay out of secluded places and parking lots at night. But this happened in broad daylight with lots of people around. I wonder if I could protect myself from an attack like this. Until now I thought that if I was smart, everything would turn out. Now I'm not so sure."

Old words appeared in my head, projectiles hurled across the room: *Useless as tits on a bull, whore who can't be trusted, should be grateful I choose not to break your bones, if you leave me, I'll find you and kill you.* Again I felt them smashing against my soul. What am I supposed to do with them? Bury them deep in the earth? Burn them ceremonially?

Sunday, May 8

IT WAS MOTHER'S DAY, and I thought about my mother, my grandmothers, myself as mother of my two boys, Brian and Sean, and how all the generations are linked in our mothering. A heaviness grew in me.

Late afternoon I raked out winter debris from the front shrubs. My neighbor Joe left his yard work and joined me. Leaning on his rake, he railed about the murder: "They said she was separated and had a restraining order, but she was crazy enough to go off with him in his car. . . . What was she thinking? Why don't women like her just leave their husbands and have the police handle it? If he'd already been violent, how could she even talk to him? Where was her self-respect? I don't get it. Boy, if any bastard gets rough with either of our girls, I'll kill him."

I came back in and collapsed on the couch. Over dinner I talked about the murder with the kids. But the queasiness in my stomach wouldn't go away. My past had come back to be dealt with one more time.

Monday, May 9

Alice Cardinal [Kelly's mother] *spent Mother's Day haunted by remorse—wondering whether a quick call to police could have saved her daughter's life.*

"I wish I had done that," she said. "She would still be alive today."

Cardinal said her daughter urged her not to call the police, even though she had obtained a restraining order against her former husband less than two weeks ago. Instead, she drove away with him voluntarily. . . .

"Restraining orders only work if they are enforced by the person taking out the restraining order," she said, adding it's also difficult for an abused partner to assess the mental stability of her estranged partner. . . .

"She was afraid. She was terrified of him," she said. "She tried to get some sort of peace of mind," Cardinal said. "But it got worse." Bruce James Stewner, 29, has been charged with first-degree murder.

–Stevens Wild, Winnipeg Free Press

I found it almost impossible to function at work. My office, with its exposed brick and art, is usually inspiring. Today, it felt suffocating. I was late for meetings, had nothing to say at the consultation, and triple-booked myself. Each time someone looked at me with kindness, I started crying. Now I know what they mean when they say "river of tears." I called the therapist who had helped me years ago and made an appointment for that evening. By suppertime, when Sean asked what was wrong, I was able to talk a bit without crying.

At the therapist's I talked about the fears the murder had awakened in me. "This murder took place at the corner of my childhood, where it's supposed to be safe. It's so close to home. This man didn't kill me, I know, but it reminds me of another who killed a sweet open part of me back then."

"How would you feel about going for ice cream at Sargent Sundae?"

"Well, maybe. No. Yes. That bastard. The park entrance is a favorite spot of mine. I'm not going to let him take that away from me. Let's go."

It was three days after the murder, and everything looked normal. The server looked worriedly at my red eyes as I ordered cooling lime sherbet. We sat eating our cones outside on the bench, gazing across the street to the darkened park. Every few minutes a car would stop by a large tree, and people would get out, stand there a few minutes, then leave. I thought I saw a human form leaning against the tree, but it didn't move. I felt wobbly but knew I had to have a look.

The single large elm across Portage had been transformed into a memorial. What I had thought was a ghostly person was actually photos, signs, and flowers attached with wire to the trunk. An eight-by-ten photo of the slain woman and a sign—"We will miss you, Kelly"—were surrounded with notes of remembrance, large cellophane flowers, and small bunches of real ones. A spontaneous memorial to a victim of violence.

A Jetta pulled up at the curb. In the infant seat sat a toddler draped over in sleep. A young couple joined us at the memorial tree. They had witnessed the murder. The woman shook her head slowly. "If only we could have done things differently. But I don't know how we could have saved her. How could he do it?"

Her husband described how things had unfolded. "I was coming out with our cones. Mary was waiting on the wood bench by the bike rack with Kristy in the stroller. It all happened in a flash—an instant from picking up two soft ice creams for our walk in the park, to this guy stabbing his wife. She didn't stand a chance, he moved so quickly. He was prancing he was so mad. Ugh! Right in front of us. I've never seen such rage."

"It was a violent nightmare that flashed in front of us," the woman added. "Then it was over. Except it's not over. The memory is so real and keeps coming back."

The man's eyes were caught by stirring in the car seat. "We're still shaken. It has taken away our confidence in life." They quietly laid a small bouquet of carnations at the foot of the thick tree trunk and drove away with their sleeping child.

Somehow, I felt much calmer. I was grateful for the memorial as a focus for my own twenty-year-old grief, here under a tree where I had played as a child.

When I tucked in Sean that night, I noticed a hammer under the edge of his bed. He said it was for protection. Sadly, I pulled up the teal comforter, his apprehensive face staring at me. It wasn't someone in his life I had been afraid of, I told him. It was someone long before he was born. There was nothing to be afraid of now.

Tuesday, May 10

AWAKE AT 4:00 A.M. AND UP AT 5:00. On *Newsworld,* witnesses described how they had tried to help Kelly. As I passed her memorial on the way to work, I didn't cry. At the office, I talked about the murder with anyone who would listen. After a quick lunch I went for a walk, looking in the bookstore and flower shop for ordinary things to calm me down. Back at the office I still felt faint, so I put my head on my desk and fell asleep. Two hours later I gave up and headed home.

Then some healing normal stuff: making Spanish rice for supper, taking

Sean to his soccer game. During the game Sean's playing got better and better. He streaked down the field and kicked accurately. He even scored. Then we hurried home to pack for his two days at Camp Assiniboia; he stuffed comics and flashlight into his duffel bag enthusiastically. He was having fun again.

Wednesday, May 11

We can't ignore this death. We can't forget it either. It's time to turn our tears into change.

We're mad as hell. We have every right to be mad as hell. And we need to shout out, to tell everyone from politicians to partners that it's time the hurting stopped.

It's time we stopped having to accept fear as part of a woman's legacy. Enough is enough.

—Lindor Reynolds, Winnipeg Free Press

Thursday, May 12

I AM SUSPENDED IN THE YELLOW SKY above Portage and Overdale. Under me the flat, black asphalted roofs of Sargent Sundae's and Sunstone Cafe cast shimmers of heat. Between them the elms of Overdale move gently in the wind. Beyond the busy avenue and lawn, the footbridge arches across the brown-green river. Sidewalks teem with people, bicycles, and strollers.

Right below I see a woman jump out of a car and run. I float closer, moving with her. She does not know I am there. I see her clenched jaw, her pale clammy skin, I hear her heart thumping in her chest as she runs. She gasps for breath. I hear her thoughts.

From above I watch a dozen people run, pull him off, hold her, chase him away. Cars are frozen. There is no sound except for frightened cries of onlookers. I hover over her. She is quiet, and I know she is dead. I weep because I can't help her. But I am still here. I will keep going. Floating up and over the chain fence, I settle on the grass by the river.

ANN ATKEY, *who has previously published in* Prairie Fire, *is completing a nonfiction manuscript about contemporary Canadian women. After living most of her life in Winnipeg, where she has held positions as an officer at Manitoba Arts Council and marketing director at Prairie Theatre Exchange, she and her two sons recently returned to Toronto, her birthplace, where she works as a freelance arts administrator.*

Her Studio Was Her Kitchen

JOYCE HARRIES

Studio I

(EDMONTON) A red and white no-room-for-a-table one where she made:
ladies' delight pickle relish (after coming home from the glorious honeymoon in the mountains where she was sick in a pub from drinking beer and tomato juice and her husband Hu had to vouch for her because she was under the drinking age of so long ago) / baby formula (because breast feeding wasn't encouraged and all her life that has been her biggest regret) / Thanksgiving turkey (and was hooked on *that* kind of smell, in *their* little house) / hermit cookies (from her mother's recipe) / apple pie (made with lard and directions from *The Joy of Cooking*.)

Studio II

(OTTAWA) In a basement suite with a wringer washer. Tommy in a playpen crowded the small studio, where she made:
fried chicken in popover batter (from a recipe in *Ladies Home Journal*.) / Minute rice (new on the market and served to

guests as the *pièce de resistance*) / Pablum (from a round blue box, good to store cookies in.)

Studio III

ON THE FIRST OF TWO STAYS at the university campus in Iowa. In the hot, muggy quonset hut where their second son was conceived, her studio's two burner hot plate and small icebox produced:

> canned tomato soup / pancakes (Aunt Jemima mix) / scrambled eggs (eggs fresh from the university farm) / potatoes, pork chops, and salad.

Studio IV

BACK IN HER HOMETOWN in a small house shared with another couple— her husband Hu only home weekends. The kitchen studio had a blue wooden potty chair, where Tommy sat and ate raisins (Cheerios hadn't been invented yet), waited till he was off the chair and his little training panties were pulled on again. This was before disposable diapers. She made:

> Junior chopped baby food, Pablum and cocoa / roast chicken or beef on weekends (and she had morning sickness and got a boil on her cheek probably from surviving on leftovers.)

Studio V

AT LAST IN THEIR OWN HOME. With a new little boy, Bruce, carriage blocked in the doorway to the dining room, where the hum of the Bendix washer processing its loads of diapers kept him happy. And then there was a little girl, Jody, and she grew to sit in the high chair and spill her milk on the battleship-green linoleum studio floor while her mother made:

shrimp mull served on rice (her first sophisticated food, she thought, for a Christmas neighborhood party) / macaroni and cheese (pre-Kraft Dinner) / real angel food cake (pre-cake mixes. Her mother showed her how to fold egg whites) / Christmas dinners (for thirty-seven years, they flowed from this studio, with flaming Christmas pudding (only adults liked it, but the children adored Nanny's warm caramel sauce.

Aunt Muriel, mentally slow, always came to visit and always overate and always threw up in the night. Aunt Ruby, a big bosomed Buddha figure, wolfed her dinner. Aunt Pearl smiled and smiled—she'd been a teacher during the First World War, and she was an active member of the WCTU, so they didn't serve wine. Other relatives, foreign university students, sat at the once-a-year damasked table. She would rather iron six white shirts than one tablecloth. And she remembered how babies would be taken from cribs, carriages, or high chairs and passed around from lap to lap, and they would put the colored paper hats from Christmas crackers in their mouths and cry when they couldn't have what they reached for, and in later years, when the children were adults, they could drink wine and lift their glasses in a toast, "Merry Christmas.")

Then the first child, Tommy, died in a polio epidemic, and she lost interest in her studio, and the whole house was sad, so she made baked custard and red Jell-O because they slide down crying throats.

Studio VI

THEN A SMALL STUDIO WAS ADDED at Hidden Bar Ranch. A dull, red trailer at the edge of a swampy poplar wood, where pink and blue hairbells grew, kitty-corner from the horse corral, and next to the single men's bunkhouse. By this time, Lori and Jeff were born, and he slept in a portable cot and Lori joined her two older siblings in the back of the station wagon. She made:

Kraft dinner with ketchup / salty Lipton's chicken noodle soup / peanut butter and banana sandwiches.

Outside, a small, round Father's Day barbecue grilled steaks (from their own Angus cattle). And they went on picnics by wagon behind a team of horses—Nick and Flick. And then another little boy, Danny, was born, and when they went to the ranch, the other four slept in a real Stoney Indian tepee they had helped paint, and Danny and his parents moved into the spiffed-up settlers' cabin just for the summer, where she cooked for university students, just for the summer, and she gave them:

> meat, fried potatoes, tomatoes, and eggs for breakfast / packed lunches of meat, buns, hard boiled eggs, and fruit / dinners of stew, baked ham, ground beef patties, chili, and pies / chiffon cakes (The hens kept laying until she thought she couldn't make another of these if you paid her) and homemade ice cream (in a hand-cranked tub surrounded with ice plus salt. One sad day, the salt got in the peach ice cream, and you'd have thought it was the end of the world.)

Studio VII

AND THEN SHE HAD A SMALL JIGGLING STUDIO in a faded green trailer in southern Alberta at the Stampede Cattle Station where she made:

> gallons of coffee and ice cubes / beef sandwiches (for the cowboy-booted men who came to drink Scotch and buy or sell the purebred Angus cattle).

And sometimes, at sale times, she cooked:

> roasts for 150 people / pancakes and bacon (from Coyote pancake mix and cooked on griddles on a long barbecue in a windbreak next to the house, across the driveway from the sale barn).

Studio V

THE GREEN LINOLEUM CHANGED to subdued gray and white vinyl bricks which showed every speck and drip. Jody and Lori had by this time become her efficient helpers. Bruce, Jeff, and Danny, not unlike Hu, though he was competent in basic kitchen maneuvers, appeared to have little interest, except for the end results. The teenagers brought their friends to sit on the long white benches at the studio table, and ate and drank:

> peanut butter cookies, Rice Krispie squares, and baklava /
> homemade herb bread / gallons of herb tea (and they
> laughed and laughed. She hovered, though not over them,
> while she prepared dinners and knew this stage wouldn't last
> long enough.)

During this period, she had three types of Christmas parties, ones for Hu's staff and for friends and business associates, and for the Faculty members, since by now he was the Dean of Commerce. (One night a professor's wife was locked in the main-floor washroom for more than an hour. She was too embarrassed to S.O.S.). She prided herself in being ahead of many food trends. She made quiches and crepes.

Before convocation, nervous young graduates came for brunch, and her studio produced scrambled eggs in her copper chafing dish, along with muffins and fruit. Many of these young people turned up in their lives years later.

Business dinners for directors from Germany included:

> smoked salmon in endive / broiled tomatoes and steamed
> asparagus / chocolate mousse (and the wine flowed, and rose
> petals dropped, and she would once again empty the ashtrays,
> load the glasses, rinse the plates and silver, soak red wine stains
> off table linen, and go to bed satisfied, though exhausted.)

And usually for Hu's December birthday dinner, when the children were older, she would make a big steak and kidney pie (and invite a few friends over).

Studio VI

BACK AT HIDDEN BAR RANCH, in a big log house they all helped build, there was room for the whole family and friends to make:

sandwiches of beef, ham, or turkey (around a huge middle island, and she could watch a crackling fire, make dinner, and see the children in the swimming pool, all at the same time) / pancakes and bacon breakfasts (for high school graduation parties) / crepe parties (with choices of fillings for sixty people, while the sun sparkled the snow, their guests drank Bloody Marys, and nearly everyone smoked.)

Studio V

BACK HOME AROUND THE DINING ROOM TABLE next to the studio, where she offered:

gallons of coffee and mixed sandwiches (to the smart young men and women who helped devise political campaigns and advertising strategy. She listened and even put in her two cents' worth, and three out of five times, not counting nominating meetings, the end result was victory).

Studio VIII

ONCE A YEAR HER STUDIO WAS OUTSIDE, next to a set of corrals, next to an old sagging gray barn where cattle were sorted, branded, de-horned, and altered. She cooked:

"prairie oysters" in bubbling butter in old black frypans on an open fire, and they picnicked from dune buggies, truck and station wagon tailgates.

Studio IX

FARTHER WEST, at the Paradise Ranch in the interior of British Columbia, on a bay looking down to the end of Lake Okanagan. Ponderosa pines swayed out the window or stood in perfect, hot stillness, and she watched Canada geese honking past on their way to the apricot orchard down the lane.

Friends Mary and Jim came every year, and Mary helped make:

> apricot chutney (whose pungent fragrance permeated walls and people, and the jars were boxed for shipment back to Edmonton in any cars going that way) / pickled cherries (wrinkled marbles with gin and juniper).

And every adult held a wineglass, and their first grandchild came to visit, and the barefoot chef in her chutney-stained apron made:

> stuffed grapevine leaves / homemade ice cream (sugarless, for Hu, from a fancy Italian machine) / leg o' lamb, ratatouille, cucumber, and sunflower seeds in yogurt / corn on the cob (picked from the back garden and rushed to the pot, the way it *should* be).

Studio V

NEWLY REFURBISHED WITH OAK FLOORS and an added greenhouse, had:

> salmon baked in foil with onion, dill and tomato (and the humidity steamed the windows, and ice formed near orchids and sprouting bulbs, and at night, the stars shone down and the moon lit the room where they drank wine and talked far into the night and felt a part of another world while they were safe in their own nest).

From this studio she hit her stride—party fare for over a hundred. The invitations read, "Please come for JUST DESSERTS." (And this was before Martha Stewart talked of "Just Desserts.") The next year, the invitations read, "Please come for MOSTLY WILD CHARCUTERIE."

Invitations for the last big Christmas party read, "Please come for COUNTRY FARE." Dishes served included:

> elk paté / tiny wild-rice pancakes with red-pepper jelly /

smoked trout rillettes (with marigold petals) / world's largest
pecan pies (cooked in paella pans and topped with whipped
cream and candied borage flowers).

(Her studio was "really cooking" now—later, she sold some of these items—
not that that was what she had intended, but when asked if she would . . . "Sure.")

Studio IX

SHE AND HER HUSBAND had their last two and a half days together, part
of the time at the studio on the lake, by the vineyards, in British Columbia
with tomatoes for sandwiches and strawberries, both bright red and warm
from the garden.

No studio in the little motel in Langley, B.C., where they spent their last
night. Next morning, her husband died in the saddle, riding his horse,
Twister, in a cutting-horse contest.

Studio V

SHE RETURNED TO THE CITY and made large floral arrangements of:
blue and white delphiniums / pink larkspurs / pink alstro-
maria / baby's breath / eucalyptus (in large white baskets for
the church where her husband's memorial service was held).
It was the first time she had cried while arranging flowers.
And from her studio, her friends catered the lunch after.

Studio IX

SHE CAME BACK TO THE B.C. STUDIO a month later, walked the hills,
and told herself, "That's it, I'll never see him here again." And she cooked
apple sauce (from early Spartans in the orchard and drank some wine).

Studio V

SHE COOKED FOR ADULT CHILDREN, who wrapped up their father's businesses. She made pasta with pesto, and they sat around talking about how lucky they'd been to have had such a man as Hu in their lives.

She catered a daughter's wedding, adding a blue and white striped tent next to the greenhouse. The three-tiered, homemade carrot wedding cake, with its trim of fresh violets, tilted, mock orange and peony blossoms dropped, the champagne flowed, three brothers toasted their sister, and life went on.

When she thought of STUDIO V, she wondered how many times had she sung "Happy Birthday" through the doorway to the dining room, and how many birthday candles were blown and how many wishes came true? She knew *her* silent birthday wish was always the same: "I just want my family to be happy."

She remembered their Tommy's last birthday with three- and-four-year olds. The favors at the tables were big red suckers with Lifesaver faces, from Picardys. They were wrapped in cello, and the children thought they could melt this off by pouring chocolate milk over the candy.

Studio XI

ALMOST AS SMALL AS STUDIO I of so long ago. She turned out:
sweet and sour pepper jelly / nasturtium, and lemon thyme
vinegars / biscotti and lemon curd / French Market Soup
mix (All under the "Through the Grapevine" label, to be
sold at craft fairs and a farmers market, along with dried
flower wreaths and arrangements.)

Studio IX

MORNINGS, ALONE IN HER STUDIO, she watched a beaver swim past each day, and forced apricot and plum blossoms in wine decanters on her studio counters. She was den-mother-cook for men from Washington who'd come to graft grapevines. When they came in for dinner, they called, "Hi Mom—we're home."

Later, she managed and cooked for a retreat for groups of writers and artists, who received instruction from Toni Onley and Mary Dawe. She offered her guests:

> whole grain homemade bread with marmalade / chicken
> breast stir-fries / low-fat prune cake / hot apple with lemon
> and almonds on low-fat ice cream / decaf coffee, herb tea,
> and local wines.

She'd thought, after reading a bed and breakfast novel, that she might have guests prowling the halls in the middle of the night, that there would be couplings or mysteries going on, but she saw no sign of this, though a guest told her some years later there was a story to be told. She was so tired, she almost didn't hear the bear's heavy breathing one night, beside three bedroom windows.

Studio XII

NOW SHE CHANGES HER ATTENTION from "food and flowers" to "food for thought."

A writer's eyrie in her crowded bedroom, filled with bed, books, family photographs, paper fax, P.C., and phone. Memories change into stories about people and events known, and people and events unknown. She goes in her head for thoughts never thought before, but now almost clear, in this her new studio.

Her first two published stories were about food.

JOYCE HARRIES, *mother of five and grandmother of fourteen, has been writing for five years and is a member of the* Other Voices *Editorial Collective. Her book,* A Wise Old Girl's Own Annual, *is forthcoming from Lone Pine Publishing.*

Eating a Jonathan Apple

JEAN HORTON

THE YEAR BEGINS FOR ME IN THE AUTUMN, as it always has. Perhaps this is partly because school starts each September. Not only have I been a student, but, for most of my professional life, a teacher. More than that, autumn harvest brings a new crop of apples. And as a girl I relished the apples my parents bought by the bushel from roadside stands north of our home. Their choice was always Jonathan apples, red and crisp, at once both tart and sweet. Jonathans made wonderful apple sauce or apple butter, which my mother canned and then fed to us throughout the winter. And there were apple pies, apple turnovers, cider, and jelly. But the apple I loved most was the one which my mother handed to me—and one to my brother—from the newly purchased bushel of fruit. It was intended to keep me quiet at the end of a long weekend drive in the days before four-lane highways. Her ploy worked, partially. I never told my mother, though, what that Jonathan apple, fresh from the orchard, really meant to me. Perhaps I didn't understand it myself at the time.

The annual first bite of a Jonathan apple was ceremonial. It signaled the beginning of the autumn, of the year, the beginning of the world. No matter that in the front seat of our DeSoto or Packard my parents were disagreeing with each other and that beside me my little brother was making faces and rude noises. I slowly ate the best apple that ever was. Beyond the car window, the sun shone, elm leaves turned yellow, oaks were orange, and maples red.

While I ate that apple, the school bully who loved to remind me that I had a moustache disappeared. My size-eight feet became size five. That apple tasted better than a Hershey bar, better than hand-dipped strawberry ice cream at Miller's Ice Cream Parlour.

I have not lived in the Midwest or been there during the harvest for more than thirty years. I make do, then, with Granny Smiths, Braeburns, and Spartans. But perhaps even the fruit stands back there do not sell my apple of choice. Jonathan apples, I was told at the Calgary farmers' market, are no longer grown; they do not ship well. Recently, though, traveling through southern Iowa in late May, I found a pile of Jonathans. Quickly surveying the nearby customers to be sure that in my ecstasy I wasn't making a childish spectacle of myself, I selected only five or six pounds of the treasure. After all, I was traveling alone; ten or fifteen pounds might be excessive without refrigeration. The check-out line inched forward. A customer two buggies ahead of me complained about the disparity between the price of Fantastick last week and the current posted store price, demanding that the manager settle the dispute. I cradled one of the Jonathans in my hand, held it close to my nose to smell it, wanted more than anything to taste it. The man ahead of me was twenty-three cents short of his bill. My eager offer of the needed funds was declined, as he searched through his groceries, deciding what to put back on the shelf. Finally, my apples paid for and in a paper bag, I left the market, walked to my car and got in, set the apples carefully on the passenger seat, started the engine, and drove to a remote corner of the parking lot to eat, after three decades, a Jonathan apple. I withdrew one of the apples from the bag beside me, twisted the stem—it came off at the letter *E*—polished the apple on my slacks, and shut my eyes in anticipation of a gustatory epiphany. I bit into my Jonathan apple.

The apple was not crisp. In fact, it was mealy. Oh, well, I told myself, these apples have probably been in cold storage since their harvest eight months ago. Any apple would lose crispness in that time. Concentrate on taste, then. Tartness? Not really. Sweetness? Adequate. The keen edges had disappeared. I was reminded of a grocery shopping trip a week after I was married. My new husband spotted a small box of dried codfish, grabbed it, and said, "Creamed dried codfish on toast tastes delicious! My mom used to make it when I was a kid. You've got to try it!" The next evening I prepared the creamed dried codfish on toast, setting it down proudly in front of my young bridegroom. I had prepared it exactly as he specified. He grinned. He tasted it. He took a second taste, then put his fork down, his face serious. "I guess my taste buds aren't what they were when I was fifteen," was his only comment.

Today, that bridegroom is something of a wine expert. Upon tasting a wine, he is likely to identify the shipper, the vineyard, the year, and to make an educated assessment of the wine. For my part, I can taste a soup or sauce and correct the seasoning. Not long ago the owner of a small restaurant asked me to try his new peach mousse. "It needs vanilla," I told him, "and a bit more salt." Later he told me that the staff had forgotten the vanilla when they made up the sample batch. And he agreed about the salt. My palate has developed through time, and I do not really want to return to age ten or twelve. But I would like to experience just once more the first taste of a Jonathan apple in the Septembers of my girlhood.

JEAN HORTON *teaches medieval literature and nineteenth-century American fiction at Concordia University College in Edmonton, Alberta. She is a quiltmaker with special interests in Amish quilts and nineteenth-century patchwork.*

Wise Blood

Rebecca Luce-Kapler

I CALL OUT THEIR NAMES to sense their presence with me as a place of beginning. And ending. "Lavanche Searls Luce." Outside the spring wind taps the lilac against the window in answer. "Martha Rentz Fenske." The sun dims with an afternoon cloud.

I wander through my house searching for artifacts: the rocking chair from Martha, Lavanche's cross-stitch of a little boy and girl, a straw purse, teacups, cookbooks marked with their handwriting in the margins, photographs, an old bullet casing. I touch each one, collect the smaller items on my desk, spill the photographs out of the envelope.

My grandmothers. Most of my life I believed they existed for me—their attention and concern directed toward my well-being. But now they are gone, and so I examine the photographs, and the trace of their belongings wanting to know who they were, their doubts and certainties, their love and desire, their womanhood.

THERE IS A PICTURE of my cousin Danny and me riding our trikes in Martha's backyard near the edge of a garden with the earth black and newly turned, a row of peas staked with chicken wire, and several large heads of lettuce. The cement sidewalk, which I know is red although this is a black and white photo, stretches down past the garden and then around the side of the house. My hair is pulled tight into two pigtails tied with satin ribbon, and I have a determined look on my face as I watch my cousin. He smiles placidly at the camera, ignoring me. With his brush cut and striped T-shirt, he could be any little 1950s boy appearing in a Kool-Aid or Jell-O advertisement.

I screech at the top of my lungs. For the third time Danny has blocked my path down the sidewalk, and I bump him, pedaling forward, backing up, and then coming forward again. He just smiles and pretends he doesn't even know I'm there. "Danny, you little devil," I cry. Suddenly, Grandma has her hands on the handle of my trike. "What did you say?" Her face is grim and her eyes sharp with anger. I know I've done something very wrong, but I have no idea what. "What did you say?" she asks again, her voice cool and insistent. "I don't know," I reply and at this point I truly don't. "Do you know what the devil is?" she asks. I shake my head because I realize that the right answer is something I don't know. "He is evil," she said. "He works against God our savior. You never call someone a devil. That is saying they're wicked. Calling up his name brings awful, horrible things."

In 1915 twelve-year-old Martha stands in the yard, looking out across the fields stretching toward the church. Behind her she hears the cries of her older sisters as they and the neighbors from down the road prepare her mother for burial. After the funeral they will go home, and she will be alone with Father and her three brothers, one of whom is feebleminded. She and God in the kitchen, her mother's kitchen. Already Father has told her she must leave school; someone has to cook the meals, wash the clothes, polish the lamp chimneys. Martha tightens her lips, determined not to cry, determined that God will show her the way. He is all that she has left now.

This is our first real dinner party. Because my husband and I are worried about how we might manage such an occasion, we invite only family. It is a time of frivolity and enjoyment, but I am responsible for cooking the food, for making sure that everyone has enough to drink, that they are looked after. I feel outside the circle of fun that rolls around and over me. I have helped create the occasion yet am not part of it. There is a transparent wall between me and the family that frolics about me, a severity in my very core, and an overwhelming sense of responsibility that I can find no source for. I wish to let go, to play, to forget about the dishes piling in the sink, the bread warming in the oven, and whether there is enough ice, but I cannot. The burden is mine alone.

WHEN MARTHA TURNS EIGHTY, she parcels out her teacup collection to her granddaughters. The three she gives me are delicate china cups with ornate handles just big enough for my index finger to slip through, although I know the proper way is to hold the edge of the handle between my thumb and finger with my pinkie raised just slightly. One Royal Albert cup has a deep teal background with pink roses and forget-me-nots; the other is green and white with a gold filigree of wild flowers. The Royal Vale has a large red rose surrounded by wood violets. The cups are the only elegant dishes my grandmother owned.

The meal set out on the table is abundant. Roast goose with orange sauce, boiled potatoes, cucumbers in cream, fresh peas delicately cooked. My grandmother nods toward Grandpa, and we bow our heads as he thanks God for the blessing of food and family to share it with. The dinner is tasty, and the careful preparation bursts through in the flavors, textures, and colors. Around the table, there is a sense of reverence for the simple act of eating. When we are finished, a dish of trifle and cups of tea follow, and when the last crumb is eaten, we bow our head again as Grandma thanks God for so richly caring for us all. Eating, living as an act of spirituality.

In 1921, BruderWeld Moravian Church arranges a week of special prayer meetings. After Martha finishes the supper dishes, sweeps the floor, and puts her brother to bed, she walks the two miles to attend the meetings. Night after night there are inspirational speakers, hymn singing, prayers, and a call to the altar to accept the Lord. The last evening, tired from the day's work, the week-long intensity of prayer, and the walk, Martha stumbles and falls. Sitting by the edge of the road, exhausted tears in her eyes, she is too self-absorbed for a moment to realize what is happening. But as she gradually stops crying, she realizes that it is surprisingly light for late evening. She looks at her arms and legs and sees that they are surrounded by a mysterious light. As she stands, her whole body seems to glow and a feeling of deep peace soothes her. She knows, without doubt, that this is God, warming her, telling her that he will be with her on her walk home and forever after.

ON THE SECOND DAY of a Buddhist meditation retreat, I walk out into the October sunset, crisp with drying leaves and cooling air. I've spent half of the past twenty-four hours either in silent sitting meditation, my body still, my breathing the only movement, or I've glided through empty halls in quiet walking meditation. I have had to break through my resistance to waiting and just being with myself. I am too used to moving quickly, going somewhere, doing something. I am surprised at how little I know myself when there are no distractions to interfere.

For the moment, however, I've left the warm, still air of the retreat center and walk about in the streets where the busyness and energy of life crash against me. I feel untouched, a sense of solidity and oneness so encompassing that I am a stream of energy forever opening up to the present moment. For this time, there is no division between my body, mind, and spirit. I rejoice in being so alive.

Grandpa lives at our house while Martha is away on a trip. Every morning my mother fills his black lunch box with sandwiches, fruit, and cookies for him to take to his job at the service garage on main street. It has been many years since they spent time together without Grandma there, and they talk about many things but mostly her. How distant she is and how without warmth. "I should have known," he tells my mother, "when I noticed there was no laughter in her home."

I struggle with the passions and emotions that often seem just below the surface. Sometimes, when I try to express those feelings, I feel like I'm trying to kick down walls of solid brick. Sometimes the irrational fear of rejection closes my mouth entirely, my lips as thin as Martha's. But they cannot be contained. For unlike Martha, who channeled it all to God, if I restrain my emotions in one instance, they explode in another, even if it is across the page. I feel what my father calls "mushiness," like his mother, Lavanche.

Lavanche. How she hated that name and insisted we call her Vantie.

Vantie and I are cooking supper in the kitchen. Well, she is cooking supper and I am tasting. "I just knew your grandfather was the one for me," she tells me. "The minute I saw him. I came down the stairs and there he was, standing beside my cousin. The most handsome man I'd ever seen."

"How do you know?" I ask. This sounds highly risky to me.

"You'll just know he's the one you'll love and marry," she said. "Your heart will tell you."

And in that moment I believe her.

ON MY DAUGHTER'S SHELF is a Hawaiian straw purse decorated with strips of palm wood in a silhouette of a tropical beach scene. The purse is over thirty years old, a gift from Lavanche when she returned from her trip to Hawaii. I have kept the purse for all this time, passed it on to my daughter because of the dreams it holds within its fuschia rayon lining: the whisper of faraway, imagined places and adventures. As long as we have that purse, we are travelers.

They have been gone for over a month. My job is to water the plants in their chilly house where the air hangs stale and breathless. No one except me and the African violets breathing the air in gulps too small to warm it. I can't remember Grandma and Grandpa being away so long before, and the loneliness of the house haunts me like an empty space.

The March day they return, they are brown and warm as Demerara sugar, melting the cold from our winter white faces. They seem different, exotic. I can smell pineapple on their breath and see white sand spilling from their shoes. When I clutch my new purse and shut my eyes, I can imagine the tropical sunset and the darkening night as the luau begins. I inhale the perfume of pink and white flowers that Grandma says she wore around her neck.

Vantie writes the chronicle of her trip in a letter, July 21, 1965.

"Long drives in the country on good roads revealed good but small homes. We saw no slums. Lots of flowers everywhere, only a few that we knew—huge poinsettia, giant hibiscus in red and yellow, red hedges and trees with red leaves, oranges, and wild banana. . . . We had a clear hot day for the boat trip to Pearl Harbor. The Japs surely messed things up there." She lowers her pen and tries to remember December 1941. Canada had been in the war for two years already, but she was still at heart an American and when the attack came so close and on home soil, her fears for her sixteen-year-old son deepened. The threat of his going to fight shadowed every corner of her existence. Fighting the Japs or the Huns.

Vantie is delighted that I am moving home with her first great-grandchild. After years of graduate school, my husband has a "real" job as a psychologist at Alberta Hospital, Ponoka. A stressful and exciting time with a move, a new baby, a house. When Grandma tells her friends over tea that her grandson-in-law has a job in the "loonie bin," I gasp and turn away, struggling with the desire to chastise her, remembering the way she sorts everyone according to differences: their color, their size, their intelligence, their income. A life tidy and arranged. Sometimes the categories come too close to me, make me wonder. Can I be good enough? And there are moments when I see someone on the street whose difference from me is obvious, when the snap judgements flood my thinking before I can stop and slow the assumptions, think again. Struggle to see the world differently.

I HOLD A BRASS SHELL CASING, slightly tarnished and dented so that the light reflected from the surface is rippling and shadowed. If I pull the point of the bullet, it opens to reveal a small penknife embedded in the top. To lengthen the handle, I can slide the nose into the body of the bullet and then use the knife to open my mail or slice my apple. This bullet is more than eighty years old. Fired during the First World War. Toward or from the German lines? I no longer remember.

Vantie places the bullet in my hand. Shows me how to find the secret knife. "This was made by a boy who lived on our street," she tells me. I wait, knowing there must be more just by the way she smiles dreamily. "He was such a wonderful boy," she says. "Good looking and kind."

"Was he your boyfriend?" I know she wants me to ask. "I suppose. We used to walk home from school together even though he was older; he asked me to write to him when he went overseas." She pulls the knife apart and puts it back together. "I wrote several times and he replied, but then he saw his brother shot and was never the same again. When he came back, I went to see him and he handed me this, but barely said a word. I was afraid to ask him what he'd seen, what had happened. The next week he moved to Seattle and I never saw him again." I hold the bullet she has handed me. With the knife hidden, it does not seem lethal at all. Was this the bullet that killed his brother? I want to ask but don't. Her eyes are closed and the story is over.

In 1920, at Coutts, Montana, Vantie turns to watch the American border retreating. From Spokane to Canada, she has been imagining life with her new husband whose smile and clear, blue-eyed gaze still stops her breath. She has envisioned the farm they are traveling to somewhere in Alberta. The white frame house, two stories with bedrooms: one for the parents-in-law who await their arrival, another for a brother, and one for her and Rowe. Their own bed is covered with her crocheted bedspread sent ahead by train in their luggage. She pictures cooking for Rowe, making pancakes for breakfast and cake for his morning coffee. The rest of his family are shadowy figures who do not intrude on this circle of light.

Once they've crossed the border, however, and chug ever closer to the farm, she reviews the life she is leaving. What might have been. How she could have been a teacher if only her father had let her continue school. She imagines herself at the front of a classroom, a pointer in her hands. She's wearing a smart navy skirt that rides just above her ankles, topped by a starched white blouse, spotless, with a tie. Her wavy dark hair is swept up onto her head, clasped with an elegant clip. She nods wisely to a student in the front row, a smile of pleasure rewarding the correct answer. Vantie sighs and opens her travel diary, writing down her dreams on a clean, white page.

For the third week I'm rising at 5:00 A.M. struggling to find time to write the novel, to tell the story that has been forming for twenty years. The incidents Vantie has described to me—her life as a girl, her journey to Alberta—become tangled in other family myth and legend, in the stories of the place where the novel unfolds, in my imaginings. When I sit in my semi-sleep, willing my fingers to type words onto my screen, I feel the dreams, hers and mine, swirling into shapes of possibility, creating a space for the story to be enacted as it never was, but might have been. She becomes a character of fiction, as airy and persistent as her spirit; someone who lives with me even during my days of teaching.

As I write of Vantie, Martha begins to call from the margins and connects to moments in the page. Snippets of conversation, old stories told around a dinner table or over tea on quiet afternoons, and artifacts that live in my home wind into the telling. When there are gaps in their stories too great to leap over, I imagine a narrative, discover meaning through writing my life and theirs, learning for myself how women who no longer shed the lunar "wise blood" become wise themselves, Crones, Goddesses of Wisdom.

Outside the clouds roll in, and lilac brushes my window as I search again for the wisdom in their living, in the memories that continue to speak through my dreaming.

REBECCA LUCE-KAPLER, *an Assistant Professor in the Education Faculty at Queen's University, does research on the role of writing in women's lives. She has had fiction and poetry published in numerous literary magazines, including* Other Voices, Grain, *and* Event. *A selection of her poems about Emily Carr were broadcast on CBC's* Alberta Anthology.

The Night the Thirty-Ought-Six Got Shot Through the Ceiling

SARAH MURPHY

THE NIGHT THE THIRTY-OUGHT-SIX got shot through the ceiling is just a continuation of all the other stories   maybe it is all the other stories except this one has an advantage this one didn't take place right down the stairs where mickey's head got kicked in this one took place all the way downstairs in the front vestibule that's three storeys down and i have no idea what happened and even if years later i once came very close to telling a family therapist that i don't handle the impact of violence too well because where i come from you know   well if someone had actually been killed that night we probably would just have buried him or her in the backyard under the ginkgo tree and carried on still that's not what i think we really did it was just so far away it's funny to think of far away in those terms down three storeys instead of one but those are the facts probably why i don't remember it nothing more dramatic than that though you never know the night seems to have a frame around it the way things do sometimes when there's something important that you participated in or were made to do that you've forgotten but it's nicer to think that it was just so far away all the way down not just too much   i don't remember any of it not when the bars closed not the screaming and shouting not bill meeting the other guy at the door with the rifle not mickey saying something about how she was going to screw him not if it was serious like the summer with johnny rice down from kahnawake to do high steel or just someone she'd brought home just to bring him home or if something really bad had gone down the way she would bring them sometimes not just come alone to tour my room but whatever it was i don't remember a thing and that's really nice   so this can be another kind of story a story with lots of description vivid writing like for a christmas present how we crept down the stairs my brother bragging that he'd heard it he always bragged about things like that because i was the light sleeper i was the one who always woke up and he never did and he'd heard it he'd heard it someone had shot off a gun he was sure bill had shot off a gun mickey had brought someone home and bill had shot off a gun so there we were creeping down the stairs like for christmas maybe to see who was dead or who was in the house but slowly slowly down the stairs to the livingroom where the christmas presents would be if there ever were any or if we didn't open them christmas eve after everyone was sufficiently loaded not to notice then sneak away to miss one of the great drunks of the year   but there we are on the stairs and we're looking into the livingroom which isn't one story down or three but two the floor above where the shot was fired and there it is christmas time confetti time even if it's summer there's confetti all over the living room small pieces of colored paper everywhere so that we smile and giggle like we were still the two little kids we knew we weren't confetti confetti confetti confetti different millions of tiny pieces of confetti because that's what happens when a thirty caliber bullet comes up through a ceiling and through a two inch thick wooden coffee table and an eighteen inch thick pile of magazines   the upper three to six inches of the magazines just explode into confetti confetti and there we are laughing and picking up the little pieces of paper and throwing them into the air and examining them closely a christmas present to ourselves without saying a word because maybe there are no words after all and no story certainly no story and who cares anyway confetti confetti whether there are any words or any story but just this moment this one long perfect moment it's a lyric poem when you can smell the summer air through the open window and see the dappling of the light along the street spreading from the shade under the trees   the dappling of the small pieces of paper spread across the bright morning light in the living room all those perfect descriptive things of a perfect moment held forever that is the morning a rifle was shot off inside the house and no one died no one died confetti confetti and if they did it certainly wasn't you confetti confetti you're still there   that's right it's a ticker tape parade and you're the astronaut returned from the moon and you're giggling confetti confetti or wherever it is that parenthesis you go to is located so that by now you've gone to the window and you're throwing those little bright colored pieces out confetti confetti with your brother while everyone else sleeps off a drunk and you laugh and you laugh and you don't even remember the story not the littlest little thing about it and why tell stories anyway why tell stories at all why not just curl up inside this one moment this one brilliant perfect confetti colored moment before time resumes   why not forever?

SARAH MURPHY, *of mixed Choctaw, English, Irish, and Hispanic heritage, is a translator, interpreter, teacher, social activist, prizewinning visual artist, and author of five books. Two collections,* Comic Book Heroine *and* The Deconstruction of Wesley Smithson, *were finalists for the Writers' Guild of Alberta short fiction award, as was her novel* Connie Many Stories. *Her most recent novel,* Lilac in Leather, *looks at the New York art world of the 1970s and friendships between women.* "The Night the Thirty-Ought-Six" *is part of a longer work,* 26 Nutmeg Mews, *which Sarah is currently developing, and has appeared in* Absinthe, *10:2* "Women Writing Lives" *and* The Text, *#8, published by The Word Hoard in Huddersfield, West Yorkshire, UK, in the summer of 1997. In the autumn of 1998, Sarah Murphy was the Yorkshire Humberside International Writer in Residence with The Word Hoard.*

Births

Lia Pas

Vishnu has caught another sparrow. My sister tries to catch her and make her drop the bird, its wings fluttering maniacally. Vishnu heads for the house, through her cat door, and into the basement. I am stepping out of the guest room when I see her, manage to catch her despite the bulk of my eighth month of pregnancy. She drops the sparrow. It flies into the guest room, fluttering against a window. I climb up on the bed and gather it softly to me with my hands outstretched. Its heartbeat is fast, frantic. I hold it for a moment and watch its eyes dart around the room, feel its small drumming heart before I go outside and let it free.

They say a sparrow in the house is a sign of impending birth. I am home from university to give birth. This will be my first child. This should be a time of celebration and joy, and it is. But it is also a time of mourning for me, as I will have to say goodbye to this baby.

"ARE YOU *sure* you haven't been having contractions?"

My doctor has done my first internal since the first trimester of pregnancy. This baby, my second, is not due for another three weeks, but Adrienne, my first, was born two weeks early.

"Just braxton hicks, nothing regular that I've noticed."

"You're four centimeters dilated, but your membranes are still intact. Any spotting?"

"No. None that I've noticed."

"I think you should go to fetal assessment just to make sure. I'll phone and make the appointment."

Ed and I call a cab and go to the hospital. The waiting room is full of tired-looking, heavily pregnant women. They do inductions here as well. While we are waiting, one woman is told her induction will have to wait until tomorrow. Again. She starts crying. Edemic women walk on swollen legs through the hallways. After half an hour, we are let into the ultrasound room.

The baby is a good size, and the technician doesn't tell us the sex, though when I'm later hooked up to the fetal assessment monitor the nurses keep referring to the baby as "he." Last time it was "she."

They finally decide I'm not in labor and send me home. We go down to my dad's office in personnel. He is surprised to see us and happily introduces us to his coworkers, lets us borrow the van "just in case it happens."

My alarm goes off at 8:00 A.M. I have a job interview at ten. I hope that my pregnant and single state won't lessen my chances of getting the job. I'll have to explain to them about the adoption.

Last night Ed's sister wanted to feel the baby kicking, but I kept having braxton hicks contractions. As I pull myself out of bed, there is another one. I look at the clock: 8:15. As I start the shower I have another. 8:20. I don't feel any pain, so I figure it's not really labor. I step into the shower, and the contractions seem to get stronger. I finish quickly and go upstairs and phone my doctor.

"You don't sound like you're in labor. Come in and we'll check."

I phone my mother, who has just arrived at work, and then

phone Ed. He's not up yet but wakes up quickly when I tell him
I think I'm in labor. He arrives on his bike shortly after my
mother gets home. We head to the doctor's office.

ED AND I HAVE SPENT THE DAY walking around Broadway. I have had so much energy all day, and now it's 1:00 A.M. and I can't sleep. I'm getting downward feeling contractions but very irregularly. I wake Ed to tell him, but he's too asleep to register anything, so I pack my hospital bag.

At 3:00 A.M. the contractions are more regular, about five minutes apart, but my water hasn't broken yet. I wake Ed and we decide to wait until 5:30 to call the doctor. I try to sleep but can't.

In the doctor's office my back starts to hurt, so Ed rubs it. My
mom looks nervous. My doctor is in with another patient, so we
have to wait. The receptionist explains to the woman in the
waiting room that she'll have to wait for her appointment
because I might be in labor.

When we finally get to see the doctor, she wants to see if I'm
dilated, so I take off my underwear and climb up on the exam-
ining table. As she's about to check, my water breaks, gushing
out of me, relieving some of the back pain. My doctor is sur-
prised how fast things are moving, checks to find that I am four
centimeters dilated and asks, "Do you want an ambulance?"

We decline but head quickly in my mother's car to the hospital.

BY 5:30 A.M. NOTHING'S CHANGED, but I call the doctor anyway. She says to go to the hospital because last time was so quick. I put on my boots and a jacket, towels on the passenger seat of the van, and we drive to emergency.

At the hospital I am wheeled to fetal assessment because I tell the receptionist I *might* be in labor. An intern asks me questions. She remembers Ed from when we were there earlier in the week. She checks and thinks I am five centimeters dilated. I tell her I was four centimeters on Tuesday. They hook me up to the fetal monitor, and the contractions are there but slightly sporadic. The intern thinks I'm in labor and calls my doctor. My doctor wants a second opinion on how dilated I am and so the nurse checks. "Five and a half, maybe six." So we're led to a birthing room.

I'm hooked up to an IV and a fetal monitor. Ed almost faints when they put the IV needle in. I don't want the sugar drip, but no one's listening to what I want. It's a nurses' strike, and they tell me most everything has to go by the books.

An intern comes in and starts asking questions. He's oblivious to the fact that I'm having very strong contractions now and doesn't seem to understand that I can't talk through them. I am especially upset when he asks me if I wear contact lenses when he can see for himself that I'm wearing glasses.

A doctor comes in and checks to see how much I've dilated. Eight centimeters now, so they move me to the delivery room despite the fact that I can't walk. They lean me back in a birthing bed and put my feet in the stirrups. I don't want my left foot in and keep moving it out, but a nurse keeps putting it back in. I think I kick her, but I'm not really sure. The fetal monitor belt moves off my contracting belly, and I move so they can't put it back on.

An engineering professor acting as labor nurse is helping Ed give me ice chips, and my mom is wiping my face with a cool cloth. The intern seems to be doing most of the work, and I get the distinct feeling he's never done this before. A tour of medical students comes through the room. The doctor who checked my dilation when I came in seems to be running things and leaves my doctor in the background.

"It's crowning. I can see the head!"

My mom puts the face cloth over my eyes and goes to see.

THE WALLS OF THE BIRTHING ROOM ARE PEACH COLORED, and I can see my dad's office window. Ed and I watch the sunrise while I pace, trying to get the contractions going. It's much slower this time. I have a few hard contractions about five minutes apart and then they stop for twenty minutes.

Two interns come in and introduce themselves. I like them both much better than the intern I had to deal with last time. Every once in a while the nurse hooks me up to the monitor, but the contractions always slow down when I stop moving.

My doctor comes to see me at about 10:00 A.M. She checks and says I'm almost eight centimeters dilated. She says that they may have to break my waters if they haven't broken in an hour.

She comes back in an hour and pokes my membranes with what looks like a long crochet hook. It's a big relief. I feel much more relaxed and less full. The contractions speed up then. She leaves again and says she'll come back when I'm in transition.

Within the next half hour, the contractions get much more painful. I don't remember them being this painful before. The nurse reminds me that they have ordered an epidural if I want it, or else they can give me some nitrous oxide. I don't want anything. I need to be in my body for this.

I don't want to walk anymore, and the male intern comes in and checks to see that I'm dilated more. He sees that I'm in a lot more pain and calls my doctor. She says she'll arrive in a half hour. I feel like pushing but pant to hold it off. My tongue is hanging out, my legs are spread wide. I feel that something primordial is building in me. I'm reminded of pictures I've seen of the goddess Kali, squatting over her lover with her tongue lolling.

In another fifteen minutes I can't hold back, and there is a flurry of activity as they prepare the birthing bed. I'm pushing as my doctor arrives, and she washes up quickly and takes over.

She redirects my pushing and the baby starts coming down a bit quicker but keeps sliding back. I push for another half hour before it crowns, sitting very painfully on my tailbone, and I lose control, crying and moaning. Ed holds me, and everyone waits until I push again.

"I think she needs an episiotomy," the other doctor says.

This is what I was terrified of and hoping to avoid. My doctor looks unsure about it and I get the feeling this is just so the intern can do one. No perineal massage, no warm compresses, just scissors. He cuts it at the wrong time and I bleed a lot.

But then the baby comes out so easily and so fast. A girl. I don't know what to do, what to think. The other doctor asks me if I want to hold her, and I have to say no. I didn't want to be asked this. The nurses wash her up, and my mother and the head nurse who had been present at my own birth are both crying. Ed sits close by and holds my hands. I am exhausted and sore. I don't want to feel anything anymore.

I START TO TEAR, and my doctor tells me that it's on my old episiotomy scar. She says she'd like to cut it again. I'd rather have a cut than a tear, so I agree. I push for another twenty minutes before the baby slides out, head and arm first. A boy. They place him screaming on my belly. He is blue and quickly turning pink. So wild and alive.

I smile at Ed, and he looks at me, unsure. He knows I wanted another girl, but sees that I am so happy and in love with this child. I touch the baby's skin, slimy with wetness from inside me, and they take him, after asking, to go wash him up.

My mother brings the baby over to me. She has a small peaceful face. I still don't want to hold her. I'm afraid of what might happen.

As the intern stitches up my episiotomy, my doctor watches closely. She takes over when he gets close to my vaginal opening. I am glad because I don't want him to touch me anymore. I want him to go away.

They move me to a recovery room and bring me some toast.

My mom goes to calls S., my social worker. Ed and I are only
there for twenty minutes when they tell me someone else needs
the room so I'll have to move. I'm not ready to stand up yet, but
Ed and the nurse help me up off the bed and blood rushes out
of me into a pool on the floor. I sit gingerly down in the wheel-
chair. I don't care about the mess. I told them I wasn't ready to
move.

They take me down the hall to my room. I want to sleep but
can't because of the sugar drip in my system. Ed leaves to get me
some real food. I sit and read bad magazines.

While he's gone the other doctor comes in with two male
interns and gives me a lecture on birth control. I don't want or
need to hear this. Yes, I know I had this baby accidentally. Yes,
I've done my own research on how to avoid it. I may be nine-
teen, but I'm not stupid. These people don't know anything
about who I am.

WHILE MY DOCTOR IS SEWING UP THE EPISIOTOMY, Ed holds the
baby. Ed's mother calls, and he tells her she can't visit until later, that the baby's
only just been born. I laugh because he doesn't even tell her it's a boy. We're not
sure how she got the phone number for the birthing room in the first place.

After I'm stitched and cleaned up, they bring the baby to me to nurse. He
latches on quickly and nurses for about a half hour. It's lovely having this
small body taking sustenance from me, it's lovely to see his small furred head
finally, his perfect fingers, to feel him against my outside skin.

The nurse asks if I want to shower there, but I don't feel strong enough to
stand up. I make it to the bathroom to pee though and then sit in a wheel-
chair with the baby placed in my arms. We're wheeled to the nursery where
they weigh and measure him, and then we leave him there, sleeping, and go
to my room, shared with one other woman and two empty beds.

Ed goes home to bathe and eat, and I go have a bath and change into my
own clothes. I remember that last time it took me longer to do this.

There are many visitors that day. My whole family, my mom's parents, my dad's mom. Ed's mom sends me squid stir-fry, which is wonderful, but the nurses find it strange. That, along with the fact that I won't eat red meat.

The woman acting as head nurse for the ward comes in and looks surprised. I grew up with her daughter. She attempts to take it all in stride, but I know I've shocked her.

I feed Adrienne. That's the name I've been calling her throughout the pregnancy, thinking, hoping, she was a boy. I feel that I could nurse her, but don't. I know it would be better for her body, but my mind already feels so weak. I sit and look at her in my lap. She sticks her tongue out and curls it up, lets me know that she really is my daughter.

A nurse comes in and tells me to go to the bathroom. I don't want to. Every time I move blood gushes out, spills onto the floor and the pad on the bed. She makes me anyways. Stands there with the tap running until I pee. Tells me it will get easier and asks if I've had a bowel movement yet. Do they have to know everything? Do they have to keep track of every single excretion from my body?

THAT NIGHT MY PARENTS VISIT. *Ooh* and *aah* at the baby's feet and hands. Take pictures. My youngest sister doesn't want to hold him, is afraid she'll drop him. My other sister won't let her picture be taken. My brother has said he'll visit later.

Ed's sister and mother come later for a short visit. *Ooh*ing and *aah*ing again. Yü-Lin reprimands Ed for not calling her before we came to the hospital. I hope she'll relax a bit once we get home, that the excitement of having a grandson will wear off quickly.

Ed stays until about eleven. We talk about names. Jarrod Griffin we think. The two boys' names we liked the best. He says he'll come again in the morning.

Finally, I sleep.

The next day I shuffle down the hall with my friend Pauline to get Adrienne from the nursery. The intern is there, makes some snide remark about how fast I'm moving. I glare at him. I want to yell at him for cutting me, for wounding me. I want to tell him to get out of this ward and leave all of us women alone.

M. and D. are coming tomorrow. We haven't seen them since we met at the adoption agency. I'm a bit nervous, but not as nervous as the staff. There are whispers going around about how strange it is, this open adoption.

I guess tomorrow I will have to wash. I don't feel like it. My hair sticks to my head, and my body smells. I wallow in it. Make excuses. Say I'm too dizzy yet. That's partially true. The blood still gushes out when I stand.

That night I bring Adrienne back to the nursery myself. There is a newborn there. Twice as big as her and covered in cheesy vernix. A thick mop of hair, an ugly croaking cry. I swear the ears are pointed. I don't want to leave her here. Don't want this demon baby near her. The nurse is no more appealing than this strange squalling infant. Large and rough with glazed-looking eyes, she shoos me off to my room. I wonder what I'm learning from this, why I have to be here.

THE NIGHT NURSE BRINGS JARROD in twice to breast-feed. He sucks voraciously. I don't mind this waking up to feed him. Don't mind holding this small hungry body in my sleepy arms.

Breakfast arrives at 8:30 A.M. I'm never awake that early. I am going to nap again, but people keep coming in to do blood tests and tell me about going home early. Jarrod feeds again and a nursing coach helps me. An intern comes in and asks if I've had a bowel movement. I have had one, thankfully, but just want to laugh at his innocence, at his scientific questions. Something incredible has happened to me, and he's asking about my shit.

Lunch is served and I eat what's there and am still hungry. My dad comes for a visit and then goes to get his lunch and some more for me from the staff cafeteria where they have real food.

While he's gone the woman in the bed across from me asks about Jarrod's size. Seven pounds seven ounces. She's amazed at how I birthed him without drugs. Her son was five pounds six ounces, her second baby. Her daughter is ten months old. I'm amazed that she would have sex again that soon after, but I don't say so. I'm so sore, but she strides around like nothing ever happened. Her baby's on formula, is getting circumcised. I'm very different from her and the other woman who has moved into the room. She sings church hymns to her baby and tells her three-year-old that babies come from God. I always thought they came from mothers. I think my black flannel pajamas and pentacle scare her. I'm scared for her children.

My father returns with a large vegetarian sandwich and some yogurt for me. Ed arrives soon after with more food. Everything feels sweet and perfect. Everything feels fine.

I finally take a shower. The engineering prof who gave me ice during labor helps me there, and I find I'm too dizzy to stand. A nurse helps me bathe, and then I sit on a stool in the shower to wash my hair. I feel so helpless, the running water makes me want to cry, but I won't. I still have her. I won't cry yet.

M. and D. come to visit. I'm happy they're here. They let me hold and feed Adrienne. They meet our families. My mom's parents feel fine about the adoption now. They know that everything will work out. The nurses still whisper about us.

ED'S PARENTS COME TO VISIT THAT EVENING. Yü-Lin insists that Jarrod can't breathe the way I've been nursing him. I let her lecture and know that as soon as she's gone I'll do it the way the nursing coach showed me. Jarrod screams when Yü-Lin does some reflexology on his feet. In China the first grandson is very important. I know that Yü-Lin wants the best for

Jarrod, and this is her way of showing love. Ed's father takes pictures.

They leave, finally. I read a bit. Ed calls and we talk. Tomorrow I get to come home.

The next day and a half are spent talking with Ed and M. and D. M. and D. attend baby care classes while Ed and I think about what's going to happen. I read and play a lot of cards. Solitaire and crazy eights. We are visited by a nun who tells us about the chapel and asks if we want to pray with her. We tell her we're not interested. My grandfather wants me to get Adrienne baptized so she won't go to limbo if she dies with M. and D. I listen and then tell him I don't believe in limbo. I have to leave tomorrow. I don't want to think about it.

ED ARRIVES WITH THE CAR SEAT. I've been dressed for the past hour, wanting to leave this stale air, wanting my own quiet bed, wanting to be alone with Ed and Jarrod. We wait for the doctor. After an hour she finally arrives, checks me and signs the papers saying I can go. As we leave the nurse says, "See you in two years!" We laugh and shake our heads. One is enough.

Yü-Lin is waiting outside. It's cold and crisp. We bundle Jarrod in his much too big snowsuit and are off. I am more nervous than ever about Yü-Lin's driving but am very glad to be free. At home I sit in bed and look at Jarrod. So tiny yet alive. We sleep with him in our bed for the first night, but I keep waking up to make sure we haven't crushed him. In the morning we fold sheets and put them in a drawer beside the bed. My friend Kim says the bassinet she's making is coming along nicely. He *was* two weeks early. I tell her we've got him sleeping in a drawer, and she laughs and says she'll try to hurry.

I am dreading today. Ed has brought me clothes and I dress slowly. M. and D. said good-bye last night. I almost fainted after they left. "Stress," my mother said. "Anemia," I said but knew it was both, and more. Too much is happening. I hate it. I want it to end.

Ed and I walk to the nursery. Adrienne's asleep. A sweet, sweet smile on her face. I lean down to kiss her and don't want to let her go. Everyone is watching and I don't care. I cry and cry and cry. Ed hugs me and says we have to go. I cry all the way home. I want Ed to stay with me, but he goes home and paints. I lay in bed and cry and cry some more.

The next morning I decide to learn how to knit, try very hard and just get frustrated. I read. I do everything I can to keep Adrienne out of my head. I register for a summer English course. My mom says it's best if I get on with things, not to linger in this pain. But I want to linger. I want her, my daughter, my baby, to feel me.

I eat as much as I can. I wait for a package with pictures from M. and D. I try to move on with my life.

THE NURSE COMES TO OUR HOUSE to check on me. Tells me we are doing very well. Others come to visit, and they all say Jarrod looks like a little Buddhist monk. I bathe, sometimes twice a day. My stitches heal quickly. I'm tired but happy. I remember Adrienne. I remember the tiredness, the depression, saying good-bye. I know I couldn't have done this mothering then. Not alone. Ed is so helpful, telling me to rest, changing Jarrod. Most times I just read and nurse him. I know that M. and D. will be so happy to hear of Jarrod, to hear that Adrienne has a brother. I look forward to their next letter, pictures of her, and being able to send them photos of Jarrod as well. I look at pictures of Adrienne and see the similarities. They look so much alike, this little brother and sister, but they are so far away. I know that one day we will meet. I know that that day is far away, but then I will be able to hold both my son and my daughter in my arms. This is a small beginning, a lovely small beginning. Jarrod and Adrienne are growing, and we are all moving on.

LIA PAS *is a composer, musician, and writer living in Saskatoon, Saskatchewan, with her husband and son. Her poetry has appeared in* Grain, Filling Station, *and* NeWest Review. *She has recently completed a poetry collection entitled* in the tongue of my hand.

The Deerhead

BEVERLEY ROSS

FOR A LONG TIME, I didn't understand why I ended up with my uncle's deerhead. I thought perhaps I claimed it out of a sense of duty. Or guilt. I remember thinking that it ought to stay in the family. Of the hundreds of animals my uncle had hunted and killed over his seventy-two years, this was the only one he had bothered to have mounted. It must have meant something to him.

Nobody else seemed to want it. All the hunting men in the family had trophy heads of their own. None of the women were interested. At the time it seemed as if my uncle's deerhead came to me by default. Now I know better.

The trophy head is a male, of course, with a huge rack of antlers. My uncle shot the buck on this land probably without a license. To go hunting up north, he always took out a license. But on his own property—"Well," he'd say, "I feed 'em all year. I figure taking one is the same as collecting rent."

My uncle was a bachelor farmer, born and raised on my grandparents' homestead, the half section of land he husbanded for over sixty years.

As a child, I often ate wild game at my grandmother's table. Moose, deer, duck, partridge, pheasant, even prairie chicken, usually from my uncle's gun. To me, the wild flavor didn't taste ragged and wind-tossed, but complex and full of mystery.

On the farm I learned about guns. Behind the barn with siblings and cousins, we target-practiced on tin cans. I was a pretty good shot, for a city girl. As a teenager, I hunted gophers with a couple of boys I was trying to impress.

I used my father's .22, an old-fashioned gun without a scope. Since gophers move much faster than tin cans, I was fairly sure I wouldn't hit anything. Then one hot afternoon one of the boys handed me his gun.

The hole is on the crest of the hill, so when he pops out and stands upright, I have a clear view of the gopher and the hard blue sky. I line him up in the cross hairs. I see his chest panting in and out in little gopher breaths. I squeeze the trigger. The explosion rips into me. Death—alive, bright, and blazing red—fills the sights of the gun. I feel as if my eyes have been flooded with blood.

All the heirlooms my uncle might have handed on to his nieces and nephews turned to ashes when my grandparents' house burned down thirty years ago. After the fire, my uncle treasured few objects. The deerhead was one.

The sight of it hanging in the living room of the new farmhouse always made me indignant. By the time it appeared, I was a young feminist, a member of Greenpeace, and a vegetarian among my friends. Among my family (especially my farm family) I still ate a little meat, just enough to avoid controversy. In a world full of supermarkets, the notion of hunting seemed arrogantly male and wasteful.

A hunter should eat what he kills—that's the only way he can justify his action. But to my newly political self, to force a dead animal into a "lifelike" pose, stuff it with who knows what, and hang it on his wall, as if killing the animal gave the hunter the right to ravage its dignity, seemed like the consummate act of hubris. Now I wonder if I was using my indignation to mask my uneasiness over a realization at which the deerhead only hinted. My uncle could look at death; I could not.

Soon after my uncle enters the hospital with terminal cancer, I dream that my cousin's son is going to be married. He calls together all the men in the family for his prenuptial party, his stag. It will not be an orgy with strippers and cheap booze. The men will gather to take part in a ritual. I want to know what will happen at the stag. I ask my uncle. "It's an old way of knowing," he says.

Visiting my uncle day after day in the hospital, I worried about what to say. Too much talk about the past or the future felt like poking my finger at a bruise. (As if he wasn't spending every day awash in memory. As if he hadn't already imagined a future beyond his own.) Many times I tried to summon the courage to tear down the taboo and talk to him about his death. I couldn't do it. It was my own terror I feared, not his.

My dream insisted that I ask him about hunting. He was as surprised (and as pleased) as if I'd asked him about hockey or about the comparative maintenance records of Ford and Chrysler half-tons.

We talked about how he learned to hunt. My grandmother would say, "Alfred, we need something for supper," and from the time he was nine or ten years old, my uncle would take the rifle into the woods or down by the lake and always come home with an animal, even it if was only a squirrel or a rabbit.

He had been a hunter for over sixty years. He knew a thing or two about the animals he stalked. Mule deer are wily; they'll circle around behind you. Whitetails, he told me, always pause at the top of a rise and look back at you. That's when they're easiest to hit, in that backward glance.

He tried to be a good hunter, to know the animal's habits, to shoot only once, and to kill his prey clean. To follow the animal if it was wounded until he found it so he could finish the job, no matter how tired he was. And if the sun went down before he found it, to go back the next day and look again. To butcher the animal properly and pack out all the meat. "Not like some of these young guys, eh?" he said. "If they can't get to the animal on their ski-doo, well, they just don't bother. Ski-doos have made them lazy. If you're lazy, you shouldn't go hunting."

He remembered the hunting trips he took up north with his buddies to the Whitecourt forest or the Swan Hills. I asked what made these trips so special. "The smell of the pines," he said. "And not having to do chores. Eating oatmeal and beans and garlic. And hunting from sunup to sundown. A little rye and cards in the evening." He was quiet for a moment. "And no chores."

When my uncle moves into the palliative care unit, my seven-year-old daughter makes him a picture. She draws and colors a still life of one of her stuffed toys, a fawn. I ask her why she chose the little deer. "I just thought he'd like it," she says.

The cancer mined its way through my uncle's muscular, compact body, leaving behind only skin and bone and eyes like bits of blue sky. In some of his lucid moments, between the pain-killer and the pain, he was wild with anger. Once near the end, he tried to leave, to pull out the tubes, to get out of bed, to get out the door. He fell, of course, bruising his knees and cutting his forehead.

"I wish I'd taken the shotgun and done the job myself," he said to me. And in that moment, I wish he had, too. Or that one of us had been brave enough to help him. Or that all of his nieces and nephews had each put a hand on a pillow and just held it there.

It's thirty below, dark, windy, and snowing. I meet one of my cousins in the hospital parking lot. He's been out there a while, crying. "I can't stand to see him like this," he says. "He wouldn't let one of his animals suffer the way he's been suffering. I can't go back in there."

We brought the deerhead home from my uncle's farm in the back of the van. I thought we'd put it in storage, but my daughter asked if she could hang it in her room. So we mounted it on her rainbow wallpaper and over the next year and a half, she festooned it with a fairy-princess garland, a Canadian flag, and an assortment of hair ribbons. I worried that its looming presence might give her nightmares or create a twitter among her friends, yet it didn't. She couldn't tell me why, but it was clear that she needed the deerhead in her room.

Then a couple of weeks ago, just before she turned nine, she came to me with a confession. "It's not that I don't want it, Mom," she explained. "I just want my room to look less cluttered. More normal, you know?"

"I know," I answered.

All summer long I cross paths with the deer in the fields at the farm, disappearing into the trees by the side of the road. One evening I meet a great buck on a mountain trail. That night in my dream, I'm crying. My uncle consoles me, holding me as I wish now that I'd held him had I been brave enough to look at his death.

Like the whitetail at the top of the rise, I pause and look back. Over the game trails and the threads on the loom I divine a connection. Yes, it's a risk. I am open now to the hunter's discretion. But I might also discover that what looked like default could be inheritance.

I'm trying to hang the deerhead on my wall. I hope it will remind me to be less normal and more brave.

BEVERLEY ROSS *is a writer, composer, and musician. Her work has appeared in a number of diverse places, from* Sesame Street *and CBC's* Sunday Morning *to festival and theater stages across Canada. Born and raised in Edmonton, Alberta, she lives there with her husband and two children.*

Reexamining
Rituals

The Day I Got My Divorce

SHARON BUTALA

This piece is dated June 3, 1980, so it was written five years after the events it describes. I billed it as a "story," meaning fiction, but in fact, it is as accurate a depiction of everything that happened that morning as I was capable of writing. I had just begun writing a couple of years earlier, and I had the idea somewhere in the back of mind that such an attempt at an absolutely accurate rendering of a serious emotional event would in itself become art. In this piece are the seeds of the writer I became, and although I might still try to do this, my writing style would be more complex, my insights (I hope) more telling, and I would work harder at laying out the metaphor more subtly.

It's now been twenty-two or more years since that morning. In fact, I believe now that I would have been unable to write it any other way—it was rejected by the one literary magazine I sent it to on the grounds that it was not properly a "story"— although I probably could do so now that so much time has passed and the wounds are less raw. But I think I handled it the right way: an event that bewildered me and stunned me with pain so that I could only dwell in the quotidian and was incapable of taking solace anywhere or even letting loose my grief for fear that it might destroy me.

I DON'T REMEMBER THE WEATHER the morning I got my divorce. I remember that I put on a blue and white plaid skirt that had a thin red thread running through it. It was an A-line skirt, and the plaid was diagonal. Then I put on a high-necked, long-sleeved sweater, which I tucked into the skirt. The sweater was perfectly white, immaculately so. From a distance it looked smooth, but actually it had fine ribbing all over it. So it must have been fall or spring or possibly winter since it was a winter outfit, and I also remember wearing my leather coat with the fur collar. I remember the coat distinctly, but I can't remember snow anywhere, although I feel sure I wore boots. I can remember walking down the street, but I cannot recall what I had on my feet. I feel sure it was boots. Still, when I think about it, the feeling I get of the day is one of early spring. I think there was a lightness in the air despite everything, that could only have been early March or so.

I don't remember how I got to the courthouse, but I do remember that I was at least fifteen minutes early. I am always early for everything, and it is a terrible nuisance but not something I seem able to change. I always get the best seats on trains and buses, but I spend a lot of time alone, waiting.

I arrived early at the courthouse, and there was nobody in authority to tell us where we could sit while we waited, and so those of us who were waiting simply stood outside the courtroom door with the number on it that we'd been told to go to by our lawyers. I think it was four. It seems to me there was another man about my age, also there for a divorce hearing, and that he attempted to make conversation with me which might have led to something more since we were both single, or about to be, but I wanted to concentrate on the thing that was happening to me. His interest in me, normally flattering, did not stir any feeling in me at all. Anyway, he seemed very bitter, and I didn't see how two people who meet in such circumstances could have anything but an unhappy relationship. He slumped against the wall and stared at his shoes, his head bent sideways.

After a while a family came, a mother I think, and two teenaged children and a young man in his twenties. There may have been a husband also I can't remember. The woman was fat, and the buttons of her dull brown coat bulged open across her chest and stomach. After ten or more minutes of waiting, which I spent walking up and down the wide marble hall and reading the signs on the closed doors since there wasn't anywhere to sit, my lawyer appeared wearing his black robe. I thought we would go in and the divorce hearing would start, but instead, he just nodded to me and went directly to this lumpy, overcoated, and indistinct family which kept merging into the shadows of the recessed doorway outside the courtroom. He put the mother and some of the children in one room on the right of the courtroom doorway and the rest of them in a room on the left. And then he kept going into one room and shutting the door behind him, and after a minute, coming out and going into the other room and closing the door. It seemed very strange, and I couldn't see how it could be a divorce hearing if both sides had the same lawyer, but I could not think what it might be about.

Just before the courtroom door opened, two more people arrived. They were men who looked to be in their fifties or maybe even older, and they both wore rumpled and nondescript overcoats with the collars up. One coat was tan, I remember, and I know that one man was bigger than the other. They both had unshaven, red faces as if they were farmers and used to being outside in all kinds of weather, or perhaps, as it occurred to me later, they were alcoholics. It would have seemed quite natural and not at all surprising if the one in the tan overcoat had pulled out of his pocket a wrinkled brown paper bag with a bottle in it and taken a drink now and then. It may be that he did do that, although I doubt it. I think they talked to each other while we waited and seemed very cheerful. Of course, they waited only a minute before the door opened. I think a commissionaire in a navy uniform with white cord dripping down his sleeve opened it, but I have to admit that previously in my mind's eye, I just saw the door mysteriously swing open and nobody there, when suddenly a commissionaire appeared in a blue uniform holding his arm against the door to keep it back. So he was probably actually there, and I didn't invent him.

We all went in very hastily, since nobody had told us what to do. My lawyer, the only one to be seen, was still busy with the family. The young man who had been talking to me, I think he had last made some bitter remark about his soon-to-be ex-wife, simply disappears out of my narrative here since

I cannot recall where he was after this. I have no recollection of what he looked like at all, just the flavor of his bitterness, which is how I know he must have been there and must have talked to me.

I sat down in the front row on a hard oak bench with an oak railing just in front of me. The room had a high ceiling, and there were several small tables in front of me on the other side of the railing, and in front of them and above, there was a large desk where the judge would sit. I had a recurring nightmare about this room, but I can't recall the dream itself, just a trace passes across my memory, and I know it was about something unpleasant being done to me in the emptiness of that room.

The judge appeared. I don't remember the mechanics of that, although now that I think about it, I do remember standing up. I hated to move. I felt that things were too precarious, and I remember mentally resisting standing up. Someone must have told us to stand.

In a moment my lawyer, who had been standing inside the railing facing the judge, his wavy white hair making wings on each side of his head, watched me walk up to the prisoner's dock or the stand or whatever the elaborate oak pulpit is properly called in a divorce case, beside the judge. I suppose I was sworn in, I think I said "yes," I'm sure I didn't say "I do." My lawyer said several incomprehensible things addressed to the judge. I think the language was archaic, or perhaps he just rattled it off very quickly as a part of the routine, but I didn't understand any of it. I really hate to say that the judge seemed bored since everyone says that, but he did seem bored. Maybe that is the official attitude of all judges, a facade of boredom so that criminals won't get the idea that they are special or in any way interesting, or maybe it is just a boring job. I was extremely embarrassed knowing that my divorce was an inconsequential matter and just another in an endless stream of divorces which, he managed somehow to convey, there couldn't possibly be any excuse for.

The first time I went to my lawyer's office, I was seated in the waiting room just outside his partner's door, and while I waited I was able to hear, unwillingly, much of what was going on inside. The lawyer would say something brief, and then a woman's voice would respond with a long monologue punctuated by sobs. Sometimes she cried so hard she couldn't talk, and I imagined him as handing her tissues. This went on the full half hour I waited, and either I could hear enough to know it was about a divorce or I could just tell. This made me realize that lawyers who handle divorces must have to go through this tearfulness with their female clients. It seemed to me to be an undignified way to behave, and I vowed then and there that I would not do that, and I didn't.

Several days before going to court, I had to rehearse the questions I was to be asked and to memorize my answers, so that I wouldn't say anything that would spoil the neatness of the divorce ceremony, I guess. It seemed silly. The afternoon I had to see my lawyer to do this memorizing, several of my friends came downtown with me, partly for moral support and partly out of curiosity, I guess. I drank one glass of beer with them before I went to my lawyer's office, and it loosened my resolve. When he handed me a document which I was to read, saying, "Your husband said this," I threw it back at him and said, "I don't care what he said." I felt really sorry that I hadn't managed to get through the whole thing without any show of emotion. But now that it is over and in the past, I rather wish I hadn't been so high-principled. After all, he expected me to behave badly, and I was paying him for the privilege, so maybe I should have.

Afterward, in the bar, I entertained my friends by telling them my answers (yes, no, a thousand dollars), but didn't tell them the questions. We had a good laugh about it while they invented questions to go with my answers.

And now that it is so long in the past, I can't remember what the questions were. The questions and answers were easy, and even though it was all very Kafka's castle-ish because nobody told us where to go or what we were to do so that we kept looking at each other for signals and finally walked into the courtroom and sat down very slowly, as though we were half-expecting somebody to suddenly appear and say no, you can't sit there, or line up, or something, despite this, I felt annoyed rather than lacking in confidence. Well, I'm dressing up my feelings by saying I was annoyed. Some part of me was, all right, but it was the sixties radical part of me which operates only out of the very top part of my head. All the rest of me was filled with bitterness that things should end in this stark, high-ceilinged room with four or five strangers watching me and nobody to tell me how to behave. I took my coat off finally, since nobody said not to, and left it on the bench when I was called up to the stand. I remember thinking, I'm not getting a divorce with my coat on. So I took it off and went up to the stand in my plaid skirt and white sweater, and I think I probably looked very nice. I had taken quite a lot of trouble with my hair. I wanted to look innocent and decent.

I was asked about my income. Then I was asked about my equity in the house I had just bought. Then I was asked about custody, which I wanted.

"Yes," I said. Here the judge or somebody told me to speak up, and I was stricken with such an attack of embarrassment or shyness or maybe it was just that I suddenly realized where I was and what was happening to me, that I panicked and thought, I can't do this, how am I gong to do this. My lawyer was no help. He stood on the other side of the railing and waited anxiously for me to get control of myself. I desperately did not want to make my divorce into something bigger than it was by crying or otherwise spoiling the ritual. And far off, in the spectators' seats near the door, the two rumpled old men sat and grinned and whispered to each other. There was someone else watching, I know, sitting just behind my lawyer but I cannot call to mind who it was. It must have been the young man who was also getting a divorce, but he is simply a shadow in that row without a face or a shape. And while I was being asked questions, the family came quietly in and sat down, but they didn't bother me. It was those two curious old men who bothered me, sitting there like a Greek chorus or like the crones who sat at the foot of the guillotine and knitted while heads rolled at their feet. So I clutched frantically for some way to carry on and found it in the gleaming oak rail directly in front of me, on which I fixed my eyes and stared hard, and didn't even look at my lawyer who stood in front of me looking up apprehensively at me.

The next question was about my husband. My answer was to have been "yes," but I said, to my own surprise, and in the good loud voice required of me, looking at the two old men, "Yes. He is living with her." I trembled at my own audacity. My lawyer shuffled his feet nervously, but the judge didn't say anything. Otherwise, I did just as I was told.

It was over in, I suppose, about three minutes, although it seemed longer. My lawyer raised his eyebrows at me to let me know that I could go, and so I stepped down and walked down the aisle to my coat, very quickly, and I think I smiled. Then I didn't know what to do. Nobody had told me if I had to stay or if I could go, and I couldn't ask my lawyer because he and the judge were into some mumbo jumbo and so I thought, angrily, that I would just go, and if I wasn't supposed to, well, that was just too bad. My lawyer turned slightly as I began to walk out, and I gave him a little wave because I thought you weren't supposed to talk in court. He gave a startled and distracted little wave back.

But when I got out onto the street, I realized that I didn't know what to do. I'd taken the day off from work because it seemed a necessary act to symbolize the seriousness of the occasion, and now I had nowhere to go. My mother and sister were meeting me for lunch, but that was hours away, so I walked slowly down the street and tried to think of a destination while all the time some bewildered and hollow feeling sat on my chest.

I had gone a block when I ran into a woman I knew.

"What are you doing downtown so early in the morning?" she asked. She was very sympathetic and insisted I go up to her office, which was nearby, and have coffee with her. And soon she began to cry and told me about her divorce, which was only a couple of months old and had been too terrible to talk about, but her children, who were all three teenagers, wouldn't even talk to her because they blamed her for the divorce and had all gone to live with their father. And so she thought she would quit her job and go out to B.C. where she had a chance at a better one.

I don't remember what I did for the rest of the morning, but I suppose I must have walked around and looked in all the stores until it was time to meet my mother and sister. We went into a restaurant and sat down. At the next table there was a man reading a book who happened to be married to a cousin of ours, and he came and sat with us, too.

"What are you all doing downtown on a work day?" he asked. My mother and sister waited for me to answer, since they had come only on my account.

"Getting a divorce," I said, and we all laughed.

SHARON BUTALA *lives in rural Saskatchewan. Her books, which are set in the prairies, include* Country of the Heart *(1984),* The Fourth Archangel *(1992), and* The Perfection of the Morning: An Apprenticeship in Nature *(1994). Her most recent novel is* The Garden of Eden *(1998).*

Pilgrimage

ANN CAMERON

T HE TRIBAL ELDER SHOOK MY HAND and peered intently up into my face, searching for something. His lined face was handsome and intelligent; indeed, he had published several books on the language of his Coeur d'Alene tribe and held an honorary doctorate. The elder said, yes, he remembered my great-uncle Ernest, once active in the politics and governance of the band, and also recalled my great-aunt Polly, who had taught him music perhaps seventy years before. Both I remembered as unusually kind and spiritual beings. He knew the whole family, no doubt better than I did: Ernest, Polly, and my grandmother had attended the same Indian mission school as his family. Was he looking for a family resemblance to them? Two generations later, there is only a ghost of the Indian genes in my face.

We were standing in front of a surprising sight: a beautiful Baroque-style church in Cataldo, Idaho, in a forest near the Rocky Mountains. This elegant mission was a miracle in itself, built by the Coeur d'Alene Indians in the first flush of their reputedly enthusiastic conversion to Catholicism in the 1840s. An Italian Jesuit missionary, Father Antonio Ravalli, worked with them to create this imposing structure from modest and unlikely materials: trees, mud, old newspapers, a little house paint. Not even nails were available at the poor, isolated mission. Together they constructed the mission church, with its Roman Baroque facade and proportions, portico, scrolls and all. Walls of adobe and hand-hewn planks perhaps, but inside Father Ravalli even managed to paint altar pieces and murals, creating images that were admired and loved. In the remote forest, the church and mission became the heart of the increasingly prosperous Coeur d'Alene community. Unfortunately for the Coeur d'Alenes, in the following generation rich silver deposits were discovered in the area. The American government reacted quickly, moving the reservation much farther south and drastically reducing its size. Ever since then, perhaps as an affirmation of ownership, perhaps as a reproach, the Coeur d'Alenes have organized regular "pilgrimages" back to this church and the country of their ancestors.

My two sons and I attended Mass on the grassy slope beside the church. The liturgical procession included warrior veterans of Vietnam, children in a casual version of native dress, a Coeur d'Alene member of the State Legislature in deerskin and blue beads. Old men drummed to accompany the ritual; young people performed ceremonial dances and rites. The only jarring note was the presence of the Bishop of Idaho. In contrast to the energy and spontaneity of the event, he seemed so pale, so weak, and so shiny in his white satin vestments. So official.

How had we come to be connected with this community? My great-grandfather Julien was a Quebec artisan who traveled west in a covered wagon to the Gold Rush of 1849, then continued on to Oregon. There, at a convent mission school, Julien Boutelier met his wife, Mary Elizabeth Chamberlain, daughter of a Hudson's Bay Company employee who was an early white settler.

Mary's Iroquois–Chinook mother died soon after her birth in one of the terrible epidemics that decimated the Indians in the West. The bereaved father then married a Coeur d'Alene woman who raised Mary Elizabeth from infancy. Julien and Mary Elizabeth eventually brought their family to Coeur d'Alene country near the Canadian border, settling to farm in an area of rolling hills, beautiful lakes, and mountains. While ugly battles erupted around them, Indians and white settlers in this remote area tried to live in harmony. Coeur d'Alene Chief Andrew Seltice shared a Utopian vision with the Jesuit missionaries; they believed that both peoples could live together, united by their faith. They seem to have thought that the few mixed race families who settled on the outskirts of the reservation could be a kind of buffer. In general, the Coeur d'Alenes and the Bouteliers enjoyed a cordial relationship which included trading game for the Bouteliers' fine fruit and vegetables. Among the families of the area, Mary Elizabeth became known for her power of healing. With no doctors in the region, sick people came to her for herbal medicine. According to family stories, she fasted and prayed, to the point of going into trances, until they were cured.

One winter day my great-uncles rescued Chief Seltice and his sons from drowning in the river near the Boutelier home. Seltice decided to show his gratitude by generously adopting the entire Boutelier family as his own: they became "his children." The two families worshipped together; their children went to school together. Chief Seltice gave my family lands adjacent to their farm and insisted that government benefits be extended to all his "family." Not all of his people were pleased to see "white" people on Indian land. As time passed and conditions for Indians worsened, it must have been galling to share scant resources with those who seemed to enjoy the advantages of both worlds. The festering bitterness erupted in an ugly murder of a similarly privileged neighbor family.

These are stories I have pieced together from reading and fragments of family anecdotes I heard as I grew up. All my friends seemed to come from easily identifiable backgrounds: English, Irish, Italian, complete with strong family nostalgia for the old country. In an age of multiculturalism, it seemed a little weak to identify myself as Canadian. And these family stories I heard seemed too exotic to be true. My father, a handsome and kind man, was comfortable in the business and manufacturing world, smiling and patient at home. His interior life, rarely shared, was deeply spiritual, a legacy of his mother and grandmother. We, his children, knew a little of the story of the Coeur d'Alenes, but without the context I found in my reading and without any sense of how he felt about it. My sons could never know him since he had died before they were born, and I wished to somehow connect them with their heritage.

As the boys matured, I began to search for my father's heritage and to understand something more of him. What do we ever know or understand of our parents, especially if they die early? Does the naive trust of a child for a benevolent parent preclude knowing him as a real person? So I began to search for my father's—and my—heritage. A book on his family's history came to light; I exchanged letters with an elderly cousin of his who lived in Spokane, who had kept in touch with the tribe. I telephoned to the Cataldo mission, did some Internet searches, and then, still puzzled and curious, I, too, made the pilgramage. From a Canadian city far to the east I made the long car trip with my boys, and here we were at the astonishing Cataldo mission: drums, sweetgrass, beads, and leather, and a lovely Roman Jesuit church on a hill in the American mountain forest. These places and people had seemed so distant, almost legendary. But I found a number of my people buried in the same mission cemetery with the elder's people. And when I heard or read the names of the places in the area, I could hear my grandmother's voice saying them. I thought of Granny and all her family, who must have come here to the Cataldo church on the pilgrimages. All of them dead, but here their presence seemed vivid. Several times during the Mass, I turned away to hide my tears from my sons.

What was on the elder's mind as he scrutinized my face? Was he recalling the complex history of generosity and resentment between his people and the adopted Boutelier children, whose ambitions had taken them so far away from this beautiful country? After primary grades at the mission school, the Boutelier children were sent away to city boarding schools. Usually seen as "white" by strangers, they easily became part of the same white society which had repeatedly humiliated his proud people. Still, I wanted to thank him for the connection which had been legally severed at my father's death. I again took the elder's hand. What could I say? I told him that it had been a great honor to meet him. The tension disappeared. His expression warmed into a smile.

ANN CAMERON *was born in Vancouver in 1948. She studied and works in the fields of art history and museums. She lives in Toronto, Ontario, with her husband and two sons.*

Anniversary
An Autumn Meditation

BETTY GIBBS

I'M NOT GOOD WITH BIRTHDAYS. They are too specific, and my memory too porous. I have my mother's birthday narrowed down to one of two dates. My father's birth date can range over about a week. Why should I remember his birthday when the month of his death is so present with me?

To be any use, birthdays need to be on the right day. A deathday changes the color of a whole month or even a season. Each year the light angles down past autumn, nights chill, and leaves abandon me. A certain kind of gray associated with the changing season hides the shortening days. I remember his graveside was raw and miserable. Snow was in the air.

I have had five decades of Octobers, and some of them must have contained golden weeks of late autumn, as delicious as stolen apples. Three of my brothers and two nephews have married in October. After harvest and before goose shooting, they say—a perfect time for farmers to get married. But when I think of October, I remember mud and bad roads, the first heavy snow coming the next day.

Each time I fly home for one of these family events, the following day I drive out to the lake. I walk past the boarded up concession stand through wet, yellow rags of poplar and willow leaves, and stand and watch the gray breakers on the lake stretching across the horizon.

My childhood beach was hot, gray sand, little frogs squashed into black leather on the road, and poison ivy in the bush. I remember with sentimental affection the noise and activity of childhood summer, and I indulge in melancholy at the October sadness. At the moment of self-consciousness, melancholy becomes useful as a means of learning.

A brother died in winter, a dear friend in July. Will I lose all of the seasons, one by one?

What are anniversaries for? For the literal-minded they cycle yearly and make a click in our year, like a clothes peg on a bicycle spoke. For some they may have a longer and more erratic period, marked only when we return to a place, re-enter a time or experience. If they are significant we count time with them—the third time I moved back to Edmonton, the last time I went home.

Why do we return? Is it curiosity or a deep tidal pull down spawning and migration routes that have a season peculiar to us? Some people go home often, on a regular and predictable schedule. Others go when something activates their homing beacon, like a disused lighthouse flashing from a distant shore—a cousin's wedding, a mother's funeral, or a family reunion. But for some it is a mystery. A pressure leans on us from an unknown source. We walk out from under it, homeward, captured by the gravitational pull of the past.

We return to a slippery reunion with the misunderstood, misplaced, and unfinished to find ourselves—like a project that may have once been intended as a sweater but now might make a good cat-bed liner or, if we happen to be pleased with ourselves, a soft sculpture of surprising beauty.

Are anniversaries something to congratulate ourselves on? We have, after all, winched ourselves away from childhood, counting the cogs on the gear. But now we hang, suspended, ready to be dragged toward old age and death on the same inexorable ratchet wheel. We are counting and measuring animals. Cycles are in our blood.

We learn to fear our own birthdays. Of course, there's nothing wrong with turning fifty, we say. It's a great age, a strong age for women, a kind of freedom. Yet there are things I thought I would have accomplished by now, and another decade has passed. Another. I'm trapped by my own expectations, my own agenda. My father died when he was fifty. Fortunately, next year will be neutral, a year like any other year. Who sorts their life agenda by thirty-one, forty-one, fifty-one?

Not every month is October. Luckily, the years roll around with the rushing joy of warm days in flowery May, bright days in golden September, and the silence of December snowfall. These days cycle through my life, buzzing with gossip of other years and offering their predictable pleasures. They also smell and taste of returning. Their multiple exposures layer over each other. The light lines up its angles, and trees grow up through it, children skip from tricycles to motorcycles, time-lapse photography.

If we can bear to, if we have the strength and discipline, we can focus on ourselves. If we can look past the fact that we feel exactly the same as we did at twenty (surely we haven't changed), we can learn. We have to look past the jowls and spreading waist to measure whether our souls have grown. What else are anniversaries for except to provide bench marks for such a survey?

Another year has passed, and I realize that although I remember a lot of details I am no longer trapped in grief. The memory of pain is at a distance. I can see back past the loss to the life, remembering his short-legged walk, his jokes, his affection for children, his cleverness with his hands. I can be glad again that I grew up with him around. I can begin to let go of feeling guilty that I moved away so early and wouldn't go home; that I took him for granted until it was too late. October now tugs at me with a warmer hand, a busy, useful, and loving hand.

BETTY GIBBS, *after a first career as a teacher and a second in educational media production, is now a full-time editor for an Edmonton educational publisher and a part-time singer/writer/liturgy designer. She has had a story and several essays published.*

The Family that Prays Together

MARY MCNAMEE

EVERYTHING IMPORTANT BEGINS LIKE THIS:

In the name of the Father, and of the Son, and of the Holy Ghost. Amen.

Every evening after supper, after the table has been cleared and the dishes washed, dried, and put away, we kneel down in the living room to say the Rosary. Every evening, regardless of where we live, we arrange ourselves in the same pattern. We face the ceramic plaque of the Holy Family that hangs above us, always the focal point of this room. The Virgin Mary gazes serenely down at the baby Jesus held lovingly in her arms, while Joseph encircles the two with a protective air. My mother and my older brother, Peter, kneel closest to the figures, eyes tightly closed, frowns of concentration lining their foreheads. My younger brother, Michael, and I kneel farther back, eyes wide open and moving, trying to catch sideways glimpses of each other. My father kneels behind us, his eyes always upon Micheal and me so he can make sure we do not lean our bodies against any piece of furniture as a prop. If Michael and I forget ourselves and lean backward to rest our bottoms on the backs of our legs, my father swings his rosary beads out in a huge arc to flick our feet. We bolt upright, startled.

Our Father, Who art in heaven, hallowed be Thy name, Thy kingdom come, Thy will be done on earth as it is in heaven.

My earliest memory is of saying the Rosary. I am kneeling on the hardwood floor in the small, white bungalow in Southend. I am four years old. Michael is three. We have our own white, plastic Rosary beads. We kneel for twenty minutes during the Rosary. Already we know how to behave, how to stay very still on our knees, how to be silent except when it is our turn to pray out loud. Our family is lucky—there are five of us and five decades in the Rosary. That means we each get to say a whole decade out loud. A decade is one "Our Father," ten "Hail Marys," and one "Glory Be." Then you start all over again until you have completed five sets. I am glad that there are more Hail Marys than any other prayer. The Blessed Virgin Mary is my favorite. I am named after her. My mother tells me that Mary is the most special name a girl can have.

Hail Mary, full of grace, the Lord is with thee. Blessed art thou amongst women, and blessed is the fruit of thy womb, Jesus.

The Blessed Virgin Mary is kind and gentle. We often call her "Our Lady." We pray to her to ask God or Jesus for things we need. Not things we want to have, like new bicycles or more friends, but things like courage and forgiveness. I ask Mary to ask God to make me good. I prefer not to ask God directly for anything. I am afraid of him. He sees everything I do, and knows everything I am thinking. He disapproves of many things and becomes terribly angry. Mary is more understanding, so I speak to her. I am devoted to her. It is a special thing to be devoted to Our Lady. The highest praise my mother ever gives is to say that someone has "a great devotion to Our Lady." This means the person is particularly holy.

Glory be to the Father, and to the Son, and to the Holy Ghost.

Glory is like when the sun suddenly breaks through dark clouds and you can actually see the rays of light shining down onto the earth. It will be like that on the Last Day. We do not know when the Last Day will be, so we must always be ready. If I am caught with mortal sins on my soul on the Last Day, God will send me directly to Hell, where I will suffer forever. My catechism book is filled with pictures of people suffering in Hell. They are burning up in flames, their bodies twisted and their mouths open, screaming, but they never die, so their pain never ends. The flames are not the worst part, though. The greatest torment is knowing you will never see God, never be allowed into heaven. No matter how sorry you are, no matter how long you suffer, it is too late—you will never have another chance.

The Five Sorrowful Mysteries: The Agony in the Garden, Jesus is Scourged at the Pillar, Jesus is Crowned with Thorns, Jesus Carries His Cross, The Crucifixion.

When we say the Rosary on Tuesdays and Fridays, we are supposed to think about the Sorrowful Mysteries. These Mysteries are dark and terrible, all about the suffering and agony Jesus had to go through because of us. Mysteries are things we cannot really understand, but we think about them anyway. My father announces the name of a Mystery at the beginning of each decade. These Mysteries always go in the same order; you cannot mix them up. You are supposed to contemplate the Mystery while you are saying the prayers of that decade. My father says this means you think about the event while saying the prayer out loud. I never really learn how to do this properly. I can't seem to say one thing while thinking another. Either I forget what I'm thinking or I lose track of what I'm saying. It is very important not to lose track when I'm saying my decade out loud in front of the whole family. If you stumble over the words, it means you are not paying attention, you are letting your thoughts stray. I pray that my thoughts will not stray when I pray. It is disrespectful to God. It is like putting Jesus back up on the cross and making him go through that terrible agony all over again.

The Five Glorious Mysteries: The Resurrection, The Ascension into Heaven, The Descent of the Holy Spirit, The Assumption of Our Blessed Lady into Heaven, The Coronation.

We say the Glorious Mysteries every Wednesday and Saturday and Sunday. Glorious Mysteries are not things you can be happy about; they are too important and full of awe for people to go around smiling about them. All of the Glorious Mysteries have to do with rising up toward heaven: Jesus rising up from the dead, then ascending into heaven, Mary rising up into heaven and then being crowned up there. The only exception is the Holy Spirit, who did the reverse, coming down from heaven to enter the Disciples, but we understand that he went back up to heaven again after that. I know that the Glorious Mysteries should mean more to me, but they don't. Maybe it's because I'm not drawn toward heaven myself. I don't really believe I'm going to end up there; I know I will never be able to be good enough to get in. Even if God did let me in, I'm not sure I'd like it. I'd have to be even more careful to be good up there, and there wouldn't be any animal friends. My mother tells me that I would be so happy up there that I wouldn't want anything else, but I find this hard to believe. And I don't think I'd be very comfortable around God. I don't understand how he would ever be able to forgive me for all the things I'd done wrong. I think he'd still be thinking of those sins every time he looked at me.

The Five Joyful Mysteries: The Annunciation, The Visitation, The Nativity, The Presentation of the Child Jesus in the Temple, The Finding of the Child Jesus in the Temple.

These are my favorite Mysteries, the ones we say every Monday and Thursday. These are the ones where people are smiling, and things turn out well. The angel Gabriel visits Mary and tells her she will be the Mother of God. Mary goes to visit her cousin Elizabeth. Jesus is born. Mary and Joseph bring Jesus to the Temple. Mary and Joseph lose Jesus and then find him. All of these Mysteries take place here on earth. All of them are things I can safely picture in my own mind. There is nothing to feel bad about, and no one, absolutely no one, is suffering. And Mary is there in all of them, gentle and kind and patient.

Hail Holy Queen, Mother of Mercy! Hail our life, our sweetness and our hope! To thee do we cry, poor banished children of Eden, to thee do we send up our signs, mourning, and weeping in this valley of tears. Turn, then, O most gracious Advocate, thine eyes of mercy towards us, and after this, our exile, show us the blessed fruit of thy womb, Jesus. O clement, O loving, O sweet Virgin Mary!

We end the Rosary with the "Hail, Holy Queen." I say this prayer with great enthusiasm because I love its extreme, dramatic words and the passionate desperation of its plea. But also because it signals the end of the Rosary, freedom from this interminable kneeling and chanting and trying not to let my thoughts stray. When I learn how to read, I find a way to make the time pass more quickly. I kneel in front of the living room bookcase, which is filled with geography textbooks, Irish novels, and books on matters of faith. I start at the top left-hand corner and read the spine of every book. My head never moves, only my eyes. They travel the length of the three shelves, over and over. Very soon I am able to recite the title and author of every book in the case, with my eyes closed. This is a different sort of prayer.

The Rosary is predictable. Except for the difference in the Mysteries from day to day, it never changes. The Rosary offers me words I can be sure of in a world where I never know what the right response is. The Rosary is the only stable pattern in the continual upheaval of our home. No matter where we live, no matter what happens, we will always kneel down at seven o'clock and say the Rosary. We will raise our voices together, the only time we can speak in one voice, my parents' Irish accents blending with their children's Canadian tones.

By the time I leave home at eighteen, I have said 5,475 Rosaries. I have said at least 268,750 "Hail Marys." I stop saying the Rosary as soon as I leave home. But I can't completely stop saying the "Hail Mary." Whenever I am frightened, whenever I have to walk down a dark city street alone, the words are automatically in my mind, playing themselves over and over until I reach safety.

When I return to visit my parents, I feel like a hypocrite, kneeling and saying the Rosary with them only because I'm afraid to say no, afraid of my father's wrath and my mother's stony silence. At some point they finally realize my heart is no longer in these prayers. After that, we do not kneel down together. My parents say their Rosary in bed before they go to sleep. When my father becomes ill and has to sleep in a separate room, he and my mother still say the Rosary together, calling out the words to each other across the hallway. When my father becomes too ill to speak out loud, my mother kneels beside his bed and says the Rosary for him. He weeps because he can no longer speak the words. She tells him it's all right, that God will understand. She tells him to think the words in his head. From another room, I listen guiltily to my mother's solitary prayer, unable to join in with her, unable to utter the familiar words that were never mine.

Mary McNamee *lives in Edmonton, Alberta, where she teaches English at Grant MacEwan Community College. Her writing has appeared in* Other Voices.

No Time to Die

EUNICE VICTORIA SCARFE

I'VE BEEN WIDOWED TWICE.

Some days I feel like the Ancient Mariner with an unwelcome story to tell. After the first death, I felt I should carry the story in silence. After the second death, I knew I must not.

Bereavement is as inevitable as death. If you haven't been bereaved, you will be, which you know of course, but perhaps can forget more easily, and more often, than I. Who are the bereaved? They are those who follow the dead to the edge of the grave. And then what? They must return. But the return from the grave is unmarked and dark. How do the bereaved find their way?

For the recently bereaved, death is more present than life. After the first death, I sat on my porch and watched people passing. "You still here?" I wanted to call out. "Not dead yet?" I was surprised that anyone I had seen yesterday or last week was still alive. Most days, I was surprised that I was still alive. I expected us all to go down like tenpins—today, tomorrow, next week.

If you saw me, you wondered what to say. You'd say, "How *are* you?" and I'd answer, "Finethankyouhoware*you*?" so fast you probably didn't understand a word. And then I'd say, "Sorry, but what is there to say?" and we'd start talking of other things.

Perhaps.

After the second death, someone who works with those bereaved by suicide said to me, "We don't know what to say to the bereaved." And I thought to myself, "Ask them. They could tell you. They know."

What did I want said to me? Frankly, I didn't want to talk about how I was. I wanted to talk about them. I wanted to tell you their story or, rather, the end of their story. I wanted to tell it fast. I wanted to tell it all.

The bereaved leave the dead in the grave; they cannot leave the story there. I now know that it is story that maps the way back for those left behind, for those left alone without companion or compass.

Twice I walked out of the house with a man into the sun of an early morning; twice I came back before noon to my home alone, while the man who had left with me went to the mortuary.

Also alone.

My husband was forty-six when he died. We had been married twenty years.

He was running along the Saskatchewan Drive pedestrian path when he was hit from behind by a Mercedes driven by a man impaired by both alcohol and cocaine. The driver, who had no injuries, was in hospital before my husband was found. The driver said he didn't know his car had jumped a curb and thrown a man forty yards into the bottom of a ravine. My husband died instantly, or so I was told when the police found me five hours later.

My husband had won two major awards the winter before he died. It meant he would be released from university teaching for three years in order to do research. His new lab, funded by a million-dollar NSERC grant, had just opened. The night before he died he said he would begin art classes again, and in September we would finally begin the renovations on our 1912 house.

My partner was fifty-five when he died. He was just beginning a sabbatical leave. We had been together for five years. He died beside me in rush hour traffic. That morning he had complained of muscle pain in his shoulder. We thought it was caused by being chilled on our late evening walk along an Alberta lake the day before. The last day of autumn. The last night of his life.

The Easter before his death, we had skiied under thin sun and the blue bowl of an April sky to the highest point on the Norwegian plateau. We had stopped for coffee with friends in a remote red cabin high above the treeline.

As evening fell, we had sidestepped down a steep cliff in the steel-gray light to make a fire in our own red cabin beside the lake, planning to spend every Easter for the rest of our lives high on this plateau, resurrecting our spirits and bodies and joy.

Nightmares still come, night after night. Nightmares in which one of them is dying in front of my eyes, and I can't save him. Nightmares replaying the details of the death. As if I could forget. As if I need reminding. As if I am to be tantalized by the hope that this time I'll succeed, this time I'll bring him home alive.

Sometimes I get the deaths confused, the deaths that cut my life in half and in half again. "Before he died, after he died." Their lives, and their deaths, were so similar. Both men were scientists. Both were university professors. Both were from "humble origins," as they say. Both were born in Europe, one in Norfolk, England, and one in Stavanger, Norway. Both were born into the suck of terror during WW II, and both remembered the years of recovery after the war. Both read poetry; both sought comfort in classical music. Both were intensely proud of their children. My husband and I had two daughters. My partner had four daughters and a son. Each man was confirmed in the Protestant tradition, one in the Anglican and one in the Lutheran. Both died young. Both died instantly. Both died with futures so filled with possibility that each wondered if there would be world enough and time.

There wasn't.

The first death, the second death. Is it any wonder that I get the deaths confused?

The first death was followed by the Anglican Service for Burial on a hot July afternoon. The second death was followed by a memorial service of music—cello, violin, organ, and choir—on a somber September evening. Both the first time and the second time, my daughters and I sat in the front pew of Holy Trinity Anglican Church just blocks away from our Edmonton home.

At the first funeral, I listened to the congregation sing the words to the Swedish folk melody "Children of the Heavenly Father." At the second funeral, I sat beside the coffin I had accompanied to Norway and listened to the trumpeter, his nephew, play the same melody from the balcony of the village church.

Though he giveth or he taketh
God his children ne'er forsaketh.

As the bell tolled fifty-five times, I was glad we did not sing the words to what had always been my favorite hymn. I felt not only forsaken but also broken in both body and spirit.

The first time, my daughters each placed one of her braids in her father's coffin. The second time, they put letters in his coffin. The two remaining braids, they said, were to be saved for me.

The first time, "Blessed are the pure in heart" was written on his gravestone in the Canadian cemetery. The second time the traditional "Thanks for all you gave us" was written on his stone in the Norwegian cemetery.

The first time, I didn't realize that I could, and needed, to have him at home before he was buried. The second time I asked the funeral home to bring him home as soon as possible. Home to where we had cleansed the room with sage and sweetgrass. Where we placed autumn leaves on his coffin. Where we could, and did, sit with him, sing for him, talk to him. Where my children and I could cry unobserved and uninterrupted.

I wish now that I had not only kept both of them at home from the moment of their deaths but had also washed and dressed them myself. I wish I had sat in a circle with women and had stitched sorrow into a fine linen shroud.

After the first funeral, I drove west to the edge of the Pacific. I went to the cabin where we had spent our honeymoon in 1968. I went alone. After the second, I drove into the heart of the Norwegian mountains to his cabin, where we had first gone together in May 1991. I went alone.

After the first death, I wrote in red notebooks with wide, black ink. I filled a dozen in as many months. The second time, I wrote nightly on email to an ex-nun a continent away who had buried both her parents in the previous year.

The first time, I searched the city's antique shops for rings with stones of significance in memory of my geologist husband. A circle of garnets for me.

A topaz set in silver for my youngest daughter. And for my eldest daughter, a Victorian mourning ring set with black jet for sorrow and pearls for tears.

Things from the earth.

The second time, I searched for items of Scandinavian origin in memory of my Norwegian partner: a blue enamel bowl, a wooden drinking cup, a Bing and Grondal plate marking the year that he died. The music of Jan Garbarek, the Grieg Trio, Annbjorg Lien, the Bergen Domkantori.

Shape and sound from the land that he loved.

The first time, I was addicted to speech, with anyone, at any time, all the time. The second time, I sought solitude. Speech wearied me. Words failed.

The first time, I set up a scholarship in his memory. The second time, I commissioned a string quartet in his memory.

The first time, I went to an art therapist and painted the unspeakable pain. The second time, I went to a Jungian therapist and entered through dreams the size of the pain.

The first time, I expected and needed people to take care of me. The second time, I neither expected nor wanted people to take care of me.

The first time, I talked to a Buddhist doctor about life on the other side. He said that the suddenly dead are startled and that the one closest to them in spirit must bless and release them. The second time, I talked to an Icelandic shaman. She said she would speak to him on the other side, and she did.

The first time, a good Christian woman told me her community had not been comfortable with my coming alone to their church, my being a married woman and all. She said it would be easier for them to welcome me now that I was widowed. The second time, I refused all calls from members of this Mennonite Church where a woman without her husband is welcome only if he is in the grave.

The first time, we planted a linden tree at the spot where he was hit along the most beautiful stretch of Saskatchewan Drive. I read from the Roethke poem I had given him just before we married: *I learned not to fear infinity / The far field, the windy cliffs of forever / The dying of time in the white light of tomorrow.* The second time, we planted a birch tree in our garden, where he had once planted spring bulbs brought over from Norway. Again I read from Roethke: *All finite things reveal infinitude / What we love is near at hand / Always, in earth and air.*

The first time, my daughters and I visited the cemetery on birthdays, Father's days, wedding anniversaries and the date of his death. The second time, distance prevented us from visiting his grave.

The first time, an insurance company contested the facts of his death. The second time, his ex-wife and five children contested the facts of his life.

Sometimes when I come home to the house in which I've lived for more than twenty-five years, I think to myself, "Two men lived here, and two men died." I think of the walls of this house as a witness. As a cradle of comfort, offering the silence and solitude I crave. As offering a mirror for the memory I carry.

I have often thought of leaving this house. I'm not sure now I can. She knows the whole story. She saw it all. She remembers. She honors with me the lives of the dead and the memories of the living.

The first time. The second time.

The first time, in those deadlike days which set in some months later, I lay in bed and read: backward through all of Alice Walker, forward through the three volumes of *Kristin Lavransdatter,* in circles through Proust's *Remembrance of Things Past,* and in bits and pieces through anything else that was thick and mesmerizing. The second time, when day after day I was unable to get up, I read through the customs and practices of other cultures, both ancient and contemporary: *The Tibetan Book of the Dead, The Mexican Day of the Dead, Mourning & Mitzvah, Jewish Insights on Death and Mourning, Mourning to Morning.* I read the loss of a spouse in *A Grief Observed, Without* and *Moon Crossing Bridge;* the loss of a child in *Hour of Gold, Hour of Lead;* the loss of a father in *A Death in the Family* and *Zero Hour;* the loss of a grandfather in *Of Water and the Spirit.*

I went to Hamlet and understood his anguish at wondering what to do for the dead. I went to Antigone and understood the horror of being forbidden to bury her dead. I went to the women at the tomb and understood their confusion at being unable to find the dead.

What was I looking for?

I was looking for how others had returned from the edge of the grave. I wanted to listen to those who had been there before. I wanted the particular stories of particular individuals. I avoided books that told me how to return, and why, and how long it would take. After the first death someone gave me Kubler-Ross' *How to Say Goodbye.* I threw it against the wall. There were none. Good-byes, I mean. Not the first time. Not the second time.

People wondered what to say to me. Whether to call or not to call. Whether to stop by unannounced or to call ahead. Whether to send flowers or food. Whether to hug or ignore me if we met on the street. Whether to mention his name or not.

I didn't know what I needed. I do know now.

The ancient Greeks believed there were three stages of grief: the death itself, the burial, and the reintegration of the bereaved. The coming away from the edge of the grave. The return to the living and to living. It is ritual for this third stage that is utterly absent in my experience of mourning and maybe of yours. There is ritual for burial but not for mourning.

How do the bereaved return from the grave? Through story, I believe. "Turn and return" I call it, a cyclical process of remembering death and turning from it; remembering death again and turning from it again.

Ritual is what is repeated. Ritual is a practice that is known and understood by a community. Ritual is a dwelling that we enter and leave, enter and leave again. Ritual is where meaning is made. Ritual is where more than one gathers together, where all participate and partake.

In the absence of ritual after the first death, I was lost and bereft. After the second death, I created a ceremony for story which may become a ritual if we choose to do it again and then again. I invited the women who had cared for me and my children, some of whom who had tended us twice, to come to my home on the evening before the first Sunday in Advent, that season preparing for the darkest day of the year and for the return of the light to our lives. I invited them to light a candle on an evergreen tree in memory of their dead. Each one told a story of the person for whom the candle was lit. We heard stories we had never heard before, even though some of us had known each other for years. "Where there is sorrow, there is holy ground;" where there is sorrow's story, there is common ground; where there is common ground, there is comfort.

After each death, I heard how other cultures and religions make room for rituals of remembrance, for the repetition of story. A Ukrainian friend told me about bringing a meal to the graves on an annual day and spending time with other mourners beside the graves. My Irish friend said the "month mind," a mass one month after the funeral, is almost more important than the funeral itself. My Greek friend said a mass is celebrated three years after the funeral, and relatives from as far away as Greece will come. My Japanese friend said the day of the death is honored on the third, seventh, and tenth year anniversaries. My Jewish friend told me a *yahrzeit* is lit on the anniversary of the death and that the spirit of the dead person fills the room for twenty-four hours. She said that saying Kaddish at the synagogue brings mourners together and that the names of the dead are read and remembered at Yom Kippur.

The Celts began the New Year on 1 November, the day they believed the membrane between the living and the dead was thinnest. In the Peloponnese, the bones of the dead are dug up by the next of kin one year after the burial, washed, and returned to the earth. (Does this surprise you? It has been done in my lifetime and yours.) In many native traditions, the stone is set on the grave on the first anniversary of the death. In Mexico, they celebrate the "Day of the Dead." In Sicily, adults give children gifts on the day of remembrance. In Norway on All Souls Day, "grav" candles are placed on the graves.

In Japan, the mourners meet every seventh day after the death until the forty-ninth day when the memorial service is held. The souls of the dead return every August, and relatives of the dead travel to their ancestral homes to welcome their return. On 15 August, the souls are guided back by lighting candles in tiny boats on the water. On the hills they light bonfires.

The purpose of all of these customs I now understand. And none was part of my tradition.

The dead die once. The bereaved die over and over and over. In story is both the first resurrection of the dead and the certain resurrection of the bereaved.

In memory of
Christopher Martin Scarfe 1941–1988
and
Karl Anundsen 1940–1995

EUNICE VICTORIA SCARFE *has graduate degrees from the University of Chicago and the University of Alberta and is a past winner of the Prism International Short Fiction prize. In 1994 she designed the first Women's Writing Week at the Faculty of Extension, University of Alberta, now in its sixth year. Through Saga Seminars she teaches writing workshops in both Canada and the United States, including the Banff Centre, Simon Fraser Harbour Centre, and the International Women's Writing Guild.*

Jesus Loved Me

JANIS SHAW

S T. ANDREW'S UNITED CHURCH. Seems like there's one in just about every town in Alberta. Where I grew up, St. Andrew's was a smug brick building with a sturdy spire topping its hexagonal bell tower. My mother started taking me there in 1952, when I was six— then seven—years old.

Nearly every Sunday, Mom and I answered the church bell's one note summons calling us to worship again, again, and again. We'd file into the sanctuary, Mom in her veiled felt hat and me, even in winter, wearing a wide-brimmed straw with a cluster of plastic cherries tucked into the band. Six rows from the front, on the left-hand side, we would take our places in the wooden, straight-backed pews—right under the stained-glass eyes of Jesus. There I learned a litany of nots. From God: "Thou shalt not covet, commit, or kill." From Mom: "Don't sit with your legs apart! Don't peek during prayers!"

From the pulpit, Reverend Martin tried to teach me to mind my mother. Twice he told me the story of *Just a Minute Mary*, about a little girl who always had her nose in a book. He looked right down at me, solemnly telling how Mary's mother asked her to stop reading and put the bird back in its cage after its exercise. "Just a minute," Mary answered back, and the cat caught the canary.

Church wasn't all rules and obedience lessons. Once, the Imperial Order of the Daughters of the Empire, in their coats of mink, muskrat, and Persian lamb, marched through the church with their full-sized Union Jacks unfurled. I was impressed. Mom, in Melton cloth, was not. Maybe that's why she said yes when I asked if I could attend Vacation Bible School at the Baptist church that summer. She even suggested that I take along my very nearly twin cousins—Brenda, six, and Linda, five.

We took to the Baptists straight away. They weren't like United Church people. They were a lot more fun! The very first morning our teachers told us we were going to have a parade at the end of the week. "Do we dress up?" I asked, anticipation coloring my voice. "Certainly," came the reply.

I could hardly wait to tell Mom. "A parade!" I said. "I'll need a costume." Mom had already turned me into a red jersey devil with a menacing rubber mask for Halloween; and she had crowned me Miss Canada for a skating carnival, dressing me in a white satin jacket and skirt, both bordered with dozens of Crayola-colored maple leaves which danced on banks of glued-on cotton-batting snow. I trusted my mother's creativity. I knew she'd do me proud! Brenda and Linda asked their Gramma Reed, who was almost as clever as my mom when it came to sewing, to make something for them.

The last day of Bible School arrived. We assembled, two by two, behind our teachers who held a neatly lettered cloth banner reading Suffer the Little Children To Come Unto Me. As we started off, marching down the dusty, gravel road outside the church, we sang out—loudly, enthusiastically—"Jesus Loves The Little Children." I believed it. I knew he loved the twelve boys and girls who marched directly behind the banner, wearing polished shoes and their Sunday best; and I thought he had very special place in his heart for the Brenda and Linda butterflies who floated, next to the end of the procession, on yellow net and sequined wings. But he must have loved me best, as I brought up the rear in my sandals, Hula skirt, and a lei of Kleenex flowers.

Mom stood at the roadside as we marched by. Her color was pretty high. She never said a word though, until Dad came home for lunch. She had trouble telling him about the parade; she couldn't stop laughing.

In the fall, she took me back to St. Andrew's.

JANIS SHAW, *with her left foot still in the domain of the mother and her right descending toward the ground of the crone, vows to write more of her story. She lives and writes in Spruce Grove, Alberta.*

The Savages

APRIL SNOW

I FIRST SAW THEM AS A FAINT GRAY PUFF OF DUST up against the clear blue skyline. Then, out of the dust emerged an old weathered wagon that had seen many more prairie miles than I. Setting the pace was a team of Indian paints—thin, dispirited horses whose dusty skin held their bones in place precariously, whose eyes held only a spark of the spirit that I saw in the eyes of my father's well-fed, well-loved team. Trust me that I would notice, that I would also notice the wire-thin arms of the four dark-skinned, dark-eyed children with long, braided hair, and hear the soft gentleness in the voice of the willowy man whose manners were dark velvet compared to my father's.

At first I suspected that they were only stopping to water their horses or their children, or perhaps for a rest in the shade of their wagon. The thin-armed children and the woman, her eyes averted and her head covered against the sun, sat silent on the wagon as the man approached my papa. It was not just a short stop. They were looking for work, and my father always had plenty of that.

So up the hill and around behind the saskatoon bushes they went with the lumbering wagon and its contents. Piles and packages of yard goods, pails, willow baskets, articles of curious shape and size that I could not recognize, deer hide robes that I thought were small animals lying in wait.

My brother got mad as hell and started crying and said, "What if they eat all our saskatoons?"

My sister got scared and cried, "What if they sneak into our house at night and steal all our stuff?"

Mama said, "As long as they stay in their own yard, it will be all right. And you kids," she looked straight at me, "stay away from the savages. Stay out of their yard. Mind your own business. Don't be a nuisance."

I, with my mind and heart plotting, planning, my face working hard to stay serious, calm, uninterested, said not a word. To have them come to live with us, on our very own land, to have them in walking distance of the farmhouse, was a joy beyond my wildest dreams. I already had my eye on the oldest girl, who was around my own age. To have a friend, not a sister, but a friend.

It was no time at all before I found my way into the only forbidden spot of our farmland. There I sat digging my feet into the warm, sifted soil that surrounded our circle of field rocks and a hollowed out hole where a cheerful fire blazed most of the day.

That plentiful summer I lied and schemed and got sneaky in order to spend time with them. They picked saskatoons, spreading them on pieces of clothing, discarded lumber or flat rocks gathered from the rock pile. The berries dried in the sun and were packed away for the winter. All the plants that we called weeds they gathered and pounded into a sweet-smelling paste, mixing berries, and the roots from cattails, and dandelions. This mixture was dried until it formed into hard cakes that could then be sucked on. Delicious! They picked red willow in the slough with a ceremony and a thankfulness that surprised me. They made baskets and stools and used the long stems for bed sprints. Everything was done in a slow, unhurried manner that was totally alien to my hurry-up nature. My mother, who was afraid of them, said it was a lazy way. I said it was a wise way. I was forbidden time and again to stray into their yard. But I was willful and cunning. My bare feet regularly made puffy, dusty footprints in the sun-warm soil that led to their yard. Just to ease my guilt, I said I was moved there, pulled by invisible pulleys tied to my feet, or as they said, Led by the Spirit who lived in the grasses and the trees and the rocks. To them, everything was alive and sacred. That, I believe, was what my mama's fear was based on. We had only one God, creator of heaven and earth, not part of heaven and earth. I began to do my own thinking about what we believed. Our one God, far away, fearful, controlling, demanding, was becoming a vexation. Their way appealed to me. In spite of all her warnings about the savages, I gave up my wish to please my mother.

When I was with them, we had time to watch every bug that crawled through the dust, to watch as he lived his bug life. We felt the wind as it caressed our faces, then sent us scurrying inside the tepee. We watched as the blades of grass danced and bowed, then swooped before the wind or stood straight, tall, and reaching for the sun when the wind was still.

Always the woman was with the children, telling stories and teaching how daily happenings were connected to the history of their people. My own mama had a house too big and too busy for that. As I sat quietly listening, I too learned to sense the spirit that moved unseen among the spindly poplar trees and saskatoon bushes. One day I asked where the juiciest berries were, as they had showed me. In the quiet, an unheard voice whispered without whispering, spoke without words. I did indeed find the loveliest berries. I gave thanks as they did, thrilled with the power.

That summer I fell in love with all the unseen, unheard yet alive parts of nature that I had not noticed before. They became companions to me. I never saw a face, I never felt a touch, but I was hopelessly in love.

As with all lovers, I wanted to share my joy with the world. I began and ended by telling my mother. I told her that I had begun to talk to god in the trees and the berries, the rocks and the leaves, that god really did have voices that were everywhere. Her face went pale. Her hands were shaking so that she dropped the silver water dipper into the rain barrel. The water splashed up into her face leaving little trickles of crystal moving down toward her mouth as she screamed and raised her hands above her head in a familiar gesture.

"I don't know what to do with you," implying that I had sinned again, implying that I was on my way to hell in a handbasket, implying that I was the curse of an otherwise decent family and would probably be the death of her. I once again received the "this is the only way we pray" talk, implying that since I was not a saint I could not hear god in the trees.

When the days of summer became golden and the stooking was done and the garden turned into a black desert with only shriveled brown sticks where the raspberries used to be, the Indian family left. Silently, with only a shy little wave from a girl named Stone. She was the record keeper, her mama said. She would always remember, but did not understand any more than I why I had suddenly stopped playing with her.

That summer I lost my first love. I never heard the voiceless voices or felt the spirit in the trees again. The great beyond that we called god moved far away up into the sky.

APRIL SNOW *lives and writes in Edmonton, Alberta. She began writing after a brain injury and subsequent cranio-sacral therapy. She has five children and thirteen grandchildren.*